BOOKS BY J. C. MCKENZIE

The Lark Morgan Series

Death Stealer *(prequel)*

Death Maker

Death Raiser

Death Taker

Isle and Eyrie Series

Cormorant Run

Heir of the Eyrie

House of Moon and Stars

The Night House

House of Chaos

Crawford Investigations

Conspiracy of Ravens

Nevermore

Queen of Corvids

The Call of Corvids

From the Shadows

Into the Fire

Dark Legacy

Embrace the Flame

CARUS

J. C. McKenzie

COPYRIGHT INFORMATION

Carus

Contact Information: jcmckenzie@jcmckenzie.ca

Cover Art: Olga Sauchenia

Publishing History:

First JCM Publications Edition, 2024

First Black Rose Edition, 2016 (Beast of All, Wild Rose Press)

ISBN: 978-1-990143-61-8 (print)

ISBN: 978-1-990143-62-5 (ebook)

To Kiidk'yaas
You will always stand tall in my memories.

You're entering the creative domain of a Canadian author. There will be a combination of British and American spellings, a combination of measurement systems, and maybe even a little French thrown in to spice things up.

This series contains explicit language, open-door spicy scenes, ghosts, violence, gore, torture, PTSD from past SA, threat of SA, murder, assassinations, sociopaths and narcissists. This series also contains death, grief, and loss.

Please read with care.

I

Molten hot magma rushed through my veins as red stained my vision. The smell of burnt cinnamon exploded in the air around me and flowed in my wake like a villain's cape. Fury boiled from inside and erupted from every pore like lava spewing forth from a thunderous volcano.

"Andy..." *Tristan's voice, normally smooth, choked on blood.* "Andrea..."

The beast consuming every fibre of my being roared. Fire ripped from my throat, burning a path through my mouth, past barred fangs, heating the air, and setting the nearby forest ablaze. The trees burst into flame, hot embers dancing along the branches.

A memory ripped through my consciousness and made me stagger.

"Hey, Tristan?"

"Yeah?" He stopped and turned to me.

"I love you." The words flowed out of my mouth, as

natural as the rain on a stormy day. Why'd I choose now to say it?

Because it was right. And true.

"I know." Sapphire blue eyes twinkled back at me. "I love you, too."

With the beast riding me hard, I stomped through the forest north of Port Coquitlam, crashing through bushes and shoving past trees. My taloned feet sank into the hard packed soil, stirring the loam and snapping fallen twigs and leaves. With the smidgeon of control I had left, I aimed for the mountains, away from humanity, before the beast took over completely. Another flashback rocked my mind.

The door to my apartment slammed open. A misplaced scent.

The rata-tat-tat of machine gunfire.

The sickening jerks of Tristan's body as bullet after bullet struck his body while he shielded me.

A soulful, anguish-ridden howl exploded from my soul as it spasmed and ached. My other animal forms had merged with the beast when I transformed, letting her take control to seek revenge for us all.

A branch snapped to my right. I froze, breath fast and shaky as adrenaline continued to course through my eight foot scaled body. My shoulders and stomach tightened, as my senses searched the woods. The cool early winter wind rustled the branches and the remaining leaves too stubborn to fall.

No birds chirped. No deer stirred. Nothing moved.

The forest stood still, frozen with fear, or abandoned after I crashed through.

A gust of wind swirled around me, and my nostrils flared, little nodes plucking signatures to mark and relay the information to memory. Rosemary and sugar. Werewolf. Wick?

No. He wouldn't be here. I'd burned that bridge, and now... I squeezed my eyelids shut but couldn't stop the memory.

Tristan paused, and his gaze sought mine. Infinitesimal shards of sapphire gems, streaked with leopard yellow to reveal the animal simmering beneath the surface, met my gaze with a need so intense it vibrated my body, my heart, my very being down to the cellular level.

Another twig snapped. Grass crunched. I tensed before spinning to my right.

The air whooshed as tiny darts flew through the night and stabbed at my flesh—impacting my body with little jabs and pinpricks.

The sickening jerk of Tristan's body...

I roared again, howling my rage at invisible foes as my internal wounds continued to fester, then hemorrhage, in a maddening cycle of seething anger. Chaos consumed my body, and I didn't care. I released my diminished hold on the beast. My wings spread wide, and I cried at the moon overhead.

Let the beast reign. Destroy. Destroy them all.

I was the Carus and the world would see my rage.

I stepped forward. And faltered. Ice flowed through

my veins, smothering the raging fire licking at the inferno of my soul. I staggered forward another step.

Pay. Make them pay. Destroy them...

My body crumpled forward. Dark figures emerged from the forest wearing black fatigues, long sleeved shirts, balaclavas, and night-vision goggles. They wielded an arsenal of badass weaponry, but no one took a shot. A wave of vanilla and honey rolled through the wind, announcing the cloaking spell employed for stealth mode.

Get up!

The ice continued to neutralize the burning in my veins. My skin itched as it receded and transformed back into my vulnerable, weak human form. I scrambled to stand, but my long, naked limbs weighed more than cinder blocks. I tumbled forward.

Move, dammit, my mind screamed.

One of my attackers stepped up to my trembling body and clicked on his headset. "We have her."

No!

My vision went black, and for the first time since I lost control, my mind went blank and rested.

2

My vision cleared slowly as a trickle of sweat ran down my spine. With one cheek smushed against cold concrete, blurry images flashed through my brain as broken memories played like a maniacal film reel.

The back of my eyes ached as I focused on the room confining me. My prison. I sprawled on the floor by the base of a small cot, tangled in a sweaty, bed sheet. My holding cell resembled something from a maximum security prison after a white-obsessed designer got her hands on it. White walls, white bedding, and white ceiling. The starkness of the room made it appear almost dream-like, surreal. But this was no dream. This was a nightmare.

A vision surged up like acid reflux.

Pain burst through my body as I threw myself repeatedly against the thick, unforgiving bars. A low drone of chiming metal resonated in the air like some sick, dark calling. I turned and pummelled the concrete walls, howling my rage. Blood dripped down my skin as my fists bled. Bones crunched.

The memory faded.

I glanced down at my knuckles to find them covered with yellow bruises and encrusted with old blood and scabs. The cotton of the white prison garb chafed at my raw human skin. At least they'd clothed me. More memories of the night they brought me in surfaced. Naked, dirty, and broken. I'd fought with every ounce of hatred infused in my bones, but it hadn't been enough. Whatever they used to subdue my beast prevented me from exerting extreme damage. Only my martial arts training remained, but I still broke bones. When they finally chucked me in this prison cell, I was covered with blood—not all of it mine.

Mountain lion? Falcon? I called out to the feras normally cohabitating my mind.

No answer.

Baloo? Kaa? Red? With command in my thoughts, I summoned the animal familiars I'd dispelled to another realm. Normally, they popped into existence when called and made inappropriate comments about my love life.

Again, nothing.

Cold slithered along my spine. No feras. No beast. Whatever they shot me with blocked my communication with the animals. Did it prevent shifting as well? I squeezed my eyes shut and tried to call a form and change. Only a headache answered. Dread flittered across my skin. Was this permanent?

As the Carus, the genetic throwback to the first

demigod progeny of the beast goddess, I caged a beast with rage and power rivalled by few, and possessed more than one animal familiar to shift into.

At least, I did until the someone shot me full of chemicals. Would I ever regain my abilities? Hear the indignant screech of the peregrine falcon? Or the lusty purr of the mountain lion? Or soulful howl of the wolf?

My heart hammered, punching bone. A buzzing sensation filled my head. The "wrongness" of my condition grated against my nerves, slicing them into slivers like a planer shucking off wood shavings.

Something in my abdomen swelled, as if the beast pushed against whatever barrier caged and hid her from me.

I'll get you out, I told her, not knowing if she could hear. *We'll make them pay.*

I looked down and sniffed. They'd cleaned me, too. Who got the sponge bath job? I'd find out and break their hands later.

After a deep breath, I clambered to my feet and pulled the white sheet from my sweaty body. Three white walls, closed off by a fourth side of thick bars, Were-proof from the look and smell. The single bed, bolted to the cement floor, appeared disheveled and rumpled. I must've fallen out with the sheet. My scent, old and fresh, clung to the bedding. How long had I been here?

I closed my eyes and opened my senses. No mountain lion. No falcon. No beast. They'd somehow blocked me from my feras, but at least my Shifter senses remained.

The scent signatures of the cell and the room outside

filtered in. Boring as paper norm scents cluttered the space from trace to strong. One stood out among the rest, one smell triggered the fury simmering beneath my skin, coiling in my bones; one stench, accompanied by overpowering, expensive cologne, made that weird pressure in my core rise and brush against the invisible barrier again.

ATF.

Agent Tucker Fucker.

The agent from the Supernatural Regulatory Division, or SRD, whom I loathed more than raisins in my butter tarts, despised more than zombie apocalypse movies, hated more than sand caked in places sand should never go.

I paused.

No, none of these comparisons expressed the sheer disgust I held for Tucker.

His scent triggered another memory.

His smug smile flashed from the other side of the bars. Pale face and hazel gaze bright with victory. The beast howled deep and low inside my core, yearning to rip his face apart. He leaned in, and his boring as paper scent coiled around me like a lasso. "You're mine, now."

Tucker's scent here, combined with my flashbacks, told me my worst fear had finally come true—I was in the SRD lab.

The place they stuck weirder-than-normal supernaturals, or supes, and essentially poked them with sticks. And beast-suppressant narcotics, apparently.

Something else tickled my nose. Fresh and old,

substantial and trace. Here and now. Vanilla and honey meant one thing, and one thing only. Witch. And from the estrogen swirling around in the scent, I'd bet my secret stash of yogurt covered raisins, a female Witch lurked close by. As a guard? Or fellow inmate?

My pulse picked up and my skin prickled.

"He-hello?" My voice cracked like someone took coarse sandpaper to it and wore it down so thin it broke.

A woman snorted nearby. "'Bout time you woke up, princess."

I staggered a few steps before reaching the bars. With not enough room to stick my head through, I smushed my face as far as I could to look around. A wave of dizziness shrouded my vision.

If only I could call Kaa, my snake familiar, I'd be out of here and kicking ass in minutes.

Despite my best efforts to cram my skull through a space half the width, the view didn't offer much information. Outside my cell, it looked like a hallway, with maybe a cell or two on each side of mine.

"Who else is here?" I croaked.

"Just us, darlin'," the woman spoke again, her voice a lazy drawl. "Not sure what or who you are, but they deemed us too dangerous to keep with the other specimens."

Fellow inmate then. "The SRD lab?"

"Mmhmm."

Animated visions trickled through and teased my neurons. Men in lab coats. ATF's smug face. Multiple injections.

Another memory rose up like vomit and clouded my mind.

Tucker's smile broadened, his teeth gleamed as he held up a large syringe on the other side of the bars.

I shook the image away. "How long have I been out?"

"This time? About a day. It's the first time you've spoken, though. Or at least the first time you've made any sense."

Her words confirmed what my healing wounds and the nausea in my gut suggested. I'd been here longer than a day. My capture hadn't been recent. With a deep breath, I asked the question rebounding in my head since waking up. "How long have I been here?"

She sighed. "Hard to track time in the lab, but my guess is almost two months. Maybe more."

"That's not possible," I whispered, confusion fogging my brain. Surely, I would've come to my senses sooner than this? Two months? I'd rolled around in a drug-induced haze for that long? Impossible. I had a monthly visit from a Seducer Demon. Surely, he would've found me by now and rescued me from this testing hell hole. Having his anchor behind SRD bars wouldn't provide Sid with any advantage. Unless... Unless the supe suppressant crap blocked his link as well.

My stomach twisted.

The woman cleared her throat.

"I'm Andy. Who are you?" I asked. Why'd I bother? No amount of chit-chat would distract the vibrating fear niggling up my spine.

"Veronika."

Veronika? Veronika...Veronika... Her name clicked into place, like the final piece to a puzzle. Laughter bubbled up my throat at the same time nausea swirled in my stomach. The fear gripping my backbone dissipated. "Veronika Klug?"

Silence.

"Your brother wanted me to find you." Heck, I would've agreed to almost anything for Lucus to work the locator spell I'd asked him for. At the time, a menacing supe had lurked at large and already having a destructive past, I wanted him found and dead, sooner than later. Lucus had located the supe in record time, demonstrating his power and finesse as a Witch. That he couldn't use a similar spell to find his own sister spoke volumes about the magical defences of the lab.

More snorting. "Hell of a way to come looking."

"Not exactly my plan." Fucking fairy tits, I'd barely had time to relax and enjoy life after the Demon fiasco before...before everything was taken from me. Finding Veronika had been on my "To Do" list, but saving my Witch neighbours from the Elders had been my top priority at the time. If only I'd known.

Tristan.

A sob lodged in my throat, and I swallowed it down. I couldn't save Tristan. Not now. Not ever. But I could save myself and still help my friends.

Ben, Matt, Patty, and heck, even Christopher, though he was still a douche.

An image of kind, soft brown eyes framed with shaggy dark blond hair flashed through my mind. Ben.

Neighbour, Witch, and one of my best friends. His brethren had messed up a Demon summoning, which ended in catastrophe. The Witch Elders had ordered the entire coven to appear and answer for their mistake. I promised Ben I'd rescue him if the Elders didn't release them, or the punishment went on too long. *I promised.*

Was it too late to help him, too?

I gripped my white shirt and my fingers dug in, twisting the cheap cloth.

"Sugar," Veronika interrupted my thoughts. "You need a new plan. There's no way you're breaking out of these bars."

Not chemically declawed, I wasn't. My skin itched as memories of shifting flittered through my mind. She had a point.

"They gave me something," I croaked. "I can't feel my feras."

A sucked in breath. A pause.

"Feras? As in plural?"

Normally, Shifters only possessed one animal familiar, one that walked beside them instead of in their mind fondling their neurons. Being the Carus, I had special abilities.

"You're the supe Richard always goes on about." Veronika moved in the cell beside me, her feet shuffling against the concrete floor while her clothes rustled.

"Richard?"

"Agent Richard Tucker."

"Ah, yes. We're well acquainted, unfortunately." ATF's first name was Richard? Always knew he was a dick, but apparently his parents foreshadowed his future quite accurately at birth.

A pause. More shuffling. She moved closer. "From your tone, I think we're going to be good friends."

From her tone, she was right. The itching across my skin eased. "A useless friend. I can't do anything. Have they done anything to you? What got you sent to the naughty corner?"

A deep sigh. The scent of canned ham churned in the air. Despair. "They took away everything, save the one thing they use me for, and that won't help us. It will only get us killed."

My brain pinged with a neurostorm of possibilities. "What is it?"

"I'm a Demon portal."

The tiny hairs on my arms stood on end. "Excuse me?"

"I can summon Demons without anchoring, calling for Hekate's power, or the new moon. I just reach across the veil between realms and literally snatch any Demon I want and haul them here. Of course, without the ability to form a summoning circle or any witchcraft to protect myself, I'd be Demon pâté the moment they materialized."

My mind raced. Relief flowed through my veins as my brain rapidly made calculations. "I know how we can escape."

"How?" Veronika rasped.

"You need to summon a Demon for me."

3

I n the distance, water dripped and Veronika's heart
thudded. Her breath came out in little puffs of air.
All else remained silent.

"Are you kidding me?" she finally whispered. Her
tone, though light, cut sharply.

"Not at all."

"The Demon will eviscerate me. Why on Earth
would I welcome that?"

"This Demon won't." This Demon better not.

Before she could demand answers, footsteps echoed
in the distance. Farther down than Veronika's cell, a door
clicked open. Feet shuffled. The door closed. I scurried
back to my bed and sat down. Though it went against my
nature to place myself at a lower, submissive position to
whomever approached, my limbs had grown shaky and
sitting appealed more than showing weakness.

The air floating down the hallway announced our
visitor. Boring as paper smothered with expensive

cologne, his norm scent put my teeth on edge before he showed his smarmy face on the other side of the bars.

Medium brown hair, Caucasian complexion, with average face, height, and weight. Even without any supernatural abilities, Tucker would've made an excellent agent, had he learned to apply himself. Instead, his perfect-for-blending appearance went to waste. His hazel eyes, the only striking part of his appearance, twinkled like a crazy crack addict as he looked me up and down from a safe distance on the other side of the bars.

Veronika scampered away, remaining mute. Only her soft breath, noticeable because I listened for it, carried through the air in between the dripping water and Tucker clearing his throat.

"Oh, hello." I yawned. Be nice to stretch for added effect, but I'd probably face plant onto the floor. Stupid, untrustworthy muscles.

Tucker's lip curled up. "*Carus.*"

"Please. Half of Vancouver already knows my *secret.* Don't act so chuffed you finally figured it out." Fifth graders probably could've connected the dots sooner. Along with abandoning the life of an assassin, and opening myself to friendship and love, I'd lost my ability to keep my nature hidden. In other words, I'd grown soft.

Former badass SRD assassin, now one giant, Carus softy. *Ugh.*

"What I don't understand is why Agent Booth withheld information from the agency." He peered at me. "I never got the impression she liked you much. Yet she promoted you instead of booting you out of the agency, and she cleaned your file before she disappeared. Why?"

A little smile tugged at my lips, and I let it show. Booth did like me. She was also an Egyptian goddess with better things to do with her time than babysit spoiled brats like Tucker. Once she got her husband out of the lab, she fled the SRD faster than a babysitter's boyfriend when the parents' car pulled up.

Booth was smart. She got what she wanted and ran away.

A sharp stab sliced through my chest. I should've taken off with Tristan. We should've gone on the vacation we always talked about. The one with the tropical beach, whiskey, and a bulk box of condoms. Now...

The air wheezed out of my lungs, leaving them dry and empty.

"Keep your secrets, then. What little you have left." Tucker sneered, either ignorant or ambivalent to my collapsing heart.

"What do you want?" My blunt, human nails dug into my palms as I clenched my hands into fists.

Tucker leaned toward the bars. If I had full strength and energy, he'd be within striking distance. One lunge using supe-speed and my hands would wrap around the vulnerable soft tissue of his neck, finishing what I started months—eons—ago. I'd give his head a few good beats against the bars, too.

Instead, I sat useless in a sweaty heap on the bed, with an upward angled shot of Tucker's hairy, yet pruned, nostrils.

"What do I want from you?" Tucker repeated my question. "Nothing that I didn't already take."

My skin prickled with the implications. What did he take? Aside from blocking my abilities, what did he do to me? Take my blood? Clone me? Turn me into a mutant ninja to do his bidding as he commanded. Sweat broke out across the bridge of my nose.

Too many Sci-Fi movies.

Tucker leaned in, gaze gleaming.

No way would I let this fucktard know how much his words freaked me out. "Then you're here to gloat."

He paused as if he had to think about his answer. "A bit," he admitted. "But more to observe."

"I'd think my hatred for you would be quite obvious by now."

His mouth twitched as if he found me amusing instead of scary like he should. "How are you feeling?"

"Your neck looks tasty."

His brows furrowed. "Sucking my blood won't give you any sustenance. You're not a Vampire."

"I plan to rip it out," I snarled.

"With what? Your dull human teeth? You can't shift anymore, McNeilly. Can you even feel your feras?" he chortled, the sound so obnoxious it bypassed my brain and went straight for the eye twitching muscle.

I gripped the crappy outfit they put me in. My jaw ached as I clenched *my dull human teeth*. "What did you give me?"

"SomaX."

"What the hell is that?"

17

"It's a derivative of somatostatin. It's the hormone that inhibits cell division and growth, except this version has none of the gastrointestinal effects. You're welcome for that, by the way." He paused for a thank you, but receiving nothing other than my best death glower, he soon continued. "We discovered SomaX while working with another experimental drug, one based on growth hormone. One I think you're more familiar with—King's Krank."

My body stiffened. The emergence of the genetic reordering drug had led to the deaths of many, including my former master, Lucien—good riddance—and my partner's wife, Loretta. My stomach dropped at the memory of my friend's pain. "That stuff's fucked up. Why would you mess with it?"

Tucker's smug smile remained on his face.

A light bulb flickered on in my head. The SRD's complacency, the KK super-supe producing side effects, Tucker's satisfied expression.

"You're working on KK with the Pharaoh."

The Pharaoh, an ancient Vampire had subtly played the supe community of the Lower Mainland for the last year, probably longer. His actions resulted in many deaths, and he aligned with Bola, the Demon tormentor from my past, which meant he had zero redeemable qualities. Guess I didn't need to ask Veronika which Demon she summoned.

Tucker straightened and pulled on his shirt sleeves. "Well, I—"

"I'm going to get out of here. And when I do, I'm

going to slaughter the fuck out of all of you." I spat. My blood boiled. "Every single person remotely responsible for Tristan's death will feel my wrath, suffer my claws, and scream as my teeth rip into them." A pause. Another annoying tilt of his head.

"The SRD had no part in Tristan Kayne's death. Although the turn of events ended up quite advantageous for us."

I hesitated. The assassins who killed Tristan lay dead on my apartment floor, or at least they had, but they acted on someone else's orders. I didn't need to investigate to know a hired thug when I saw one, and these men had gone after me before.

When I found out who sent them, I'd rend their flesh from bone.

Tucker snorted. "If you're going to fling empty threats and curse the SRD, at least get the reason correct." He spun on his heel and sauntered down the hall, pausing briefly at Veronika's cell. He didn't say anything, but her breathing quickened. Tucker's healthy pulse sped up as he wordlessly watched the Witch. Until, without warning, he walked away. Nervous? Attracted? Just his normal sicko self? What did he plan for my Witch neighbour?

The door finally clicked shut on Tucker's fading footsteps, leaving me and Veronika to the near-silence of our prison cells, lost in our own thoughts, trapped with our own internal Demons.

Images of Tristan kept running through my mind like an old video feed stuck on a loop. I'd failed him. He'd given his life to save mine, and I'd turned into a monster while the person or persons responsible for his death roamed free.

My arms warmed as if Tristan ran his hands along them, as if he sat right beside me, holding me. As if he'd materialize if I closed my eyes and willed him into existence hard enough.

But Tristan wasn't in my prison cell. He wasn't anywhere. He was gone, and I was alone. The silence of the moment allowed the weight of my reality to settle on my shoulders, pushing down until my body and soul threatened to crumple under the pressure.

Tristan. My love. My mate.

Even though we hadn't completed the mating bond, we would have, given time, given the freedom.

Good things come to those who wait? Hardly. Only more pain and suffering. More chance and possibilities of unknown factors popping up to knock me down.

Well, one good thing would come from waiting.

Tucker might think my threats empty, but I'd see them through. I'd crush them all.

After all, revenge was one dish best served cold.

"I'll do it." Veronika's shaky voice whispered down the hall.

I shook my head, wiping the tears trailing down my cheeks, and swallowing the sob lodged in my throat. "What?"

"I'll summon your Demon."

4

A slew of emotions bubbled up to swirl around the base of my throat as if fate cackled gleefully while it stirred the pot. Excitement, fear... everything fluttered around, simmering, waiting to get out, while the grief—dark, ominous and with a mind of its own—continued to lurk a layer below, knowing it didn't need to rage around with the other emotions, knowing it would always be there to haunt me.

If Veronika was willing to summon a Demon, it left only one question. "When?"

"After George brings us dinner."

My stomach rumbled. When was the last time I ate? "Is it any good?"

"I feed my cats better."

"Great." I withheld the crazy cat woman barb. Who was I to judge? Besides, Veronika planned to rip a Demon from the nether realm for me. Great time for me to keep my mouth shut.

"I think they drug the meal to make us sleep."

"Just gets better and better..." I muttered.

"Don't eat any of it."

"But you've done such a great job selling it."

She snorted.

I peered around my room, taking in more details, including the chipped paint in the cement on the far wall. I'd thrown myself at it. The scent of my blood and anguish still lingered.

A small toilet jutted out of the wall. Beside it, a small sink with a soap dispenser.

Well, isn't this...cozy?

Personally, I was a "keep the bathroom door shut" kind of girl. Not that I tried to deny what happened in there, but geez...maintain some kind of mystery.

Whomever, whatever George was, he needed to bring our food and scram so we could get our escape on.

Just as a whine trickled up my throat, the door at the end of the hall banged open and a large norm wheezed and lumbered down the hall. Something jingled with each step. Keys, probably.

"Here *ladies*," he drawled. Something clattered on the concrete floor. I turned in time to watch beige-coloured sludge in a shallow metal bowl slide under the bars. He must've kicked it over. The congealed slush slopped over the sides, and the edge of the bowl smelled of dirt. I've seen dog chow more appetizing.

The guard didn't travel down the hall far enough for me to view his foul, oily-smelling self. The shuffling of his feet grew distant, the door banged closed, and Veronika and I were once again encased in silence.

"Real charmer," I noted.

"Yeah. He was one of the guards who brought you in. You pulled out of the drugs a bit and thrashed around. Gave them a good fight, even though you were heavily dosed. They call you hellcat." She paused. "Anyway, you bit him, hard. He bled all over the hallway. It was pretty awesome."

My shoulders straightened, and I smiled.

"He's a jerk and totally deserved it. Even though you've been mostly comatose, he keeps his distance from your cell."

I glanced at the slop in the bowl he'd kicked under the bars at me. "Fucker."

"Mmhmm."

A thought flashed through my mind. With a little release of the animal magnetism I held from my part-divine nature, I could've lured him over, knocked him out against the bars, and grabbed his keys. I'd pulled off more challenging feats. "I should've grabbed his keys."

"Wouldn't do any good."

My elation and internal planning came to a screeching halt. *Huh?*

"Our cells are magically locked as well as physically."

I grunted. Bloody magic. Always messing up my plans. "Well, let's get this party started. Do you need me to do anything?"

"Just keep quiet while I'm summoning. Once he

arrives, though, you better yell something so he doesn't smite me for my insolence."

"This one's not much of a smiter." More of a sex-mojo, orgy-inducing pervert, but I kept that detail to myself. She might get second thoughts.

"Who is he? It is a *he*, right?"

I groaned internally. Why did she have to ask? Now she'd definitely get second thoughts.

"Sidragasum. I call him Sid."

An image of the seven-foot Demon with olive skin and a dark promising gaze flickered into my mind, followed quickly with a recent memory of him choking on banana nut loaf in my kitchen. A smile broke out across my face. Sid might not be a friend, exactly, but he wasn't an enemy, either.

"What's his role in the nether realm?"

"Err..." My voice trailed off as I mentally scrambled for ways to rebrand the Demon.

"Andy." Veronika's tone turned hard.

I cringed. Well, crap. I should tell her everything. I'd be pissed if the situation was reversed and someone withheld pertinent information. And heck, all Demons could be fickle and nasty. She already knew that. "He's known as Sidragasum the Seducer, and he's Satan's assistant."

Veronika sucked in a deep breath.

Fuck. She was going to back out. Ice seared through my limbs. I'd be stuck here as the SRD pincushion for the rest of my extended Shifter lifetime.

"He won't hurt you," I rushed to say. "Promise." He was more likely to have her swooning at his feet begging for an orgasm. Him and his stupid sex mojo. He usually turned it off around me, but I sometimes had to threaten his junk.

"Well," she sighed. "At this point, death by a Seducer Demon is a far more preferable way to go than..." She shuddered hard enough for the air to vibrate. Her breathing picked up. "Than whatever hell Tucker has planned for me."

"I hate that douche." Unlike sadistic Shifters and Weres, whose form of unpleasant torture and domination normally held a sexual undertone of some sort due to their brutish animal nature, Tucker was a norm, and I'd never picked up "rapist" in his asshole vibe. I had no idea what pain and suffering the agent planned for Veronika, but knowing his inferiority complex and insatiable need to overcompensate, it wouldn't be pleasant. I'd take the Seducer Demon way out, too.

"Agreed."

"What's the deal with you two?" I asked.

She paused and tapped her fingers on something. "We dated and I made the mistake of telling him my secret."

I sucked in a breath. I'd assumed ATF was asexual until now because he never reacted to my animal magnetism. On reflection, that wasn't very fair to the ace community. But knowing he betrayed his significant other to lock her up in the SRD lab...that fit.

"He's even worse than I thought," I said.

"He's the vilest thing I've met, which says a lot since I

summon Demons. Now, shush. Summoning in progress."

The hairs on my arms and the back of my neck stood on end as the air swirled into a large vortex. My spine prickled from the dip of my lower back to the base of my skull. The air continued to move, spinning as Veronika's magic sucked it into her cell.

With no view of her room, my imagination went wild. Most likely, the vortex formed as it did with a regular summoning, but Veronika murmured no chants, nothing verbal to ground her to the mortal realm, and the air grew hot, as if a dry prairie wind blasted across my skin.

The scent of Veronika's sickly sweet fear rushed through the bars of my cell. The hollow pit in my belly churned when no feras perked up with predatory delight.

The air popped as the portal snapped in place. Almond everything flooded my senses. Normally, smelling a Demon either pissed me off or caused me to worry, but this one meant freedom. This one meant Sid. This one was the best stinking Demon I had ever smelled before in my life. *I needed out of here.*

"What a delectable treat," Sid crooned at Veronika. Hidden from my sight, his silver-tongued voice was unmistakable. "A tasty morsel to whet my appetite."

Veronika's sharp intake of breath and the musky coconut of her induced lust snapped me out of...well, whatever I was doing, or not doing.

"Sid, you perverted whore," I screeched. "If you so

much as eye-grope her, I'll wring off your nuts and use them for shark bait."

A long silent pause, like the one where wolves freeze when the wind shifts and they catch the scent of prey, or when the sea draws back like a slow caress before it pounds the shore with a destructive wave; that moment of perfect stillness before chaos erupts.

"Andy?" Sid's voice cracked.

"Who else?" I muttered.

"You're the only one I know who hasn't realized slut-shaming is juvenile, and so last decade."

Another smile spread across my face and my tense muscles relaxed. "If I'm juvenile, it's because I'm dropping to your level. We're in the SRD lab. You need to get me and Veronika out. Like ASAP." I really hated talking to a concrete wall. The white painted cement held no answers and gave me no information on facial expressions.

What was Veronika doing? Thinking? Was Sid eye-groping her as we spoke? Did I need to punch him in the nads for being a snake, or did he axe the sex-mojo and switch to his best behaviour?

Sid grunted. Some shuffling. Some mixed emotional scents from Veronika.

"I can't leave this cell," Sid said, his tone deep and gritty, as if spoken through clenched teeth. "Why can't I leave?"

Veronika cleared her throat. "The SRD created some sort of magical shield around this wing. Magic just rebounds off it. I assume magic can't get in, either, or my brother would've found me by now. My portal building still works but only because they haven't figured out how to block it."

Hmm... That might explain why Sid hadn't visited me on the new moon before, but if Veronika could form a portal, logic followed I could as well. Or was it because Sid actually formed it from the other side? Or did it have nothing to do with the SRD and everything to do with what they gave me to block the beast? A zillion questions zinged around in my brain.

"What is your name again, Witch?" Sid asked, his tone surprisingly soft.

Another long pause. Minimal scent signatures to tip me off. I'd love to be a fly on the wall to take in the visual cues ping-ponging between Veronika and Sid. He better not harm her. "Your balls—"

"Veronika." Her tone, husky and low, interrupted my threat.

Oh, for fuck's sake. If they started humping, I'd lose it.

"Demon, if you—"

"Save your idle and ridiculous threats on my junk, woman. This Witch will come to no harm by my hand."

No harm, he said.

I snorted. After Lucien, I learned "no harm" was a relative term. "Just cut the crap, stop using your mojo on Veronika, and get us out of here."

"I can't get you out of here from within."

I slapped my palm against my forehead, grunted, and

flopped face-first on my bed. The thin mattress did little to cushion my fall, and the hard springs dug into my body as my head smacked the rough surface.

"Fear not, little one." Sid chuckled, as if he saw the epic fail at flailing. Jerk. "I'll get you out of here."

I believed every word. Having his free ride to the mortal realm void of encumbrance and the control of the SRD played to his advantage.

"Please send me back, Miss Veronika," Sid crooned, his tone full of promises and seduction. "I will see you soon."

Gag me.

"Of course," Veronika breathed. The air snapped with her power as she opened a portal.

"Goodbye my lovelies," Sid said.

I didn't catch Veronika's response, the whirlwind of the demonic streams of hell so strong, they drowned her out. When the portal snapped shut and the air settled, Veronika let out a long dreamy sigh.

I rolled my eyes. "He's a Seducer Demon," I reminded her. "Don't fall for his act."

"Act?" Veronika tittered. "Have you seen him naked?"

Plenty of times. More times than I'd like. He always showed up to summonings naked—all part and parcel of his Seducer image. Sure, he had a ridiculous eight pack and swung his impressive wang around like he knew how to use it, but I'd never held any personal interest in the Demon or interacting with his nether bits... Well, that was a lie. I thought about kicking or kneeing them from time to time, especially when Sid got saucy.

"I'll take your silence as a yes," she chuckled.

"He doesn't appeal to me in that way. He just pisses me off, mostly." No, another man appealed to me. A man slightly taller than six feet, with broad shoulders and the athletic build of a rugby winger.

My heart convulsed, and I curled up into the fetal position. The pain radiated out to my limbs before it sank deep like rotten waste into the pit of my stomach.

Tristan...

I wiped my wet cheeks and took long shuddering breaths.

Get a hold of yourself, McNeilly. I shook my head and cleared the painful memories. Focus. Here. Now. "Why didn't you summon a Demon sooner to escape?"

"Are you crazy?" Veronika whispered. "He would've killed me if it weren't for you. And he's one of the least crazy. I couldn't trust any of them not to rip off my head before I had a chance to broker a deal."

Huh. "Good point."

"Can we trust him?" Veronika asked. "He could sell us out to someone even worse than the SRD."

"True, but I don't think so."

"He's a Demon, Andy."

"Also true." I took a deep breath. "But I'm his anchor. He'll want to keep me safe."

Veronika gasped. She took a couple of quick breaths and seemed to collect herself before speaking again. "Well, at least he's easy on the eyes."

"You should stay clear of him."

"Oh, I plan to." The stench of her lie curled around the bars of my prison cell.

5

The ache of resetting bones thrummed through my body as blood and tears trickled down my face. The bars of my cell remained unblemished from my failed attempts to break out by sheer force.

Tucker's smug face smiled at me through my blurred vision as my memories replayed Tristan's death over and over again. My stomach twisted, and I curled up on the cold cement floor.

"Please... Please, just kill me..." I begged.

"Never. Besides, one of my associates would like to meet you. Again." Tucker tilted his head back and laughed like a bad B-list actor.

I bolted upright in bed as Tucker's fiendish laughter echoed in my head and faded away. Stark white cotton sheets stuck to my sweaty body as the nightmare—no, memory—slipped away.

Had I seriously begged Tucker to kill me? Nausea coiled in my stomach and surged up. I gulped. Fucking hell. That prick did not deserve to see me so weak, so broken.

When we first met, Tucker had assumed I was a regular Shifter and asked where my fera was. Considering the majority of Shifters were eradicated during the Purge by norms killing their feras, a fate worse than torturous death, Tucker's question hit a super-sensitive button. The fera bond was sacred. A fera's death meant the death of the Shifter, and this method was a terrible way to go. The worst way.

As an SRD agent, he knew better, too. Despite how much I detested Tucker, he wasn't stupid.

Of course, I could've handled my rage a bit better. But at the time, anger took over, and I lunged across the interrogation table and tried to squeeze the life out of him.

We'd been enemies ever since.

I pulled the rough thin sheet over my clammy skin and flopped back on my hard pillow and mattress. Sweat cooled and dried on my face and body.

Maybe I should eat the drugged food. Sleep did not come easily, and when it did, nightmares plagued my mind and shrouded every corner. Drug-induced delirium sounded pretty good right now as I stared at the dark ceiling and counted the cracks. Twenty-eight so far.

The door at the end of the hall creaked open. I jolted upright, again. Sitting in my bed, I pushed the sheet aside.

Footsteps padded down the hall toward our cells. Not the lumbering stalk of George the guard. The beams of multiple flashlights bounced off the stark walls. I slipped off the bed and crouched into a fighting stance. My muscles screamed from neglect, and sweat sprang from every pore. I licked my dry lips. The air rushed in and announced the late night visitors.

A big sigh escaped my lungs and my shoulders relaxed.

Soap and leather—Stan, my partner in fighting crime.

Scrumptious almond—Sid the Seducer Demon.

Vanilla and honey with a side of sass—Lucus Klug, Veronika's brother.

And...

Unease flowed through my body and froze me on the spot. Breathe. Just breathe.

Sugar and rosemary ran along my skin in a sweet caress to seep into my bones—Wick, the Werewolf Alpha whose heart I'd broken when I chose Tristan.

"Rescue never smelled so good," I whispered.

Stan snorted as he came into view. The sight of my middle-aged friend and his rotund belly from too many beers and donuts washed away my unease. His flashlight brightened my personal prison, but he kept the focus off me. His smile widened and his snaggled teeth gleamed in the dark. His teeth reminded me of bacon grease, hopping in different directions in a hot frying pan. I'd never been so glad to see that warped smile in my life.

"You look like crap, McNeilly," Stan said. "Nothing a shower won't fix. The same can't be said for you." I moved toward the bars and Stan's chuckling. "How'd you find me?"

Stan shifted on his feet and cast his gaze sideways to where the others stood out of sight. Magic always put him off-ease. His face said it all. We both turned toward Veronika's cell, though I couldn't see beyond the bars of my personal prison.

Lucus whispered quietly to Veronika as she whimpered in her sleep.

"Ronnie!" Lucus hissed, louder.

She snarled something before a large thump sounded in her cell. "Ugh," she groaned.

While my hearing strained to follow what occurred next door, the rosemary and sugar scent drifted closer to me, giving a split second warning before Wick came into view to stand beside Stan. I gulped. The space in my mind which used to fill with howls and heavy panting whenever this Alpha drew near, remained a silent void, making my soul ache even more.

"Veronika," Lucus crooned next door. "We're getting you out of here."

"Lucus?" she whispered, her voice trembling. "Lucus?"

She started crying and rushed to the bars, her bare feet padding lightly against the cement. Lucus crooned as she sobbed. I envisioned them hugging through the bars.

While the brother and sister reconnected, I turned my full attention to the Werewolf Alpha vibrating across the bars from me. Standing well over six feet, with solid muscle, broad shoulders and powerful legs, Wick always reminded me of a Norse god with his height, stature, and blond hair. His chocolate brown eyes still threatened to drown me in their softness. I hadn't broken it off with him because of any fault of his own. Not really. I ended it because I loved him and refused to allow a power-thirsty crazy Master Vampire use us against each other.

I hadn't known at the time his wolf wouldn't accept another mate, even if I left and chose another.

Nor could I have foreseen the Pharaoh assassinating Lucien, the aforementioned Master Vampire, which resulted in Wick's freedom.

"Andy." His whiskey and cream voice filled the room with its deep timbre. His Alpha power pushed against my skin, but no fera answered. Nothing remained inside save a hollow chasm.

"Hey, Wick," I said.

"Enough of this mortal drama," Sid huffed. "Let's get these *women* out of here."

I growled at his tone. "Women" was not a bad word like his tone implied.

Wick and Stan turned toward the booming Demon and nodded. Veronika's lock clicked, and the barred door slid open. Lucus walked over to my cell, and after a brief once over, presumably to ensure my well-being, he nodded and repeated the same voodoo-hoodoo Witch mojo crap he did with Veronika's cell. Without a pause, he reached forward and used a key on a large ring to turn the lock. The keys smelled of George, and blood.

When my door slid open, I stumbled out and fell into Stan's open arms.

"Glad to see you, too, partner," he whispered into my ear and squeezed me tight. "You missed our B&B sessions."

I laughed, but it choked off as a sob tried to escape. I swallowed it down and hugged Stan back. How many beer and bitch sessions had I missed? A lot.

"We need to leave," Wick said, tone gruff. His lips compressed as he took in Stan and I hugging. The air turned sour around him. Something inside me shredded, as if my feelings tore in two. The part of me still in love with Wick wanted to sink into the heat of his hard body and let him hold and protect me. The other part balked at the idea. We chose Tristan. We mourned Tristan. Besides, would Wick even welcome the contact?

We didn't have time for me to address the hurt I caused Wick. We needed to leave. I needed to be free, to hide, and plan my revenge.

Lucus, a middle-aged man with a bald head and soft belly, reluctantly released Veronika so Sid could pick her up and cradle her in his arms. A long, heated look passed between the Demon and Veronika.

Yeah, that wasn't good.

"Can you run?" Sid asked me. Seven feet of sexual energy loomed over me. At least he'd put some clothes on for the rescue.

I paused long enough to take in Veronika's appearance as Sid carried her. Petite, with thick wavy black hair, a pretty full-lip pout and angular face, she looked like a cute pixie doll. She turned to me and our gazes locked. Maybe a pixie who'd fry me on the spot if I crossed her.

In unison, we nodded.

I stretched my limp unused muscles. The beast stirred beyond the barrier, but after flexing seemed to fold in on herself, quiet and dejected. My limbs grew heavy, and I imagined myself standing on a precipice, having to decide whether to fall into the deep end and sink to the same gloomy depth as my beast, or to throw my chin up to face of this situation. It took little time to make a decision.

Feras or no feras, running free cleansed the soul. Could I run?

I pushed past the men and ignored my screaming muscles. "Try to keep up."

6

We ran through abandoned hallways, ripe with rat feces, oil, and the residue of intensely acrid, peppery, chemicals. Water continued to drip somewhere in the distance. Green and black mould painted the gray walls as nature attempted to reclaim the area.

"What is this place?" I puffed, arms pumping. "Abandoned substation. There's several levels. You were on the lowest one," Wick said as he loped beside me. Jerk didn't even break a sweat.

"How'd you find us?"

"Donny," Wick answered.

The name of my old handler at the SRD sent both warmth and worry through my body.

Wick glanced at me as he kept jogging. "Don't worry about the wily old coyote. He gave us the information and wisely disappeared. He said it was time to retire, anyway."

The knot in my stomach untwisted a little.

Stan wheezed and grunted as he fell behind. I slowed my pace.

Abandoned substation. That made sense. This place looked like something pulled from a sci-fi or dystopian movie. Insects chirruped in the cracks of the walls. Rodents scurried away as our feet slapped the cold, wet concrete and metal flooring. Goosebumps sprang up along my skin as ice leached into my veins.

Any second now, an alien would leap out from one of the confines, and spray me with corrosive green slime.

I jogged beside Stan and caught my breath as he continued to lumber. He shot me an annoyed glance. Whatever. Like I'd leave him behind. As the only norm in the rescue team, he didn't benefit from enhanced physical traits, like speed, stamina, or strength. Plus, he hit the donut shop and fed the cop stereotype along with his belly.

We hopped over knots of cables and discarded machinery. Beneath the rust and grime, rested a once functioning substation. Now, aside from nature, it lurked in a deep, eerie silence.

The same quiet rattled my bones and sent an itch screeching up my spine. How many supes were held captive here? To be forgotten and illegally tested on without the public's knowledge? A shudder racked my body. Everyone presumed the lab existed, but like the boogeyman, people rarely sought information or went looking in dark corners for nightmares.

A particularly pungent smell of moss, mould, and

dirt filled the air as we climbed the stairs. George the Guard sat slumped against the wall at the top, his neck at an awkward angle, blood dripping down his face. His key ring no longer hung from his belt.

We passed more than a few guards, some dead, some in a magically-induced slumber, their soft snores drowning out the trickling water and the scurry of rats.

"It won't last forever," Lucus warned. Sweat dripped down his face. "We need to move before they wake."

"How is it even possible? Surely there's a protective charm over the compound?" To lay a sleeping spell over an entire compound, one with magically contained cells like Veronika's and mine demonstrated an amazing amount of power and control. "Only on some parts like your cells," Wick answered. "They probably wanted to avoid detection. We killed any guards we came across in the protected areas."

Huh. That meant some guards might still lurk about. I grabbed Stan's arm and hauled him with me as I picked up the pace. His weight pulled me off balance. Wick dropped back and bent to pick up Stan.

"Fuck off!" Stan spat. "I've got this." He shrugged off both of us and put his chin down. Sweat glistened on his pasty skin and soaked through his shirt as we reached the next set of stairs.

Wick exchanged a glance with me. We shrugged in unison.

The soft din of a city trickled down the stairwell as we rounded the corner. The faint glow of artificial light surrounded the exit door like a halo.

"Where did you say this substation was?" I whispered to Wick as we climbed over a supersized pipe, slick with dew and clotted grease.

"I didn't."

We stepped onto a tiered plaza of sorts, illuminated by nearby street lights. I blinked until my eyesight refocused with the change in lighting. We faced a large, ornate church, and the familiarity of it slapped my senses. We were in downtown Vancouver somewhere.

Thick concrete pillars rose from the ground to surround us on all sides, while steel beams made a prison-like cage above and cast the platform we stood on in shadow.

"What took you guys so long?" Sid huffed at us, with Veronika still in his arms. He hadn't broken a sweat. And he hadn't put Veronika down, yet, either. He turned away before we could answer and walked toward the park's exit carrying the petite Witch with him.

Stan and Lucus followed, jogging across the overgrown lawn and around a shallow reflection pool. The water smelled of tepid urine and looked worse than an abandoned Chernobyl fish pond. Leaves lay on the bottom along with dirt, cigarettes, and who knew what else. A putrid odour lifted off the surface of the stagnant water and slapped my face.

"Ugh." I pulled my shirt up to cover my nose.

Wick turned and smiled at me. "I know."

His gaze moved to over my shoulder, at the same time a boot scraped against the concrete slabs.

I turned in time to deflect a blow to the head.

A guard I didn't recognize renewed his attack, his dark gaze narrowing. His uniform swished with each movement. I staggered back as my arms and legs ached from blocking his brawler-style strikes. My muscles screamed in agony from neglect and struggled to react.

Wick shoved me out of the way, grabbed the man's hand mid strike, and growled. The guard's eyes widened. One punch and the man was down and out. From the sickening crunch of his skull, he'd likely remain down.

Wick turned to me.

"Thanks." I scratched my head. Normally, I would've bristled and claimed I had that, but it would be a lie, and Wick would know.

His nose flared and he hesitated. After a silent pause, he nodded, grabbed my upper arm, and steered me toward the park's exit. "The spell must've worn off, or we missed some of the protected areas. The spell is hard for Lucus to maintain. He took Sid's blood to cast it."

We moved quickly across the jungle-length grass through the park. Cool air licked my skin, and a gentle wind rustled the nearby trees lining the street. The city lights provided hazy lighting, and the unseen pollution in the air blocked out the stars.

Before exiting, I glanced back at the entrance to the SRD's lab. This park had been left to deteriorate, hiding the lab in plain sight. The concrete columns and the overhanging metal marked the entrance to the lab. How many people assumed this place was just an ugly remnant from the past? How many cursed its clashing style with the opulence of the nearby church, or called it an eye-sore before moving on with their day? How many people plodded along the sidewalk on their daily commute, like lemmings, with no idea a government lab illegally imprisoned supes beneath their feet?

We exited the park and stepped onto the street. Escaping the SRD lab with magically-induced sleeping guards and hacked cameras ranked the same on the difficulty scale as sneaking out at night to play hanky-panky with the boyfriend at the beach while my parents watched the news.

If only Tucker had been close by.

Well, it wouldn't have been very satisfying to have Tucker served on a platter. That man had to pay, and it wouldn't—couldn't—be quick.

Anger boiled in my blood, and the pressure pushed against the barrier housing the beast.

Stan helped support a barely-standing Lucus. The Witch looked like he'd drop without the use of Stan as a crutch.

A van pulled up and the side door slid open. Clint?

With massive shoulders and a smug smile, Clint's presence was unmistakable, even in the night-shrouded abandoned streets of downtown Vancouver. With slicked hair the same deep sable as mine, Clint's big-as-a-tractor shoulders made most girls want to take up farming. Except me. My field didn't want to be plowed. At least, not by him. Instead, I wanted to rip him apart and sell the scraps.

As the former human servant of the douchebag Vampire who'd caused me to sever ties with Wick, Clint's presence, though unmistakable, was unexpected. As was the driver's. Allan, the new Master Vampire of the Lower Mainland.

Allan turned his formidable muscled bulk to wink at me. "Hop in, Carus. We need to talk."

Not one to argue in the middle of an escape, I jumped into the van, and the rest of the rescue team followed. Wick turned to help Stan get Lucus in. Sid leaned over and slid the door shut, almost catching Stan's foot. The police detective scowled at the Demon.

The van peeled down the vacant road, slamming the lot of us against the interior siding. My body crashed into Wick's.

"Sorry." Allan's tone said he wasn't sorry at all.

"Sorry, not sorry," I grumbled, righting myself and pulling away from the heat and scent of Wick's body.

"I've always wanted to do that," Allan admitted.

As the largest Japanese man I'd ever met—not overweight, just all muscle—I was surprised he fit behind the wheel.

Allan chuckled and shook his head at me in the rearview mirror. My powers might be synthetically muted, but Allan could still read minds. Vampires developed special powers over time. The older ones, like Allan, held particularly nasty skills.

Obviously, Sid recruited my known associates to aid him with the prison break. My eyes stung as I surveyed who'd stepped up to answer the Demon's call. Their presence made sense. Well, most did, anyway.

"Not that I'm not appreciative of the help, but why are you here?" I asked Clint and Allan.

The rest of the van remained silent.

Clint smirked and shrugged his massive shoulders. "The Pharaoh is making a move."

Allan's fingers tightened on the steering wheel.

"And you wanted the big bad Carus on your side?" I asked.

Clint shifted and his gaze cut away.

Allan chuckled. "You're on our side, regardless. Don't try to deny you'll go after the Pharaoh. Your anger is potent and barely contained. Even if I couldn't read your mind, I'd read your face."

I closed my eyes and sank against the cold metal of the van's interior.

Wick's warm hand covered my arms. "Can you guys hold off on your diabolical plans for later? Andy needs to heal."

Heal. Not rest. Wick knew. How did he know? My eyes popped open, and I turned to Wick.

His hard gaze met mine and his brows furrowed. "Something's off with you."

I nodded. When I tried to explain, a sob lodged in my throat. No way would I break down in front of these guys. I blinked back tears rapidly pooling in my eyes. I would not cry.

"They pumped her full of drugs," Veronika whispered.

Everyone's attention swivelled toward the Witch, except mine. I stared at my useless, pathetic norm hands, with *dull* fingernails. Tucker's smug smile flashed across my vision.

Allan sucked in a breath, gleaning the truth from my brain before everyone else.

"She said she couldn't feel her feras," Veronika continued.

I winced and everyone's gazes turned back to me. Silence filled the van as cold seeped through my veins, leaving me weak and shaky.

Wick squeezed my arm. "I'm sure you'll find a way to fix it."

His confidence surprised me. The hollow ache of uncertainty ballooning in my chest didn't.

7

With my apartment as the site of Tristan's death, and still technically a crime scene, albeit an old one, I'd rather kiss Tucker's feet than step foot in the place of my nightmares. I needed someplace else to go. Technically, I still had a safe house on Vancouver Island, but without wings, I'd have to wait for the first ferry to leave Vancouver—six hours from now. I needed a place to hole up.

Stan had a small apartment, but he had to go to work and didn't want me left on my own. When I suggested a hotel, everyone in the van grumbled. Obviously, Stan wasn't the only one worried about my solo activities.

How many had I killed or harmed? A growing pit sank low in my stomach. My beast rampage, now only flickers of memory, must've been pretty epic, and my assurances of the beast's containment fell on deaf ears.

So where could I stay?

Veronika and Lucus wanted privacy to catch up.

Besides, Veronika needed to heal as much, if not more, than I did from whatever hell she'd endured in the lab.

Clint and Allan's places respectively were out, because, well, Clint and Allan. Enough said.

"You'll stay at my place." Wick's tone bordered on an order and made my skin bristle.

Not able to raise a proper objection aside from "awkward," I nodded and kept my gaze down.

When the van pulled into Wick's West End driveway, the silence blanketing the vehicle grew heavier.

"Thanks everyone," I mumbled at the floor.

Clint snorted.

Allan nodded.

Lucus, now mostly recovered, mumbled, "Mmhmm."

Sid acknowledged me with a brief nod before resuming his not-so-subtle observation of Veronika.

Stan grunted before pulling me into a big bear hug. He kissed my temple. "Take care of yourself, Andy. The wolf has a new phone for you. Use it."

I nodded and turned to Veronika. Her dark gaze met mine and a silent understanding passed silently between us. We'd get revenge. Just not now.

"Come on." Wick slid the side door open and hopped out. He turned to offer me a hand.

"We'll speak soon," Allan whispered. Even without feras, my Shifter hearing picked up his words and the assurance woven into them.

My pulse increased with the promise of vengeance, retribution, and making those who'd hurt me and

Tristan pay with more than the blood coursing through their veins.

I placed my hand in Wick's large, calloused one and scrambled awkwardly out of the van. My joints and muscles creaked and moaned at the movement. The run had completely sapped my strength. As adrenaline left my system, my whole body cooled and stiffened.

The door slid closed behind me, and the van peeled off into the night.

"I think he agreed to help us just so he could do that." Wick watched the van's path down the dark street. "That and he filled up on a month's supply of blood from the guards he took out by the entrance."

"Yeah," I said.

Wick turned to me, and his gaze bore into mine. As if only realizing now he still held my hand, he dropped it, like my touch burned his skin. He raked his fingers through his blond hair. Though he'd grown it out a bit, the longer hair did little to detract from his good looks.

"I'm glad you're okay," he said, voice gruff. "I'm sorry about Tristan."

"Yeah." I looked away from Wick's intense gaze. In the centre of Kitsilano, a couple blocks away from the beach, Wick's house epitomized taste and class, yet somehow stayed true to the Alpha's wild nature. Worth well over a million dollars, the Parisian blue heritage-style building had multiple levels and a covered front patio. As a building developer, Wick had updated and modernized everything, top to bottom, inside and out, while maintaining the nostalgic feel of the older home. When I first met Wick, he'd held me captive here on the demands of Lucien, the Vampire Master. During my stay, I'd dominated the leading pack-bitch, sprayed dog repellant on the pack's second-in-command to escape, and I'd fallen in love with the Alpha.

"There's been a few changes since you've been here," Wick grumbled.

The only time I'd visited Wick's home post break-up had been to ask for help on a case. Searching for the killer of Stan's wife, and wanting to ease my friend's pain, led me to take desperate measures, including visiting an ex I still loved. Along with answers, I discovered Wick had replaced my absence with my least favourite female Werewolf—Christine. Given the sour tang to the air, and Wick's shifting feet, his uncertainty meant one thing.

"Christine lives here now," he said.

And there it was. The knowledge bomb. Yet, it didn't cut like it might have a month or two ago. Even with Tristan by my side, it had hurt to see Wick move on and to see who he chose to move on with. Now, just emptiness met his words, and a little unease.

"Is she okay with me here?" We weren't exactly besties, and Mel, my Werewolf friend in Wick's pack, had once warned me to watch my back where the she-bitch was concerned.

"She's not happy with the arrangement, but I'm still the Alpha of this pack." His voice steeled with his response. "We are capable of protecting you until you get on your feet. And the SRD will not look for you at your...ex's house."

My soul ached a little at the truth in his words. Why would the SRD look for me at Wick's? Most would assume he'd hate my guts. Part of him probably did.

"Andy." Wick ran his hand through his hair again. "You should also know..."

"We're going to mate to break your control over his wolf." A female voice fractured the night. Tall, willowy, and attractive in that model-skinny, sucked-on-a-lemon way, Christine stood in flashy clothes, probably designer, with a hand resting on her bony hip.

Her scent took longer to reach me than her words, and by then, my mind reeled so hard, the nauseating impact her scent signature normally had on me held little effect.

Wick and Christine mated? Or soon to be?

I'd never like any woman Wick chose, but Christine wasn't a good match for him. Had she been, Wick would've mated with her long before I flew into the picture. Why now? Was the pain of his wolf pining for mine so bad he was willing to tie his life indefinitely to *Christine*?

"Um, congratulations?" My gaze flicked to Wick.

He watched the street instead of us. "We should get you inside."

"Yes," hissed Christine. "Welcome to *our* home."

I smiled faintly at her. Too bad I couldn't shift my fingers into claws to swipe off her smug expression.

My mind ached, hollow, devoid of feras.

I climbed the stairs, each footstep weighing more than the last, and walked through the door of Wick's home. A niggling feeling crawled up my spine, like little goldfish pecking at the food on the surface of water.

Had I replaced one hell for another?

As Christine's innate scent swirled around me, I closed my eyes and braced myself for what was to come. Wick shucked off his shoes and brushed past me. "Make yourself at home. You'll be in the guest room at the end of the hall. It's Were-proofed. We'll lock you in at night for your safety."

"And ours." Christine's jeering tone in my ear acted like a screeching alley cat issuing a challenge. She stood beside me. "After the destruction you caused, it's more than a precaution."

Truth. Her words rang true. I squeezed my eyes tighter and clenched my fists. How many lives had I destroyed? My mind tried desperately to access and replay memories from my beast's warpath. "How many?"

"How many what?" she asked.

"How many innocent lives did I take?" The words burned my mouth. I'd killed before, but not innocents, not knowingly. I had to know the truth. Did I even deserve protection?

"Well..." Christine hesitated.

My eyes popped open to find her calculating gaze trained on my face.

"No one's sure—"

"None," Wick interrupted.

We spun to find him standing at the end of the hall. His formidable frame tense, his hands on his hips.

"None?" I sucked in a breath.

"You caused a lot of property damage and scared the shit out of people, but you harmed no one." He paused. "Well, aside from your attackers. You annihilated them."

An invisible weight lifted off my shoulders, and air rushed out of my lungs.

"There must've been enough of you left to stop the beast from outright chaos." His chocolate gaze flicked to Christine. His jaw clenched.

Christine stiffened beside me, and her thin lips compressed.

After an awkward silence and whatever cerebral conversation Christine and Wick had through their pack bond, Wick nodded at both of us and walked away.

"Whatever," Christine muttered, more to herself than to me. She flipped her perfectly coiffed hair. "Personally, I don't see why we're helping you. They say we need you to stand against the Pharaoh, but I just don't get it. Why should we fear him? He killed Lucien and set us free."

The Pharaoh was also responsible for the deaths of a lot of people, many not guilty of anything besides being in the wrong place at the wrong time. The Pharaoh's control over the area instead of Lucien's did not bode well for anybody, including the Werewolves. Christine was too short-sighted to see the big picture.

"Sleep well." Christine smirked, probably knowing perfectly well the nightmare-riddled rest I would get tonight.

I watched her bony ass saunter down the hall to follow Wick.

What she didn't know was I would find a little comfort tonight. The darkness still plagued me, but at least I wasn't a true monster.

No, I hadn't joined the ranks of the truly deplorable, but I still planned to cut my enemies down.

All of them. Every. Damn. One.

8

*S*trong fingers slid through my hair, coming to rest
on each cheek, cupping my face.

*"Beautiful," a silken voice whispered. A purr
rumbled through the air and vibrated against my body.
"Beautiful."*

*My eyes popped open, and the intensity of Tristan's
sapphire gaze bore into my soul.*

"Tristan," I breathed.

His lips tugged up at the corners.

*"Tristan..." My face heated. The tender expansion in
my chest, the one I associated with my love for the
Wereleopard Alpha, grew, almost painfully, and pushed
against my ribcage. The pressure squeezed my lungs.*

Tristan's smile froze. The corners dipped down.

His eyes widened.

*I wrenched back. My arms morphed into my beast
limbs, black and scaly, cradling a broken, dying man.
Oozing with blood, cold against my beast lap, his body*

racked with each shuddered breath. Would this be his last?

Please Feradea, No.

"Andy..."

A sob bubbled up my throat.

"Andy. I love...you."

And just like that, the warmth of sunlight I had grasped for only a brief moment slipped through my reach. Tristan's last breath shook through his body, his purr now gone, his warmth forever leached away. With the sweet air expelled from his mouth, his citrus and sunshine scent, the one laced with honeysuckles, the one that reminded me of sex on the beach, faded...faded and turned to something dark, something morbid and sad. Death.

"No," I whispered. The beast pushed.

"Noooooo!" My talons dug into his dead flesh. The beast flowed through me, over me, everywhere, as fury slid to replace the overwhelming sadness. The beast took over.

My resistance gave way as I surrendered to her.

I stepped within myself, sealed the steely doors on my loss and let her reign.

Together, we roared.

JOLTING AWAKE, I BOLTED UPRIGHT IN THE foreign bed. Warm hands squeezed my bare shoulders and gently pushed me into the bed.

"Shhh...Andy, you're having a nightmare. You're safe." Wick's whiskey and cream voice rolled over me and soothed the goosebumps prickling along my limbs. His scent soaked into my skin and settled my rattled nerves. "You're safe, and you're okay."

"There's nothing okay about any of this." My voice quivered. Weak. Pathetic. My stomach churned. I promised myself never to be a victim again. Yet, here I was, drenched in sweat, stuck to sheets while the remnants of my nightmare slipped away and left me drained. Soothed and comforted by my ex, whose heart I'd essentially ripped out and stomped on, made my self-loathing all the more poignant.

Wick's kind gaze widened as I turned to him.

I didn't need his pity. I didn't need, or want, any of this. "What are you doing here? I didn't pick you." I regretted the words the second they passed through my lips.

Wick recoiled. Something tender and vulnerable flashed across his gaze before it darkened. The burnt cinnamon of anger rolled off his body. His hands flew off my bare skin as if acid leached from my pores instead of sweat.

"I know you're hurting, Andy," Wick said, gaze hard. "So I'll forgive you for that, but don't forget who the real enemy is."

I sucked in a deep breath.

"Everyone will be here in an hour to discuss a plan. Get dressed. Things changed while you were gone." He jerked up off the bed and stomped away. The door shut softly against his palpable anger.

STAN, LUCUS, VERONIKA, WICK, CHRISTINE, Mel, and a few more of Wick's pack sat around the living room watching me, some with smiles, and some with scrutiny. I had an epiphany of what zoo animals must feel like. Clint also made an appearance, but he stood off to the side, sneering at his non-premium whiskey. Of course, Wick had the good stuff; he just didn't share it with Lucien's former human servant.

Apparently, Sid told the Witches not to call him until it was time for action. Or maybe he intended his comment solely for Veronika.

Hard to tell with that one.

I ignored Christine's glare and Wick's anger; choosing instead to focus on Stan's face as he talked, and Mel's warm presence beside me while she held my hand.

"So, I'm fired?" I asked Stan. My lungs constricted. Sure, I'd slaughtered a number of mercenaries in my apartment before going MIA for two months. Obviously, that warranted some sort of disciplinary action with the Vancouver Police Department. To fire me without notice seemed a bit too efficient for a VPD termination process. They loved paperwork, meetings and mandatory sympathy training.

"Not yet. But *if or when she gets her shit together...*" He deepened his voice and added a little sauce.

"Quoting Lafleur?" Lafleur was the precinct's chief, and he'd taken a huge, unprecedented step to hire me for my supernatural skills. The first known supe hired by the VPD since the Purge, which occurred over eighty years ago. And I'd blown it. Fuck.

Stan nodded. "There'll be some sort of disciplinary hearing. But I wouldn't get my hopes up."

My mind raced. Maybe there was a way to salvage my career. I was part goddess, after all. Surely, that could impress a few of the upper brass.

"I'm not sure any amount of sweet talking can convince them to keep you." Stan eyed me as if he read my thoughts.

Wick cleared his throat before commenting. "Being sweet is not exactly your strong point."

I winced, catching his tone and his reference to our earlier conversation.

"I'm not sure I can return, even if I wanted to..." I said.

Mel squeezed my hand. Christine smirked. Most looked away.

"Well, your nature is no longer a secret." Stan shifted in the large chair. He looked ready to spring up the second any of the Werewolves snarled at him.

I bristled at his words as unease crept up my spine.

"Like, at all," Mel piped in.

Stan nodded. "After you thrashed around like some hopped up wrecking ball, the *experts* started researching and appearing on the news. And then..." He trailed off, and his face pinched inward.

Not good. "And then?"

Stan took a deep breath. "And then the documentaries started. You'd already *disappeared* by then, but the crime scene at your apartment and the path of destruction leading away from it not only gave away your connection and identity, but the cause of your fury." He looked down at his laced fingers, obviously uncomfortable referring to Tristan's murder.

Or maybe the inhuman growl rippling through my throat made him twitchy.

"You're somewhat of a celebrity now," Jess, a female Werewolf in Wick's pack said. "Weirdos hold vigils outside your apartment, waiting for your return."

"Man, that must've pissed off the boys." The words fell out of my mouth. I froze.

As soon as my brain recalled my Witch neighbours, Ben especially, my body stiffened. A sickening weight sank in my stomach. This whole time I'd felt sorry for myself. I hadn't once thought of my Witch friends and what kind of trouble they might be in.

"Andy—" Stan said, then abruptly stopped.

Oh, Feradea! I knew. His tone and scrunched face told me everything. Ben and his coven had handed themselves over to the Elders for punishment over three months ago for a botched Demon summoning and failure to report. At the time, I agreed to be patient for a month or two, but if it took longer, I promised to get them.

"Oh, god. Oh, Feradea. I failed him. I failed them all." Everyone. Including Tristan. "Where is he? Where's Ben?"

Lucus hesitated before answering. "The Elders still have the entire coven."

I lurched from my seat and staggered toward the exit. Everyone stepped back and created a path. My head pounded. My vision swam. My heart lodged in my throat. I failed them.

Wick's strong hand closed around my upper arm, and stopped me a few yards from the front door. "What are you going to do?"

"I promised him! I promised I would come for him." I sagged against Wick. "I've already failed Tristan. I can't fail... I *need* to get them."

His hand relaxed its hold, his warmth soaked into my skin. "And you will, but not like this. He'll understand, Andy. You can't attack the Elders in your current condition," he whispered into my ear.

"Broken," I spat.

He hesitated. "Damaged. Take the time to heal and form a proper plan."

Wick's strong arms closed around me. His body relaxed and his burnt cinnamon scent smoothed away, replaced briefly by lavender and hope, before he shut it down. I clung to his shirt and his solid chest beneath, and cried as Wick continued to comfort me with his silent presence.

After an eon, the sobs eased and the pain withdrew, not gone, but cleared so I could think. The beast pressed against the barrier and for a split second, her wail trickled through my veins.

Had I imagined hearing her?

Could she be reached? Had the drugs finally worn off?

I needed her.

Beast? You there? I called out.

My core vibrated as if I tried to hula-hoop without the hoop, but no answer came.

Cat? I called for my mountain lion. Only silence answered. I'd gone through this before, but some sick compulsion drove me to try again, crying and hollering for my feras, one by one.

Red? Summoning the fox fera I'd dispelled long ago resulted in eerie quiet as well. My shoulders dropped. Surely, the drugs the SRD injected me with should've worn off by now. Or was this permanent?

I swallowed another sob before it bubbled out of my mouth.

"We'll find out where the Witches are, and when you're good, we'll make a plan," Lucus said somewhere behind me.

I stepped back. Wick's arms tightened briefly before releasing me. Christine's venomous glare bore into my face from over his shoulder. She clutched her fashion magazine with a death grip, knuckles white.

"What if I can't fix what they did to me?" I asked.

An ache seeded in the middle of my chest and grew outward. If I somehow managed to heal the damage the SRD inflicted on my nature, I had the means and allies to extract the Witches from the ultra-powerful Elders.

Stan came to stand beside me and rested his hand on my shoulder. "You'll fix it."

"What if I can't?" I snapped.

Silence filled the room. The traffic outside hummed with a constant rumble. Laughter from the nearby park trickled in, while everyone in Wick's house remained frozen.

The Andy they knew never doubted herself. The Andy they knew never admitted defeat.

"Then we revise the plan," Wick's voice rumbled, he squeezed my arm before walking away.

The group dispersed, and Clint moved from his corner toward the door. His silence for the majority of the meeting made my skin itch. I caught up to him before he escaped.

"Why are you and Allan really helping?" I asked.

Was it just because of the Pharaoh?

He paused with his hand on the door handle and turned to me. "Maybe we just want to see your pain."

I shook my head. Clint was his own brand of asshat, but his words didn't quite fit. "Not that."

Clint shrugged. "You've pointed out more than once how I like to break women."

Clint's previous comments and actions clicked into place. Yes, he was rough with the ladies. Even though they were willing participants, Clint held an unhealthy attitude toward women, and I despised him for it. I stepped forward. "I think you like to break women, so they don't have a chance to break you."

Something flickered across Clint's face. "You know nothing."

"I know damaged goods when I see it."

Clint snorted, but his eyes cut away and confirmed the truth. I reached out and touched his arm, which stiffened at the contact.

"Like recognizes like."

Clint turned to me, and something softened at the corner of his eyes before his lips formed a hard straight line. He slowly removed my hand. "If you're going to throw a pity party, I'm not attending."

"Fine. Why are you helping?"

Clint sighed and pulled the door open. "Because you're our best and only chance to take down the Pharaoh before he assumes control of the entire Lower Mainland and every supe within it."

I froze. Dangit, I kind of knew that, but his words sent my stomach twisting into a knot. Sweat broke out along my skin. Ben wasn't the only one counting on my recovery. Everyone did.

"Heal fast, Carus." He walked out the door and closed it softly behind him.

9

*S*harp *beast talons shredded through weak human flesh. Blood splattered against smooth obsidian scales and the soft black fur covering my belly. The life force of my victims trickled down my face.*

Dead. All of them dead. Ripped apart by my fury and rage. Useless guns lay strewn around their limp, ragged bodies. Their familiar scents drowned in blood and death. This group had attacked me before. The shirt of one of the shooters lay ripped open, exposing scars from a previous mountain lion attack.

In the centre of sprawled bodies, Tristan lay dying. His chest shuddered as he struggled to breathe and his Wereleopard nature tried desperately, vainly, and unsuccessfully, to heal the damage wrought by the machine guns.

In the distance, sirens wailed.

I stumbled to Tristan and gently collected him in my large beast arms, before shifting back to human.

His sapphire eyes opened to look at me with an unfo-

cused gaze. His mouth twitched in an attempt to smile. He coughed, and blood bubbled out to coat his lips.

I tried to breathe. I couldn't suck in any air. The oxygen lodged in my throat.

Stuck.

Smothered.

My eyes popped open. The remnants of my nightmare slid away as my brain reeled and attempted to make sense of...what?

A pillow-top mattress cushioned my body. Something large and soft covered my face. A familiar rosemary aroma filled the room. The scent that always smelled off, a little sour, as if her vindictive, jealous nature tainted her very essence.

"You should've died that day," Christine seethed, pressing the pillow down harder on my face. "It should've been you."

My arms flailed. I brought my legs up and kicked her off my body. She sprawled backward and fell off the bed.

I sat up, dragging in quick, ragged breaths. My vision blurred before clearing. Christine staggered to her feet and clutched a large pillow, skeletal fingers turning white from the pressure.

"You?" My brain clicked into gear. Mel's warning to watch myself. Multiple attacks from mercenaries. The last attempt, laden with their familiar scents as I brought them down, one by one, beside Tristan's dying body.

"You!"

Christine snarled, chucked the pillow to the side, and launched herself at me.

As a Werewolf, Christine possessed uncanny strength for a woman who looked like a sneeze would snap her in half. As a Shifter, stronger than a norm, yet weaker than a Were, my strength was dwarfed by hers. I had training on my side though.

And rage.

As fire raced through my veins and red stained my vision, and we grappled on the bed, I quickly gained advantage.

I'm going to kill this bitch, I hissed at Wick through mental communication. One Carus perk not stolen from me by the drugs.

With a combination of hand, elbow, and knee strikes, I knocked the wind out of Christine and sent her reeling back—far enough to allow me time to stand. My chest burned as I sucked in quick drags of air. My muscles ached from lack of use in the lab. My knuckles popped. The beast pressed against the barrier. Her caged roar echoed through my bones, but the artificial barrier held.

The cool night air blew through the open window and caressed my hot skin. I wouldn't shift to a falcon and fly away. Even if I could, no way would I let Christine live through this night. Every breath she took was one too many.

My lips twisted as I envisioned my claws ripping into her smooth, flawless, spa-pampered flesh.

"This won't be quick," I promised.

Christine scowled and shifted her weight forward.

She'd lunge low again. She always did.

Before she launched another attack, the door flew

open and slammed against the wall. Wick stepped into the room, his presence filling the doorway. Wearing only boxers, his muscle-rippled skin gleamed in the moonlight, and his bed-tussled hair stood in all directions.

"What the hell is going on?" Wick boomed. Christine jumped. Her gaze widened. She hesitated before turning her glare to me. A second later, she moved.

"No!" I screamed. I lunged forward, but she blew by me.

Christine ran and dove through the open window. Her body hit the ground, one story down, with a heavy thump.

I ran to the window and looked down. A prickling sensation enclosed my scalp and ran down my spine. Christine twisted to snarl at me. She lurched to her feet and shook out her limbs as they cracked back in place with her fast Were healing. I stood useless by the window and watched her run off into the night.

If I could shift, I would've followed, and she'd never get away.

"No." The sight of Christine alive and running while I stood pathetic and helpless to prevent it, boiled my blood and burned a place in my memory.

IO

Cool air from the open window travelled through the room. A warm hand clamped on my shoulder. I jumped.

"Andy, what the hell is going on?" Wick demanded.

I turned, muscles tense and ready to fight. His expression, a comical mix of anger, confusion, and concern, diffused the fire racing in my veins and cleared my red vision. I straightened and sucked in a number of deep breaths. "Don't mate with her."

Wick hesitated. "I already called it off."

All tension unexpectedly released from my muscles, and my limbs grew heavy, and weak. "Good," I sighed, and glanced back at the window. "I don't want you hurt from the backlash when I rip out her heart." *With my bare hands.*

"What the hell?" Wick growled.

Anger returned like the flip of an emotional switch. My pulse quickened as my vision clouded again. The very muscles craving a warm bath seconds ago, now screamed for action again. If my falcon had been present, she'd demand I peck out some eyeballs. "She's the one. She's responsible for Tristan's death."

Wick's eyebrows pinched in. "That makes no sense. She was thrilled you picked him over me."

My hands gripped the hem of my shirt and twisted. A loud ripping sound filled the room as I tore it to shreds, acting out what I'd really like to do to Christine. "He wasn't the target."

Wick's gaze widened. Then understanding hit. His mouth pinched. His jaw clenched. A growl rumbled from his chest, and his gaze flashed Werewolf yellow. His muscles tensed as if, with one word, he'd leap through the window and run after her.

Good. Though I doubt he'd catch her now, even if he sent the pack to track her.

"She tried to kill you," he stated.

Not sure why he bothered saying it out loud. Her actions spelled everything out.

"Three times." Twice through mercenaries, and now the last time on her own. And like a coward, she'd attacked me while I slept and was most vulnerable. I moved away from the window and the cool breeze.

Wick's hands folded into two clenched fists. He vibrated as burnt cinnamon rolled off him in waves.

"This is my fault," he said.

Unexpected laughter barked out of me. "This is not on you. At all."

Wick cast me a pained look, and paced in front of

me. "When you first lost control and started rampaging, I tried to get to you first. Even tried to tranq you, but the one shot I got in wasn't enough, and you got away. When I caught up to you again, I was too late and without backup." He shook his head as he looked down at his trembling fists. "I watched the SRD take you."

No longer flushed with rage, my skin grew cold and clammy. I folded my arms across my chest and looked for a sweater. Anything to buy time from my reeling thoughts.

A distant memory, one of detecting Wick's delectable scent during a rage-fuelled rampage, flickered through my mind. At the time, I dismissed the possibility of Wick's presence. Why on Earth would he care about the woman who broke his heart?

The answer smacked me in the face.

He never stopped caring. Heck, his spot on my rescue team confirmed it. My scalp prickled with warmth. My mouth grew dry. What should I say?

"I appreciate the effort, I do," I mumbled. "But what does that have to do with Christine?"

"She was angry. I sensed her hatred through the pack bond. I thought she was pissed I tried to help you, and she was, a bit, but it must've also been from her failed attempt on your life. I should've seen it. I should've known."

"Still not your fault." I took an extra-large sweater from the dresser and pulled it over my head. It smelled of rosemary and sugar. The clothing must've come from Wick's personal stash.

72

He shook his head again. "Even before I told her I wanted to wait on mating, she knew. She saw it, felt it, when I hugged you earlier. My heart's not in it. Never was. And my wolf chose you a long time ago."

The mattress dipped as I dropped onto it. "Well, that answers why she attacked me tonight."

Wick nodded and sat beside me, fists still clenched. "Your death would've hurt me, but it wouldn't have changed things with Christine. Those feelings were never there for me, not before you and I met, and not after. I guess, in my grief, I let her convince me otherwise. Seeing you again made me realize how pointless mating with Christine would be, and how unhappy it would make me. It would destroy the pack."

"And she sensed it all through the pack bond."

"Exactly."

I reached out and squeezed one of his clenched fists. A pack bond didn't work like mind reading, it transmitted emotions, not thoughts. Wick really had no way of knowing the extent of Christine's hatred, nor her plans. "Still not your fault."

"I wish I believed that." Wick stood and shook out his limbs. "Come on. I have another guest room."

I followed as he walked stiffly through the house. Sure, he could've handled the Christine situation better, but I couldn't, and wouldn't, hold that against him. My rejection had cut him deeply. Who made logical decisions when they were hurting?

Certainly not me.

The only thing I knew for sure, logical or not, Christine had to die. I wouldn't rest until I made her pay, painfully, for the life she stole from me.

II

The cold, unfeeling stone stared back at me. *Tristan Leonardo Kayne.* The date of his death, a red flag to the angry beast lurking inside. Freshly laid grass and soil covered the rectangular patch in front of the gravestone. The scent of his body, the citrus and sunshine laced with honeysuckle, had diffused away long ago. Departed with his soul and everything that made Tristan who he was.

Did his parents name him after Leonard Da Vinci? No wonder he never wanted to tell me his middle name. Although, he should've known I'd think it was awesome.

I kneeled in front of the stark stone and placed the roses at the base.

"You shouldn't have left me." I trailed my hands lightly along the smooth stone as if it was Tristan's porcelain face. "You shouldn't be dead."

Tears trickled down my cheeks, and I sniffed as my nose began to run. The moisture from the soil soaked into my black pants. Knee-high black boots protected me only a little from the dampness, and although the thick jacket with its fur-lined hood battled the cold, it did nothing about the ice emanating from within me.

"You should be full of life and laughter." I leaned forward until my forehead butted against the cold rock.

Stan brought me to this place of death. He'd picked me up from Wick's house and without a word, headed toward the cemetery. "You need to grieve," he'd said. "Not as a beast on a death-mission, but as a human."

Although misery and stiff air clung to his pores, Stan seemed a lot better than he had in a long time. He left me at the gravesite to visit his wife's on the opposite side of the cemetery.

The tears flowed unhindered down my face and dripped off my nose and chin to splatter on the grass. I breathed deeply. Grass and loam. Grass and loam.

A sob shuddered through my body, and my lungs constricted. As if someone tied a rope around my heart and tugged it tight, the pain intensified and burned.

I'd never feel Tristan's arms around me again—no kisses along my neck, no warm hand holding mine, no body heat to caress my back as we lay spooning in the early hours of the day.

I twisted a little to take in more of the surroundings. Tristan's prowl had chosen a plot on the top of a hill, where the sun hit for most of the day.

Tristan loved sunshine. He loved basking in its warmth. The prowl made an excellent choice.

Pain lanced through my lungs as they constricted

again. I drew in unsteady breaths. Tristan was gone, and it was all my fault. Did his prowl blame me? Hate me?

Probably. They should.

The cool air drifted by, bringing messages of the land and the emotions of others visiting the cemetery. I closed my eyes and envisioned Tristan beside me. What would I tell him? What should I say?

"I love you," I whispered.

His face would've brightened like it had the first and last time, the only time, I said those words to him.

"I miss you," I sobbed.

The cold ground provided little comfort as I curled up on Tristan's grave, unable to say the one thing I should—goodbye.

Unwilling.

Time passed. The sun faded. The air turned from refreshing to cold. The birds sang their lament to the dying light. How long had I lain here? How could I possibly leave?

The grass rustled as a couple made their way toward me. Their familiar citrus and sunshine scents gave away their identities—Angie and Olly, from Tristan's prowl. Olly, second in command, liked me as his Alpha's soon-to-be mate. Angie on the other hand... Well, she didn't.

I stiffened on the cold ground as I continued to lay curled up on Tristan's grave. Had they come here seeking revenge?

Their scents were closed off and gave nothing away of their intent.

"If you came to kill me, don't bother," I mumbled into the dirt. "I'm already dead." *Inside.*

They stopped walking a few feet away. Olly stiff and motionless. Angie huffed and shuffled her feet.

"We're not here to harm you." Her soft, bell-like voice trilled, but for once, it didn't grate against my skin, and I no longer had a mountain lion in my head hissing at her.

I half-rolled over. They stood far enough away to offer respect, instead of appearing intimidating or threatening.

A pint-sized doll with unnatural curves stared down at me, her perfectly coifed hair, slicked back and more severe than usual. With a grim expression and stiff posture, Angie didn't appear to have murder on her mind. She had loved Tristan, and I always suspected she loved him as more than her Alpha, but we'd never physically fought over him.

Olly shifted his weight from where he stood beside Angie. A beefcake with no neck, Olly looked like he spent every spare minute in the gym. In actuality, he spent day and night working for Tristan and his security company. Heat rose off his shaved head into the cold air, and his soft gaze flicked briefly up to meet mine.

With their heads bowed and hands clasped behind their backs, they showed me something I'd never seen from them before—deference. They postured as they would toward their Alpha or their Alpha's mate.

My eyes stung. I blinked rapidly and staggered to my

feet. Brushing my pants with both hands did little to knock off the wet dirt, but I had to try.

"We came to give you this." Olly pulled a thick, business envelope from his jacket's inside pocket and held it out.

"Thanks." I stepped forward and plucked the envelope from his hand. It smelled of Tristan. I clutched it to my chest.

Angie cleared her throat. "I know we never got along, but you should know—" Her voice trembled and cut off.

My head snapped up.

Angie's full lips trembled and her eyebrows dipped down. She blinked rapidly. She took a deep breath, stared at her feet, and continued. "You should know, Tristan loved you. Very much. We could all feel it through the bond."

More tears leaked out of my eyes, but I ignored them. Tristan had said those words to me. Only twice. They were the last words to slip past his beautiful lips.

"You helped him continue on after Ethan's rule over us. You helped the whole prowl heal, whether you know it or not," Olly added, his tone deep.

Angie sniffed and nodded. "He was content when he died."

I sucked in a breath.

"He was thankful to protect you and calm. At peace. He died for something and someone he believed in."

I winced. My skin prickled, and my lungs shrank. Tristan sacrificed everything for me. Was I even worth it?

"If there's anything you need," Olly said. "Let us know."

I nodded and bit my lip. Either that, or start crying again. The Wereleopards inclined their heads in another show of respect before turning and walking away. I clung to Tristan's letter the entire time I watched Angie and Olly carefully navigate around gravesites, and make their way to the cemetery's exit.

Glancing around provided no intel on Stan's location. With my phone safely nestled in my pocket, I could call anytime. I glanced at the letter. My hands grew clammy, the sweat moistening the envelope to give it a sticky feel.

With a deep breath, I forced my tense muscles to relax and ripped open the seal. The cemetery's lighting, the early evening light and my Shifter nature provided me with the means to read the handwritten words.

My Love,

If you're reading this, then my worst nightmare has sadly come to pass. I wanted to stay with you forever, for always, but it must not have been written in the stars for us. I am so thankful I found you. Though I won't know when you receive this letter, I know with absolute certainty I spent the rest of my days in supreme happiness.

What you didn't know about me, and what I dreaded telling you before we mated, was my age. I am, was, very long in the tooth. Some would say too long. I have lived to see all three of Catherine de' Medici's sons become kings of France.

Though we hate to admit it, leopards are no different than house cats in some ways. We seek solitude when it's our time to depart this Earth. Before my leopard set eyes on you, he longed to leave and find our final resting place. My time has long been up, but Ethan prevented me from ending my life, and then I met you.

You breathed new life into me, and my prowl. You gave me a purpose, a goal, and time to set things right. My prowl almost broke under Ethan's rule, and because of you, we all had time to heal and mend the ties that bind us together. I no longer craved the eternal slumber.

I wanted to stay with you forever, surrounded with your love, until the end. We never know when Feradea will call for us, though. But one thing I am certain of is whenever she calls for me, it will now be too soon.

Your happiness is the most important thing, as is your survival. Survive me.

If we've mated, you'll feel the pull to join me. Please don't. Resist the call. A mate isn't half of one soul, but a match for it. The chances of coming across a gift like you in a lifetime, even one as long as mine, are extremely rare to say the least. To find two, is almost unheard of.

Don't squander the offering fate has given you, against all odds.

Live. Find happiness. Find love. Enjoy a long, full life, and know I will always love you.

~Tristan

SOMETIME DURING MY READ, I'D SAT DOWN NEXT to Tristan's tombstone. My hands dropped, and the letter fell. I shut my lids over stinging eyes. My thoughts spun. Time slowed around me, as if only the letter, now blurring through tears, existed.

He'd wanted to die? He knew he'd essentially die if I'd chosen Wick over him? And he never said a word. Instead, he kept quiet to remove as much pressure as possible.

That was so…Tristan.

I blinked back tears. My breath formed little white puffs in the frigid night. I ran my hand down Tristan's gravestone, ignoring the tears as they now streamed down my face.

The words of his letter replayed in my head, over and over as the cold continued to attack my skin and seep into my bones.

Whenever she calls for me, it will now be too soon.

Tristan was gone, and I could do nothing about it.

Except accept it. Cherish the moments, though short-lived, that we shared together, and try to do as he suggested—enjoy a long, full life.

I snorted.

I had one single focus right now and it had nothing to do with my happiness. Christine needed to die. Vengeance needed to be served.

But there was something I could do now.

Deep breath.

My heart punched against my breastbone so loud my hearing became consumed with the thudding sound. My body warmed as if Tristan held me in his strong arms, knowing what I planned to say, and providing me with the courage and strength to say it. "Goodbye, Tristan."

A sob escaped and more tears fell. I swiped at my running nose. The rope tied around my chest that tugged and burned pulled hard until it snapped and fell away. My lungs expanded, filling with cold air. The ice-like sensation crept through my nasal passage, cleansing not only my body, but my soul.

A few more papers were included with Tristan's handwritten letter. A copy of his Last Will and Testament with a highlighted section. He gave almost everything to the new Alpha of his prowl—Olly. It made sense. His lifetime accumulation of wealth belonged with his prowlmates.

To me, he left an unlimited lifetime of services from Kayne Security Solutions, a share in the company, and a bulk payment from his savings. My eyes widened at the estimated worth.

I'd never have to work again.

A picture of my partner Stan's snarled smile flashed through my memory. And my stomach sank. I shook my head. I'd make that decision later, save that fight for another day.

The last paper made my breath catch in my throat. An icy chill crept along my spine and goosebumps tingled my flesh as they spread across my skin.

A name and an address.

Tristan had highlighted the name in yellow and in the margin, with his lovely scrolling handwriting, he'd written in blue ink, "Your brother."

12

Cold and numb, my mind reeled as I staggered to the cemetery's entrance. A Norse god lookalike stood sombrely in tight-fitting denim jeans and a warm bomber-style winter jacket. His hands were shoved in the pockets, but he quickly pulled them free when he saw me approach. Frosted air plumed from Wick's nose as he exhaled into the cold. Behind him sat his twin cab truck—engine already running with a loud hum, as if he'd anticipated my arrival.

I pulled up short.

Wick shifted his weight from foot to foot and looked unsure of what to do with his hands.

"Where's Stan?" my voice croaked, worn, and tired from being wrung through with emotion.

"Got called in. Asked me to drive you back."

I cringed. "How long have you been waiting?"

His eyebrows pinched in, and he rounded his shoulders as if shielding himself from the cold. With his Were heating system, this night would have little impact on him. "Long enough."

Great. With his Werewolf hearing, he'd probably heard every sob and sniffle, including the Wereleopards' visit and those moments when I thought I was alone and spoke to Tristan's grave.

I cringed, again. "Sorry."

His gaze softened, and the tension around his mouth eased. "You have nothing to be sorry for."

I nodded. Cold air wound around me, crisp and cutting. A great night for flying. The sun had set behind the trees and the clear sky turned to midnight blue.

"Come on." He stretched his hand out. "Let's get you home—" He winced.

Not the best choice of words. I smiled, or at least tried to. My stiff face twitched, and the corners of my mouth remained tight. When I took Wick's hand, he squeezed in response and walked me to the passenger side of his truck.

The ride back to Wick's house in Kits was long and quiet, Wick smart enough to leave me to my thoughts.

A brother. I already knew he existed, but hadn't built enough emotional strength to look into who he was, or whether this sibling survived the Purge and still lived.

Tristan found him.

He probably kept the information of my brother's whereabouts to himself until I was ready. I let out a long shuddered breath.

Wick glanced at me as he navigated the late rush hour Vancouver traffic.

My brother.

Would he want to meet me?

How come he never attempted to find me? I'd been a baby, not capable of remembering a sibling, but from Tristan's recollection, my brother had been a young boy, old enough to know I existed.

Maybe he wanted to forget. He would've come home to our dead parents and my disappearance. My nature had nothing to do with the murders, but I'd vanished. Maybe he grieved me, thinking I died that day. Maybe he blamed me.

Another deep breath. I hugged Tristan's letter to my chest. Wick's gaze flicked over to me a number of times during the drive, furtive, sideways glances, mostly aimed at my face, but sometimes to the papers I clutched.

"Tristan wrote me a letter," I whispered.

Wick tensed, his hands tightened on the steering wheel. He nodded, shoulder-checked, and made a right turn. "Want to talk about it?"

I pursed my lips.

"Might help." He turned down the next street and glanced at me again.

You're my captor, not my therapist. Words I'd spoken to Wick from a long time ago echoed in my head. I had opted not to confide in him that night, despite the overwhelming urge to. The assassin life was a lonely one, and although the SRD provided shrinks, I never trusted them. They might claim to maintain confidentiality, but one slip about my beast nature, and I'd end up in the lab.

Well, been there, done that.

"Andy?"

I hesitated. One flick of his dark brown gaze, and my resolve to remain an iron vault crumbled. Wick would keep my secrets. "He said...he wrote... God, do you have any idea how old he was?"

Wick nodded, again. His jaw clenched. "I have an idea."

Oh, that's right. They'd fought once. Tristan had been winning and by more than a little. Both Alphas. Both predators. But age brought power in the supernatural world, Weres included. Had they been similar ages, it would've been a closer match. If I hadn't intervened, Wick wouldn't sit beside me today. Probably not something the big bad wolf liked to think about.

Wick slowed for a red light and turned to me. "Is his age the reason you smell of lemon and pepper?" He named the smells associated with shock.

I shook my head, and ignored the dull ache in my bones. "No."

The light turned green, and Wick refocused on the road.

"And along with money, he left me the address and name of my brother."

Wick slammed on the brakes. My body whipped forward. I flung out my hands to brace against the dash. Cars honked and swerved around us, but Wick's wolf-yellow gaze remained trained on me. Lemon and pepper tinged with burnt cinnamon rolled off his skin. It started to rain outside. The pitter-patter of large raindrops hitting the windshield added to the commotion outside.

"Brother?"

I nodded. "Turns out Tristan's history with me goes a bit farther back, but that's not the point." I had no desire to tell Wick about Tristan's involvement in my parents' deaths. At least, not right now. It would only aggravate his wolf more, and he was already on the edge of control.

"You have a brother?" He flicked on the wipers.

Typical Vancouver. The clear sky never lasted long. "I have a brother."

Wick pressed the gas and maneuvered the truck down the road and away from angry motorists.

"What are you going to do?" he asked. We'd once talked about siblings, and how I longed for them, so he understood the impact of this news.

I shrugged, and idly played with the armrest. "If I don't go, I'll never know and always regret it."

The rain picked up and splattered heavily against the windshield. The wipers couldn't move fast enough to clear the field of sight completely.

"But?" Wick prompted.

"I'm kind of on a revenge path right now."

"Revenge is a dish best served cold and you need to heal to be effective, anyway," Wick said. "But that's not really what's making you hesitate, is it?"

Wick was right.

"What if he's dead? What if he hates me? Or blames me for our parents' deaths? What if... What if I don't like him? I'm not sure I can take any more heartache right now."

Wick's chin dipped, and he turned down his street, driving the truck up the driveway without saying a word. The engine idled with a loud hum as we sat in silence. The rain continued to hammer the cab of the truck.

I finally turned to Wick and found his gaze had returned to their melted chocolate depths, the wolf receding and relinquishing control.

"So?" I asked.

"So?"

"You're not going to tell me what you think?"

Wick shook his head. "I'm not going to tell you what to do or what I would do in your place. This is your life, Andy. Your choice. You already made the decision not to have me as a part of it."

I recoiled. His words little stabs to the body. I'd made that choice because I thought it would be better for both of us. What the hell? Why had he offered to listen if he planned to just throw it in my face?

Wick turned off the truck, popped open the door and hopped out. I mirrored his actions. The rain instantly doused me in cold water, my hair and clothes plastered to my clammy skin.

"Wick..."

He halted halfway up the driveway.

I caught up to him, and we stood in the same place

we'd shared our first kiss. The memory glinted behind my eyes, and a flicker of recognition flashed across Wick's expression. My stomach twisted.

"Wick."

He shook his head and peered down at me. His hair slick against his face. His eyes flashing yellow again. "I don't want your pity."

"It's not pity, it's—"

"Do you think this is easy for me?" Wick asked. "Knowing that you chose him over me?"

"Wick." I reached out to sooth him, but he jerked his arm away. "You know why I couldn't pick you."

"No. I don't." The rain threatened to drown out his words.

"Yes, you do. Lucien kept using us against each other. Would you have wanted to keep going on like that? He would've hurt you repeatedly—"

"Yes!"

"What?" The torrential downpour hammered down on us, splattering hard against my face.

"Yes, I would have. I would've allowed that monster to gut me repeatedly. And yes, I know he threatened that. I would have endured any pain if it meant we were together, that you were mine. Anything, Andy."

Cool prickles spread across my skin as my stomach lurched. My vision wavered. The truth of his statement crept along my bones, found my heart, and squeezed relentlessly.

"But you wouldn't have done the same," Wick whispered. "And that's what cuts the deepest." He stalked away from me. The heavy rain parted for his exit and continued to slam down in sheets and bounce off the pavement. Thunder rolled in the near-distance, and water ran down my face, but all that consumed me was the sound of my pulse beating against my eardrums and the empty ache in my chest.

13

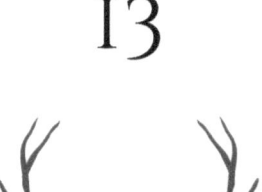

After a scalding hot shower and a long pity cry, the weight pushing down on my shoulders lightened, and I mustered enough courage to venture downstairs for food. Part of me wanted to forgo eating altogether. Who cared that the last thing I ate was a blueberry bagel slathered with butter for breakfast? The other part of me, namely my stomach, groaned in protest and threatened to claw its way out of my gut if I didn't shove something down my gob soon.

Maybe Wick would already be in bed, and I could avoid an awkward encounter.

As I tiptoed down the stairs and turned the corner to the kitchen, I realized my error.

Wick stood in the unlit living room, staring out the window at the stormy night sky. The blinds were up, and the curtains pushed to the side. Lightning flashed across the sky to cast shadows across the room and Wick's body. With his back toward me, arms crossed in front of his chest, legs shoulder width apart, he cut a fine figure, even in the sparse lighting.

Wick's body tensed, and my plans to sneak unnoticed through the house were thwarted.

"It wasn't fair for me to dump that on you," he said, still facing away. "I'm sorry. You are going through enough as it is without dealing with my crap."

I stiffened and contemplated an escape route. What could I say? I wasn't even sure how I felt. "It's okay, Wick. I know I hurt you, and I'm sorry."

He nodded, his back still facing me. "Have you decided what you're going to do?"

"Find my brother."

Wick slowly turned to face me, his face a hard unreadable mask. "Let me help you."

My thoughts reeled. Why would he possibly want to help me? I didn't deserve him and his presence only served to taunt me with what I would never have. "I searched the address on the Internet. It's up north. A couple of ferry hops or a flight away."

"And who knows what awaits for you on the other end."

I glanced around the room. Given his anger, why would he help me? "Wick—"

"Andy. Let me assist you with this. We might no longer be together, but I still care for you and don't want to see you taken down because you were blindsided. The SRD will be after you, now, too. And..." He trailed off and turned toward the lightning-stricken sky.

And I'm vulnerable.

He didn't need to say the words. They hung heavy as the unspoken truth in the room. Without shifting abilities, or my beast, I would rely solely on my combat and weaponry skills—good enough to take out some threats, but not all, certainly not an SRD retrieval task force, or an angry mob of Shifters. After silence settled on the room like a lead blanket, Wick turned away from the night sky and studied me again, jaw clenching.

I watched dark shadows play along the hard lines of his face. "By land or air?"

Wick's expression cracked a little as his lips tugged up in one corner. "Land. More feasible escape routes."

I returned his smile while internally my mind raced at the possibility of needing escape routes. I hated when Wick was right.

THE WINDSWEPT, UNSPOILED ROCKY SHORE drew my attention as I waited for Wick to come back from checking us into the hotel. The dark water lapped gently against the rocks and reflected the bright stars above. Had my falcon still cohabitated my mind, she would've screeched for release, to soar above the dense forest and picturesque shoreline.

I sighed. That wasn't going to happen. Not now, and maybe not ever.

On the remote north end of Vancouver Island, Port

Hardy was the last hint of structured civilization. I didn't really want to stop here. I cursed the ferry schedule. What an unfair interlude. Forget all that crap about life being the journey not the destination. I wanted to see the end game. Now.

The long, awkward, four-hour drive, in near silence with Wick might have something to do with my motivation to reach the end. I had a lot of time to contemplate —everything from how to deal with the loss of Tristan to how Wick's speech had evolved to use contractions now. And if I dwelled on that thought, I had to acknowledge how his way of talking had been changing for quite some time.

A guilty lump sank in my stomach. Wick had made an effort to improve himself, probably for me, and I hadn't even noticed. What an ass.

I didn't deserve him, and Wick finally figured this out. Amidst my thoughts, I couldn't shake the itch Wick impatiently waited to get rid of me, like he only carried out this good deed because of some misplaced belief of responsibility, and when he completed his task, he was free. Free of me.

Ugh.

The wind sliced past me, and I folded my arms across my chest. Nine hours of sleep before we could pick up our journey again.

Wick's soft footsteps fell on the frosted grass behind me. "Got the rooms. Ready?"

I nodded and hopped off the large rock. When I reached Wick, he handed me a key card.

"Our rooms are next to each other." He turned to walk with me toward the hotel.

We continued to stroll in silence, our feet crunching the frozen ground, until we reached the side entrance of the building. Wick leaned forward to get the door. The rustle of gravel behind us sent a silent alarm.

I spun in time to dodge a wire around the neck. Adrenaline pumped through my body. I slipped to the side and delivered a blow to the unknown man's solar plexus. His dark gaze widened. With a number of swift, efficient strikes, the man collapsed to the ground.

My muscles screamed in tune with my lungs.

Sweat broke across my brow.

Shadows moved across the building. There were more. Another large man with a shaved head and blond eyebrows leapt from the night and attacked. My arms groaned as I blocked the assassin's attack and sank his own knife into his thigh. As he folded forward, I yanked the weapon out and plunged it deep into his chest.

I spun around.

Wick stood over three more accomplices. Their eyes open and glazed over, their necks at odd angles. Without a word, Wick plucked the bloody knife from my shaking hand—from exhaustion, not nerves—and took care of the unconscious attacker at my feet. He'd never get up now.

"Think we should move?" I asked, my skin prickling.

"No," he grunted, and pulled the bodies to make a neat pile. "We're in the middle of nowhere. They won't send another team tonight, and by the time the next retrieval unit arrives, we'll be gone."

"They might figure out where we are headed and have someone in place to ambush us when we disembark."

Wick shrugged. "That doesn't affect whether we stay here tonight or not. One step at a time. Besides, for that to happen, we have to assume this retrieval team followed protocol and reported our position before they attacked. I'd bet your secret stash of chocolate-covered almonds, they didn't anticipate losing. No one knows we're here."

"Back off the almonds."

Wick smirked and held his hands up in mock surrender.

I scowled at him and bent to lift one of the bodies. "Let's get this done."

We worked in silence to dump the bodies off a nearby abandoned dock, the night peacefully silent. If anyone saw us, they wisely kept their mouths shut.

This time when we approached the hotel, nothing significant happened, and we walked through the side entrance without incident.

"That's you." Wick nodded at my door. He hesitated. "Will you be okay?"

Normally, I'd fling an insult at anyone who dared suggest I couldn't be alone, but Wick had already woken to my screaming nightmares. My limbs shook from the overexertion, despite having only hauled one body to the water while Wick juggled the remaining four.

"I think so," I lied.

His nose flared, but he didn't comment.

"You don't have to do this, you know."

His brows pinched in. "Do what?"

"Be nice to me."

"Andy," he said in warning.

"I'm serious. You're not responsible for me. I'm not your problem."

Wick stiffened, and his chocolate gaze turned cold. "Do you always spit in the face of kindness?"

My shoulders dropped. "I'm not trying to be a bitch. I know this can't be easy for you. I'm trying to let you off the hook."

"Well, stop." Wick swiped his card, and the lock clicked open. He turned the handle and pushed in the door. He paused and turned stiffly toward me. "If you need me, you know where I am."

I nodded numbly. My limbs grew heavy at my sides. The world around us seemed to slow down as unsaid words hung between us. "Goodnight, Wick."

"Goodnight."

I copied Wick's actions and stepped into the stale air of my hotel room. The silence weighed down on my shoulders. I hesitated and turned back. Back to what? Where would I go? With a deep breath, I forced my muscles to relax and let the solid door close behind me, trapping me in a quiet tomb. With the room so still, the air seemed to buzz around as I got ready for bed. Meditation did little to settle my nerves.

After staring at the ceiling, and tossing my sheets this way and that as I sought a more comfortable position, I gave up and bolted from the bed. Pacing back and forth on an imaginary fifteen-foot runway, I bit my lip as my mind raced around with empty thoughts. If Wick hadn't been with me, the retrieval team would've kicked my ass. Fatigued muscles still ached. I would've lost and ended up in another SRD compound, or worse, in the Pharaoh's control.

I shuddered.

The hair on the back of my neck remained stiff and uncomfortable, sending chills and unease.

Vulnerable.

I was vulnerable. Not safe. No feras in my head.

No Tristan beside me. *Alone.*

My stomach rolled, and I picked up my pace. What was I doing here? I should be out looking for Ben. Or figuring out what the Pharaoh planned.

I paused.

Or killing shit.

I certainly shouldn't be pacing in a three-star hotel room.

A sharp knock on my door stopped me in my tracks. I held my breath and waited. The knocking stopped after three taps. Rosemary and sugar squeezed through the less than stellar seals of the hotel door.

Wick.

What did he want? He knocked again.

I turned toward the entrance and paused by the door.

"Andy." Wick spoke softly. No need for him to shout with my Shifter hearing and bad seals.

"Yes?"

"I hear you pacing. Can I come in?"

What the hell could he do about it? I swallowed my cutting words. He was trying to be nice, to be a friend when I had few.

I sighed, unlatched the door, and swung it open. Wick shifted back on his heels.

I waited.

He ran his hand through his blond hair.

"I didn't realize I was stomping that loudly," I muttered and moved to the side.

Wick stepped in, and I closed the door behind him. "In your defence, the walls are paper thin." He offered a half smile. "The couple in the room on the other side of mine are having a lot more fun than either of us."

Thin walls and Were hearing meant little privacy.

"Couldn't sleep?" Wick's brows pinched together. What the heck? We'd barely been in our rooms long enough for me to attempt sleep.

"Thought a bit of pacing would tire me out."

"Andy."

Geez. He said my name as if it activated an internal truth serum. I stared at my feet.

"You've been pacing for hours."

"Hours? Bullshit." My head snapped up and met Wick's serious gaze. Well, dang. I yanked my phone from my pocket and checked the screen. No shit. I'd wasted almost three hours of sleeping time.

I sighed and plunked my butt heavily on the edge of the bed. Wick sat beside me, the mattress dipping under his weight. He folded his hands on his lap. "You haven't slept well since we got you out."

"It's so quiet. So empty."

"The room?"

"My head."

Wick paused as he contemplated my words. "You miss your feras?"

"I feel weak and vulnerable and alone without them." Instead of my body running into a hyper drive of wariness, my tired muscles slackened and my arms hung loose. My pulse slowed to a healthy, normal pace.

"You're not alone, Andy."

I started to protest, to explain what I meant, but Wick turned to me and the seriousness of his gaze trapped my words in my throat.

"I know it may feel that way," he said. "But you'll get your feras back, and you have friends, people who care about you. You're never truly alone."

He hesitated before reaching out and placing his palm on my chest, over my heart, not in a sexual way, but in a tender and sincere gesture.

"You will always hold those you've loved and lost here." He tapped my chest. "They will always be with you."

Tristan will always be with you.

I blinked rapidly and squeezed my eyes shut. No crying. I will not cry. I'd already lost it once around Wick. *Keep it together.*

Wick removed his warm hand and stood. "Come on. Get into bed."

My mouth opened, but he growled.

Growled. Going all Alpha on me, and not allowing any protest. My wolf would've loved this.

I snarled but did as he said. He pulled the blanket to my chin and walked around the room, flicking off the lights before locking the door and shucking off his shoes. The bed dipped again as he climbed on to rest beside me, on top of the sheets, a giant Werewolf paperweight. The familiarity of the moment pinged a distant memory, one from a lifetime ago, one from the moment when I started to fall for the Alpha Werewolf who lay beside me. He rested on his back with his head on his folded arms. So close, yet so far away.

"Go to sleep," his whiskey and cream voice vibrated the air. "You're safe and not alone."

His protective presence reassured the part inside of me twitching with uncertainty and anxiety. My lids grew heavy, and the energy leached from my limbs as I sank into the mattress.

14

The mist parted as the ferry pulled into the bay toward Skidegate Landing, the water so still the surface appeared smooth as glass. A recording blared through the speakers, and the announcer asked everyone to return to their vehicles on the car decks below for disembarking. I wasn't ready.

With the crisp ocean air slicing past my cheeks and whipping through my hair, I closed my eyes and inhaled the salty atmosphere, relishing the welcoming smell where forest met ocean—heavy scents of Sitka spruce, red cedar, shore pine, hemlock, and alder mixed with water-logged sand, rich soil, and dense moss—the signature smell of the untamed North Coast of British Columbia.

Home.

I shook my head at the random thought. My mind played tricks on me, drawing its own conclusion because a brother roamed around these old growth forests somewhere.

It.

Like my brain was a separate entity. When I'd shared the vacuous space with three nut-job feras, it certainly felt that way. They all wanted different things and pulled in opposing directions.

But now... Now, I had no excuse.

The ocean lapped the sides of the ferry. Cloaked in the earthy scents, foreign, yet familiar, I couldn't completely disregard the suggestion of home. As streams of mist curled around the vessel, and the cold air sank into my bones, the restless part of me—the one on edge from the loss of my feras and the constant feelings of vulnerability—settled. A wave of calm lathed my nerves with each drag of air. My shoulders sank and the stiffness flowed from my tense muscles.

"We should head down." Wick's raspy voice sounded behind me.

He'd silently stood behind me this entire time, like a stone guardian keeping vigil, and protecting me from potential danger. Or maybe he worried I'd jump.

The only real danger on this trip so far had been the falling missiles from the seagulls. My falcon would've loved teaching them a lesson. She hated seagulls.

My stomach twisted.

Falcon would've screeched at the birds and demanded release. My mind, however, remained quiet, and I found my head not nearly as entertaining or comforting.

The attack at the hotel had amounted to little more than a few sore muscles and one nasty bruise on my forearm. If Wick hadn't been there, the damage would've been more formidable.

"Andy?" Wick leaned in.

I turned and faced him. His chocolate gaze searched my face. For what? Hopefully not answers, because I had none. I nodded anyway, walked past him, and headed toward the car deck.

THE HAIDA GWAII.

The unceded territory of the Haida First Nation. The indigenous people from this area were known for their nautical prowess in canoes, beautifully told myths, and artfully constructed totem poles. Historically, they raided villages along the coast so proficiently the other groups feared the sound of their war drums.

An influx of small pox and other diseases from foreigners in the 1800s brought their success to a tragic end. Now abandoned and desolate villages lined the coasts, virtually reclaimed by the harsh elements and wild nature of the forest.

Some called the Haida the "Vikings of the Pacific Northwest." Most knew they needed no other title, no other name, nor someone else's worn label. They were, and are, Haida. A fierce and proud nation with a rich heritage.

I had always been drawn to the Haida culture, and explained the baffling allure as simply craving a connection. Though the adoption papers never specified the origins of my mixed-race appearance, the possibility of belonging somewhere tempted even the coldest recesses of my soul. Now, knowing the location of my brother, the appeal of this place and culture made more sense.

Driving north along the highway, with the windows up and the heat cranked to combat the damp cold, I soaked up the wild nature. As we drove, miles of untamed forests and ocean bordered the two lane road. Two bald eagles soared above, as if tailing our truck's progress. My chest expanded, opening to warmth for the first time since Tristan's death.

After pulling out of the drugged daze in the lab, clarity spanned my memory, piecing together the lost time, and filling in the two months spent under the SRD's control. But, despite the passage of time, the loss of the Wereleopard Alpha sometimes cut like it occurred days ago.

Wick's gaze flicked to me as he drove, but he remained silent, as if he sensed my need for solitude, for reconnecting with a place I didn't know I had any real link with until now.

A section of my mind cried out. I should be looking for Ben. Scooping up the bad Witches, and bopping them on their heads. I should be hunting Christine to rend her flesh from bone. Or knocking down the Pharaoh.

My skin prickled.

No. Without my animal familiars, I couldn't do much right now, even if we knew the location of the Witches, Christine or the Pharaoh. The Witches, Stan, and Kayne Security searched for them. They had better resources and contacts in the supe world than I could ever hope to have. I needed to trust them to get the job done. In the meantime, I had to recover my feras and beast. Reclaim my badass skills. Until then, I was useless. *Vulnerable.*

When the road tapered off and ended with the Naikoon Provincial Park, Wick pulled the truck to the side of the road and parked. I hopped out and tore off my shoes. Even with the cold, damp soil beneath my feet, energy zinged through my body. I tilted my head back and opened my senses. The salt-laden air from the nearby beach rushed to me. Wind clawed at my skin and whipped my hair. Unease of the unknown should've stabbed its way along my spine, but instead, despite the cold, a comforting warmth engulfed my body.

Home.

An eagle screeched above and circled along with another before they took off farther east.

"Bit chilly," Wick mumbled. He yanked the zipper of his winter jacket to his chin, pulled his head down and crossed his arms.

"Is it?" I barely noticed. My veins pumped with liquid heat and urged me forward. The darkening forest called to me. Staring into its depths provided no answers, but the darkness pulled at my soul.

I glanced over my shoulder at Wick. He nodded slightly. Without a second look, I ran.

Twigs snapped under my feet, sharp jagged rocks cut my soles, and branches reached out to snag my flowing hair, loose down my back. The wind and I wove as one around large trunks of old growth forest. All the while, the harsh elements of the Pacific Northwest beat at my body and burned my lungs.

Home.

Rushing along a broken path, I pushed to go faster, farther. The cold air continued to burn my throat, sweat broke across my face and my skin grew numb.

Faster. Farther.

Home.

A cabin sat in a protective cocoon of trees with smoke puffing out of the chimney. The soft lapping of the ocean trickled through the woods. I stumbled on the frost-hardened soil and fell to my hands and knees. My breath came in raspy gasps, burning my trachea, and puffing out in little plumes of condensed air.

Something blocked the moonlight and cast shadows across the clearing. The ground around the side of the cabin crunched, and clothing rustled.

I lifted my head, and froze.

A strong, shirtless man stood tall before me. His bronze skin shone under the soft moonlight. Hair, dark as midnight, fell straight to his waist. Broad nose, high cheekbones and a wide, soft mouth gave away his Haida heritage. His pine and sea scent gave away his eagle Shifter nature. Was this Sonny, my brother? Excitement vibrated along my body at the same time dread tried to squash the reaction. Would he accept me, or hate me?

With a dark obsidian gaze, the man assessed me in turn.

Would we stay frozen like this? Forever watching each other? What did he plan to do?

"*Háw'aa*," he spoke softly.

An eagle swooped down and landed on the man's shoulder. He didn't flinch or stagger. The bird's talons didn't sink into his flesh; instead, the large predator perched precariously, yet comfortably, in an act that must've been practiced time after time. The man glanced at his fera and took a step forward.

A growl vibrated from the trees to my left seconds before a large black Werewolf leapt into the clearing. With a white-tipped snout, white socks and mitts, Wick's Werewolf form would've been adorable as a cub, but now, he was the most intimidating Werewolf Alpha I'd ever seen, which said a lot.

Wick lunged to insert his large presence between the man and me. Spinning to face the eagle man, Wick's hackles stood on end. Saliva dripped from his snarling mouth and barred fangs. His protectiveness pulled at something inside me.

The eagle fera launched off the man's shoulders and moved to a safer perch on a nearby tree limb.

I clambered to my feet, as Wick continued to growl. Warmth spread out to my limbs and tingled my toes.

Wolf? I called to my fera.

Silence met me where my wolf would've howled in answer, before I sent her away, before I lost her.

The man on the other side of Wick pulled up short and held his hands up in a non-threatening gesture.

"Easy." The man spoke with a deep voice, rich like spiced sandalwood.

Wick's growl deepened.

The man sighed. His shoulders dropped. He looked upward again as if asking for divine intervention. He crouched in front of Wick, and muttered, "Weres."

Wick's snarl faltered. His head tilted and his black ears pinged forward.

"I'm not here to hurt your woman, wolfman."

I bristled and ignored my racing pulse. I was no one's property.

Wick's fangs gleamed under the moonlight.

"I am her blood." His obsidian gaze flicked to me.

I stiffened, and held my breath.

"No harm will come to her so long as she does no harm." The man watched me as he spoke.

No harm. These two words echoed in my mind.

Too many times I'd heard these exact words uttered, only to have them danced around. But the truth in his words and the sincerity of his gaze gave me hope.

Wick plunked his butt down and watched the man.

The eagle Shifter stood from his crouch and walked around Wick's large form. He stopped a few feet short of me and hesitated for the first time. His brows furrowed as he studied my face.

The sour tang of all our nerves spiralled in the air. He said no harm but would he welcome me or send me away?

After what seemed like hours, it appeared the man wouldn't make any move at all. I held out my hand. "Andy."

The man glanced at my stiffly jutted out arm and open palm. He shook his head, his long hair flowing back and forth to shroud his handsome features. With two large steps, he closed the distance between us and enveloped me in a tight hug. The warmth of his skin shielded me from the cold wind and his long hair flowed around me as a fragrant blanket of pine and sea.

"My name is Sonny," he rumbled. "But to you, and only you, I am *dáa*."

Brother.

15

The cedar planks of Sonny's North Beach cabin creaked with each gust of ocean wind rolling off the nearby crashing waves. Sonny, dressed in simple blue jeans and a worn black T-shirt, set steaming mugs of coffee in front of me and Wick as we sat around his small, unfinished pine table in the kitchen.

Any tension that remained from our unannounced arrival had washed away when I practically did the pee dance in front of both men and asked to use Sonny's washroom.

Now, a sense of calm settled over me with each sip of delicious coffee. If my feras still cohabitated my mind, they'd curl up for a nap right now, no longer bickering or pacing. The cabin permeated the smells of all my favourite evergreens—cedar, spruce and pine—along with coffee and oatmeal.

Home.

Sonny placed a third mug down on the table and

joined us. He'd forgone the caffeine fix and went for camomile instead. His eagle fera, Tank, hunted outside, away from the warmth of the cabin, but safer. I'd never harm another Shifter's fera, nor would Wick, but Sonny didn't know us, and his precaution spoke of common sense, not mistrust. No Shifter needlessly risked his or her fera's life. Sonny's caution didn't upset me, but his easy identification did.

"How'd you know?" I blurted out.

Sonny paused before settling in his seat. "A vision. The images showed a woman traveling toward me."

Was he one of the eagles following us during our drive north?

"But how'd you know I was your sister?" My body vibrated at the implications. I took deep breaths to calm my racing mind. Had he known all along? And still chose to stay away?

Wick shifted in his seat but took a long drink instead of commenting.

Sonny stared into the depths of his mug before answering. "As soon as I saw the news coverage, I knew."

I frowned. What news?

Stan's comment floated through my memory. There'd been documentaries and stories on the news after I went beast and rampaged around the Lower Mainland. *That news.*

"You're the spitting image of our grandmother." He nodded to a portrait in a golden frame hung on the wall over his tattered two-seater couch. Looking at the worn image sent pain through my chest. Although her skin tone was much darker and her eyes obsidian black like Sonny's, the woman resembled an older reflection of me in a mirror. I sucked in a breath.

"Why'd you never look for me?"

Sonny placed his mug down and thumbed the thick leather wristband he wore. "I was a child."

"Well, obviously not right away, but later."

Easy, Andy, Wick mindspoke to me. *You sound accusatory.*

I shot him a dark look.

He returned it, unflinching.

Maybe, I am, I replied.

Sonny sighed, unaware of our private conversation. "After the Purge, and losing both our parents, and thinking I lost you as well...I lost myself. It took a long time for me to find my way back. By then, all traces of you were gone, and I gave up hope you survived."

I bit my lip and looked away from his sincere gaze.

Dammit. He spoke the truth.

Stop looking for someone to focus your anger on, Wick said.

Obviously, my previous dark look made little impact, so I turned my best death stare on him instead.

He shrugged.

Sonny's gaze flicked between the two of us, but he said nothing more. Instead, he rubbed the leather band. His chair creaked as he sat back to take a deep sip of chamomile tea.

The wind continued to howl and batter against the wood cabin.

What am I doing here? My chest constricted and a fuzzy sensation settled into my brain. I should be out looking for Ben and the boys. Or knocking heads off douchebags.

Doing...something.

Not sitting around a stranger's table in awkward silence, wanting...wanting what, exactly? An apology? This man owed me nothing. He was as much a victim as I.

I sighed again and pushed back from the table.

Obsidian eyes met mine. "I know your thoughts."

"You couldn't possibly know what's going through this hot mess." I tapped the side of my forehead with my finger and stood up.

"You wonder why you're here."

I paused a second before flopping down in my chair. How'd he know that? Could he read minds like Allan? Had I lost my assassin's touch so much that my emotions showed on my face to strangers? I narrowed my gaze while my skin itched to shift. "Maybe."

Sonny glanced at Wick.

"Your wolf told me a little of what's going on while you were in the bathroom."

Wick's seat creaked as he shifted again. He didn't correct my brother on the label.

I started to object. Didn't Sonny know my mate had been killed?

My brother held his hands up. "You need to heal. Don't deny it. There's a dark, thunderous cloud over your soul."

I growled at Wick.

His eyebrows shot up. "I didn't say that much."

What the hell? I'd never heard of someone seeing souls before. I paused. Well, now, hang on. The Purge revealed just about everything that went bump in the night. Was a soul-seer that far-fetched? Suddenly, Sonny's explanations seemed less bullshit and more plausible.

"You're restless," Sonny continued. "Like you need to be somewhere else, even though you just arrived."

My shoulders dropped as if the weight hovering over them slammed down. I had always wanted a sibling. Yet now that I found mine, even though he welcomed me with open arms, I itched to leave. Why?

The truth slapped me in the face.

Because I failed Tristan. And I didn't want to fail Ben as well. Worse. If I grew close to Sonny, I might fail him, too.

"Why don't you tell me about it?" Sonny interrupted my dark thoughts. "I won't betray your confidence."

Truth. Every word he'd spoken rang true, with no hint of a lie. That didn't mean he omitted crucial information or talked around something he wanted hidden. Could I trust him? I peered into his dark gaze. I'd just met him. Not betraying my confidence didn't mean he couldn't deceive or hurt me in some way. When I glanced at Wick, he nodded, so slightly, the movement almost unnoticeable.

"My friends," I croaked. "I have friends counting on me."

"Yet, you came here, instead. Why?"

"I can't help them as I currently am." And we had no idea where the Elders held them.

Sonny's dark brows shot down. "Why not? You're the Carus."

I wrangled my fingers together. Twisting my hands on my lap. "The SRD did something to me. I'm not sure it can be reversed."

Sonny froze, unblinking, unresponsive. Without warning, he shot out of his seat.

I exchanged a look with Wick. Well, that was... unexpected.

Sonny paced his small kitchen, hands opening and closing, jaw clenched, shoulders tense. Burnt cinnamon rolled off him in waves.

Suddenly, Sonny stopped and turned to me. Without a word, he stalked to where I sat and took my face in both hands.

Wick growled.

Sonny ignored him and closed his eyes. He began to hum. His hands grew warm against my cheeks, and my pulse slowed to meet the beat of his tune.

As abruptly as he started, Sonny stopped and his gaze focused on my face. "We will fix this. But it will take time, and an open mind."

"But my friends—"

"Can wait." Sonny's warm hands dropped from my face. Cool air flowed across my cheeks.

"What if they can't? They could be in great danger."

"You don't know that," Wick spoke up. "Their punishment with the Elders could be longer than they thought. Lucus agreed with what Ben told you. The Elders won't kill them. They value Witch life too much. Servitude, yes. Killing, no."

"But—"

"We don't know where they are held," Wick said. I grunted and folded my arms across my chest.

Wick reached out and placed a large warm hand on my shoulder. "I know you want to save them, but there's nothing we can do until we know their location. The Wereleopards and Stan are more versed investigating this sort of thing, so you may as well stay here and take this time to heal."

Sonny nodded.

Well, crap. It was hard to argue against logic.

16

The evening sun shone over Dixon Entrance, a brilliant red-gold through sage-coloured moss and hanging lichen. The ethereal light emphasized the lush stillness of the forest, and the ocean beckoned in the distance as I walked with Sonny toward the beach. On clear days, Alaska could be spotted from these shores.

Tank soared above, easily keeping pace. As we stepped away from the protective cocoon of the forest, the high wind on the beach blasted us. Cries of eagles calling their mates filled the air. Down the white sand, Taaw Tldáaw rose from the sea spray, shrouded with mist on one side, while the sheer rocky surface facing the setting sun basked in the dying light and reflected the golden rays.

Sonny and I fell into an easy silence as we watched Tank swoop ahead and play in the air flows above the ocean. Though only two weeks had passed since my arrival, we fell into a comfortable routine, which included going for long beach walks after Sonny got back from working at a nearby lodge. His company held a calming effect, and the fear of failing him had washed away.

"Your mind runs faster than a swift river," he said without glancing my way, his face to the ocean. The reflected light danced along the harsh angles of his beautiful face. The wind played with his unbound hair and cast the long strands across his face.

"You said you couldn't read my thoughts."

"I can't."

I pursed my lips, grumbled a little, and turned back to watch the waves crash against the shore. The surf wasn't big today, but I always found something therapeutic in watching the ocean push forward then retreat with each wave.

"Your face tells your story, even if your words and mind do not."

I nodded, as if Sonny's cryptic way of talking made all the sense in the world. And it did. He read me well, too well for someone I'd just met weeks ago. This ability of his must be part of the soul-seer skill set, but whenever I asked him about his capabilities, he'd just grin with a twinkle in his dark eyes and shrug it off.

Instead of his uncanny perceptiveness putting me on edge, though, I welcomed it. Something else that should've raised alarm bells in my mind, but didn't. After waiting all this time to meet my brother, there should've been more tension, more unease of the unknown, more excitement. This immediate acceptance clashed with the Andy Status Quo. Generally, I assumed everyone was a douchebag until they proved otherwise. Had Sonny worked some family mumbo jumbo on me?

"Why does my soul sing when you're near?" I blurted out.

A smile tugged at Sonny's lips, and he turned to me. His large hands gripped my shoulders, warm and soothing. "We are blood."

I frowned. "It's more than that."

Sonny tilted his head. "We are blood, and we are Shifters. As brother and sister, we are as closely tied genetically as relatives can be. Our innate natures recognize each other. Even though we have different feras, and some feras aren't pack animals, it doesn't matter. Ultimately, we are children of Feradea, and she gifted us with a family tie stronger than a last name. Even if your face hadn't been plastered across the news on every channel for weeks, even if you didn't resemble our grandmother, or showed up at my doorstep like a lost kitten, I would've recognized you anywhere." He released one of my shoulders to tap his chest over his heart. "Here. I would know you here."

My eyes stung, and I blinked rapidly. Unsure of what to say, I smiled instead. His words echoed through my body and sank in as truth, as right, as *home*. I would've recognized him, too. The moment he appeared outside his cabin, I *knew* him.

Tank swooped down from nowhere and landed on my shoulder. I staggered forward and winced. What the hell? I straightened under his weight and waited for the pain of punctured skin, but it never arrived. I craned my neck and gaped at the beautiful fera, so regal and trusting. The depths of his eyes, so much like Sonny's in some ways, stared back at me.

We are family, he sang in my mind. Sonny's fera had never talked to me before, let alone touched me.

I...ugh...

Tank's beak parted in what looked like an eagle's smile. His weight sank down, dropping my shoulder, before he launched back in the air. His talons whispering against the fabric of my jacket without ripping the material.

I turned to Sonny, mouth still open, words stuttering, heart spasming with something words couldn't describe nor do justice.

"You are safe when you are with us." Sonny, as sharp as always, pulled me in for a hug, his sandalwood scent curling around me and staving off the salt of the sea. We stood like that for a long moment as the light from the setting sun continued to fade.

Sadness tinged the outer layer of my happy bubble. Sadness for the time I'd lost with Sonny, and with Tank. Sadness for the loss of knowledge. Sadness for not understanding Shifters carried this bond between family members, and not only had I lived in ignorance, I'd lived without it.

My brother released me, and we turned in unison to watch the soothing movement of the sea, the wind at our faces. I closed my eyes and let the cool breeze flow over me.

"Will you promise me something?" Sonny asked after a long, comfortable silence. His hesitant words stirred me from my standing meditative state.

"Depends what it is." I opened my eyes to peer up at him. Though Sonny would never cause me harm, it didn't mean I'd throw caution down in the sand and bury it for all eternity.

"Don't go on a death rampage."

"What's that supposed to mean?"

Sonny paused as if to select his words carefully. "There's a reason people say fools rush in. Don't run headfirst into revenge. You won't survive."

"I don't care." Did his soul-searing skills tell him that? Anger flared up and chased away the calm previously nourishing my soul. The rage grew hotter and continued to burn. My skin itched to shift, even if the ability had been stolen from me. "At least if I die, I'll be with Tristan."

Sonny sucked in a breath. "You don't mean that."

Guilt and shame instantly flooded my body after the words tumbled from my mouth. Part of me meant everything, longing to be in Tristan's strong embrace again. The other part wanted to bash the first part's head in, because I also craved another man, a man still alive, still breathing, still potentially interested, and sitting in the cabin not far from this majestic beach. A man who'd spent every night lying beside me as the perfect gentleman to offer me comfort. I wanted to live, yet anger spoke the harsh words for me. "I—"

A branch snapped on the path behind us. We both froze. Sonny shot me a look that bordered somewhere between sympathy and pity.

Downwind, Wick's rosemary scent and the sound of his feet against the path reached us only moments before he appeared.

Crap. Had he heard any of our conversation?

He stepped onto the beach and made his way to us. "Can I join you two? Or is this a brother-sister bonding moment?" An easy smile spread across Wick's face as he looked at us. The dipping sun cast a shadow across his gaze.

Or was his expression, normally smouldering, simply dark because his smile failed to reach his eyes?

"Of course." Sonny smiled. "Why don't we walk back to the cabin along the beach, we can cut through the forest instead of taking the path back."

My muscles refused to relax under the watchful gaze of the Werewolf Alpha, but I managed a smile. "Sounds good to me."

Wick nodded.

"Besides," Sonny said casually. "From the sound of Andy's stomach, if we don't get back soon for dinner, she might snap and eat us."

Tank screeched agreement and angled toward the cabin.

Wick laughed, and I forced a chuckle. It wasn't my

stomach bleating like a lamb led to the slaughter, but rather my conflicted heart.

17

The cold air chaffed my lungs as I sucked it in, breath after raspy breath. The time spent in the lab had done me no favours with conditioning. Sonny had already sentenced me to a morning run each day before he went to work, and now, after nearly dying on each run, it appeared Wick was determined to brand me with a different form of torture.

The large hill with a face of sheer rock, a constant backdrop to my morning runs with Sonny, grew larger as I ran along the beach with Wick. Taaw Tldáaw, also known as Tow Hill.

Wick hadn't mentioned my conversation with Sonny the night before. Probably a good thing because I had no idea what I'd say. My head and heart were swirling with mixed emotions and I welcomed the physical activity to take my mind off of...well...everything.

Wick turned to me, evil smile firmly planted on his face. "We're going to climb it."

Rising around four hundred feet above the sand, Taaw Tldáaw towered over North Beach. A light mist obscured the base, and unease settled in my gut. With my chin down, I pushed harder and aimed for disaster. It beat thinking about Ben's captivity or what evil the Pharaoh planned.

The trail was beautiful. Following the Hiellen River, well maintained boardwalks and stairs led through a mist-shrouded forest, thick with huckleberry, salal, and ferns. Moss hung from the snaggled branches of the trees while the salt from the nearby ocean curled along the path.

The feeling of impending doom had been unwarranted. The path rated as easy to moderate for a norm, which meant painless for pre-lab Andy.

"I'm not letting you off this easy," he said, gaze twinkling.

We ran the loop multiple times, stopping only for sets of burpees, lunges, mountain climbers, and squats. Wick didn't pull any punches.

Jerk.

With sweat dripping down my entire body, as if I'd taken a dunk in the ocean instead of a "light workout," Wick called an end to the training when we reached the summit for the umpteenth time.

The view stunned me.

Framed with the crisp green peaks of evergreens, North Beach sprawled beneath us with its easy curve and gentle rolling waves. The wind brushed against our faces, and my breathing slowed, going from heaving gasps to mild air-sucking.

Wick turned to me. His skin glistened with a thin sheen of sweat. It would disappear soon, but the sight gave me comfort. Perspiration dripped off my face and ran down my spine to pool on my lower back.

My body sang with energy. For the first time since escaping the SRD lab, a sense of composure, of returning to my former self, slid through my body. I shot Wick a wide smile.

Tristan's words from a life time ago, from a moment in my life when fate placed me in a position to choose between two potential mates, and they both actively pursued me, called to me: *There is more than one potential mate in the world. More than one person can complement our predator and self. A mate is not half of one soul, but a match for it.*

Wick's gaze smouldered.

I glanced as heat flushed through my body.

Tristan had been ripped from my life almost three months ago, after only a short time together. The sudden finality of it all still hurt, like a festering, deep stab wound. Sometimes, when I lay in bed, a scent so similar to his, the one laced with honeysuckle on a warm summer's day, trickled into my room and surrounded me. Almost as if I'd open my eyes to find him standing by my side. Yet, every time I bolted upright, aside from Wick curled up protectively beside me on the bed, only an empty room greeted me. Even if it was Tristan's ghost, I didn't sense anything malicious about the presence. I felt approval, warmth, and love.

Tristan's written words from his letter tumbled back

to me. *Find happiness. Find love. Live a long, full life, and know I will always love you.*

Tenderness spread through my body. Wick moved closer, his arm less than an inch from brushing my sticky bicep. His rosemary scent swirled around me like a caress, mixing in with the salt of the sea and pine of the nearby trees.

I squeezed my eyes shut.

"Andy?"

"Mmmm?"

"Can I ask you something?"

My eyes pinged open. Without glancing over, I knew Wick watched me, but instead of turning toward him I took in the mist below as it rolled in with the tide, and whispered through the forest. "Shoot."

"Did you mean that?" Wick asked.

"Mean what?"

"What you said to Sonny last night. On the beach?"

I froze. So Wick had heard the conversation with my brother. Since he hadn't spoken of it, I'd hoped he hadn't. Of course, he had Were hearing, but we'd been far enough away from the path when we stopped talking. Or at least I thought we had been. My brows pinched together.

What exactly had he heard?

"I heard Sonny caution you about running headfirst into revenge."

My shoulders drooped. One, I hadn't realized I spoke the last thought out loud, and two, I remembered what I said next. Wick shouldn't have heard that.

The Alpha continued. "You said that you didn't care. That if you died, at least you'd be with Tristan."

Silence met his statement as I continued to stare at the long expanse of beach from our high vantage point and refused to meet Wick's intense gaze, the one threatening to bore a hole through the side of my head.

"Did you mean that?" he pressed.

"Yes." I looked down at my hands. "No." My fingers had twisted together on their own accord, almost knotted to the point of pain. "I don't know."

Wick waited.

"At first, yes. I loved him, Wick. I still do. And a part of me always will. But..." *He wasn't the only man I loved.*

"But?" His voice cracked.

My throat clamped up, and I couldn't say the words echoing in my soul. I swallowed and continued. "He wouldn't want me to just wither and die. He said as much in his letter. He wanted me to go on and make a new life. And I feel guilty for saying this, but..." I looked up through bleary eyes. "I want to make a new life, too. Not just because Tristan wanted me to, but because I do." I patted my chest. "I'm not broken. I refuse to be. I —I have more to give. I have... I'm not..."

Wick stepped forward and pulled me to his body, pressing me against his tense muscles. His warmth sank into my numb skin, and his strong arms wrapped around me. His chest vibrated against my upper body with his heavy heartbeat.

As he held me and blocked the cold elements, his limbs relaxed and tension released from his body. Originally, I'd thought this hug was for me, to comfort and console. The longer we stood at the lookout, with Wick's face buried in my neck, breathing in long drags of my scent, the more I realized this moment was just as much for him as it was for me.

18

With my skin slick with moisture, half from the bone-numbing rain, and half from the cold ocean spray, I stumbled into Sonny's cabin, exhausted, yet refreshed from my morning run.

Wick stood in the small living room, his packed bags waiting at his feet.

I came to an abrupt halt. Sonny, who'd been running close behind, crashed into me. We both staggered forward with a thud.

"Wha—?" Sonny caught himself on the corner table and stepped to the side.

Wick's mouth twitched, but the humour didn't reach his sad, chocolate gaze.

"You're leaving?" I asked, between deep breaths. Maybe some of that moisture was sweat. Maybe more than a little.

Wick nodded. "I have arranged for you to keep the

truck as long as you require it, but I need a lift to the airport."

"I have to go to work," Sonny said. The lodge he worked for sat on the Tlell River, and although he headed in the same direction as the airport, he wouldn't make it there and back in time for his shift.

Both men turned to me.

Sonny shifted his weight from foot to foot, his brows furrowing. More than once, he glanced at the window. Probably wanting to fly away. I didn't blame him.

Wick couldn't leave. I—I needed him here. He'd spent every night since the hotel sleeping beside me—his large, warm presence reassuring and calming the restless, lonely part of me that craved my feras. He never tried anything, never gave the impression he wanted to. No, he'd simply offered comfort, and safety.

Wick cleared his throat.

"Yeah," I mumbled, now numb from something other than the weather. "Of course. I'll drive you."

Wick picked up his bags. They swished against the plain wood flooring. He turned to Sonny and held his hand out. "Thanks for putting up with me."

Sonny clasped his hand, but looked as confused as I felt. Sure, we'd been here for a month, but with no news from back home, we didn't have any information to act on. Why did it seem like Wick now had somewhere urgent to go?

THE SILENCE IN THE TRUCK'S CAB THREATENED
to choke me with its thickness. Wick's sugar and rosemary scent filled the confined space, but carried little of
his emotions. If I didn't know any better, I'd think a
sociopath sat beside me.

His gaze flicked to me as he drove, and his knuckles
whitened as he clutched the steering wheel, yet his lips
remained firmly pressed together. When he pulled into
the small airport, he put the truck in park, left the keys in
the ignition, and turned to me.

I took a deep breath and angled my shoulders toward
him. My skin prickled and if my falcon still lived in my
mind, she'd screech. My mountain lion would pace, and
my wolf would howl. Wick had been a friend in my
darkest hour. Someone to depend on. And now, without
warning, he planned to rip himself away like a used and
unwanted bandage.

Confusion rippled through my mind. Our moment
on Taaw Tldáaw had been a couple weeks ago, and
although nothing notable had happened between us
since, certainly nothing bad occurred, either,

Wick dropped his hands from the steering wheel, and
his shoulders relaxed. A small smile played at the corners
of his full mouth, but once again, the emotion didn't
reach his chocolate gaze.

"Andy..." he started.

I waited, frozen, not wanting to breathe. Wick acted like this was goodbye forever, not just for now.

Maybe it was. I gulped.

"I think you are in a good place," he said.

I nodded while my mind reeled. Why shouldn't Wick leave? It's not like I gave him any indication he had reason to stay. I had nothing to offer him, nothing to give but a broken shell. Why would he stick around for that? Did I even want him to? Wishing for Wick to stay was selfish.

"I need to go home for work, but I know you will be okay here. Heal here." He reached over, grasped my hands, and gave them a squeeze.

"I think so," I stammered. "Thank you for helping me and for being here." I gulped.

"I helped you because I care for you."

"I know." Where was he going with this?

"I didn't help you because I expected you to repay my kindness in some way."

"I would never think that of you." Frankly, I was a little insulted he felt the need to voice this.

Then again, I had thrown a lot of mean comments in his face. I winced. If only I could take those words back. Wick didn't deserve getting hurt.

Wick nodded and released my hands. He ran a hand through his hair. "I want the best for you."

But.

He hadn't said that word, yet, but something in his tone implied its eventuality and made my muscles tense.

"I'm a call away if you need help."

I nodded, body still shocked. It hadn't recovered from the run followed with the surprise of Wick's leaving.

"If you need a friend."

My head jerked up. Wick's dark gaze focused on me, unwavering, unyielding in its sad resolve. A friend, and nothing more.

My soul ached.

Again, what did I expect? Again, what did I want?

No miraculous answers came thundering down into my mind. Instead, I remained hollow and numb.

I nodded like an emotionless bobblehead, feeling a cold wave of fuzzy prickles spread from my spine out to my limbs.

"I want to be really clear, Andy," Wick continued. "I will always care for you, and my wolf will always want you, but I'm not waiting for you. You're still healing and I respect that. I want you to do what's right for you. But I also need to do what is best for not only me, but the pack. They can't afford to have me here any longer while they remain vulnerable. Now that you are safe, I can return to my responsibilities."

His wolf flashed yellow in his gaze. Those words must be cutting Wick up inside. Despite how he might feel as a man, his wolf had already declared me his mate. If Mel gleaned information from the pack bond correctly, his wolf would never accept another so long as I lived. If Wick wanted to move on, it meant putting distance between his wolf and me.

"Andy?"

I nodded, yet again, and sniffed. "I get it, Wick. I do. I never wanted to hurt you. You deserve the best for you and your pack."

Something flashed across his gaze, his eyes narrowed for a split second. Had he anticipated a different response? One more agitated? Argumentative? Had he wanted another response entirely instead of my spineless one?

He shook off whatever emotion hounded him and somehow blocked the responding scent from escaping. He popped the door open, and I mirrored his actions. We met at the back bumper.

"Thanks again," I mumbled.

Wick pulled me in for a brief hug, took a deep breath, and quickly stepped back.

Had he smelled my hair?

Before I could ask, he reached into the back and hauled out his luggage. The bags scraped against the metal.

"I'll see you soon," he said.

I sighed, and some of the tension flowed out of my muscles. My brother had the land rights to build a resort in a beautiful area on North Beach. Once he got his act together after losing our parents and bouncing from foster home to foster home, he started saving. With an extended lifetime, he finally had enough. He planned to leave his job at the lodge and start building in a couple of months.

For our entire stay, Sonny had hashed out his plans

with Wick, a very successful building developer, and the two hit it off. Wick probably planned to help with the project in some capacity, so this wasn't goodbye forever. It couldn't be. I was probably overreacting.

None of this rational thinking explained the sense of finality clinging in the air or the sinking pit in my chest as I watched Wick walk away from me. Again.

19

Another month passed without word from Veronika, Lucus, or Wick. Kayne Security Solutions and the Wereleopards answered all my calls with great patience and understanding, but even through the phone, their strained voices gave away their frustration. Maybe calling them every day for an update on their investigation was a bit much.

"We'll contact you as soon as we hear anything," Olly said, tone soft and reassuring.

"Okay, thanks." I said goodbye and hung up. Avoiding Sonny's knowing gaze ranked pretty impossible given his small accommodations.

"Cozy," is how he referred to his home, and as a bachelor, he felt he didn't need more. I agreed, and although we bumped into each other more than once, I'd grown to love this place, with its quiet energy amongst the raging elements outside.

"Where's Tank?"

Sonny laughed. "Playing. He finds these storms amusing."

I nodded and silence descended on the cabin again.

"You need to let it go," he said.

"Let what go?" I kept my back to him and turned the kettle on to make some tea. Tea! This crazy brother of mine had me on a detox to cleanse my body and soul. When he suggested dropping my morning coffee, I snarled at him. Must've been pretty scary because he dropped the subject and never brought it up again.

Come to think of it, he tiptoed around me in the morning and didn't speak to me until I finished my first cup.

Huh. Smart man.

I pulled the mugs out.

"All of it," Sonny answered after a long pause.

"All of it?" I whirled to face him, mugs in hand.

"Is there an echo in here?" Sonny raised a dark eyebrow. "Yes, all of it."

As if his words flicked an invisible switch, rage flooded my body. "Just let Christine go to rejoice in the pain she's inflicted?" I shrieked. "Forget my friends and let them rot wherever they are? Leave the Pharaoh to concoct another master plan for world domination?"

"Yes." Sonny stood in one smooth motion. He closed the distance between us and gently plucked the mugs from my hands. He placed them on the counter.

Did he worry I'd smash them? As my breathing grew shallow and my veins warmed, Sonny moved out of striking distance.

Smart man, indeed.

"Are you fucking kidding me?" I seethed.

"Hear me out."

I took a deep breath and forced the tension from my muscles.

"Ben and his coven are responsible for the deaths of many, many people. They might not have killed anyone directly, but the mistake of Ben's apprentices and Ben's lack of supervision cost a lot of innocent people their lives. The Elders won't kill them because they didn't intend for the deaths and were tricked by a powerful Demon, but many, especially the friends and families of the dead, would argue they deserve punishment. What is a few extra months compared to the death of a loved one?"

I snarled. His question hit way too close to home. Sonny smiled sympathetically. He spoke the truth, but it didn't make it easier to hear.

"And Christine?"

Sonny nodded. "Your anger blocks your ability to heal."

"My anger." I thumped my chest. "Is what connects me with the beast."

"That sounds like a dysfunctional relationship."

I rocked back on my heels.

"You need to truly embrace the good and the bad aspects of the beast. You're not separate entities. You are one."

I am you. You are me. We are one. The mantra of my feras echoed through my veins. As Feradea explained it, the beast, and all my unique skills were essentially remnants in my DNA from my divine heritage coming out to play. Or have a laugh.

"You can't keep the beast caged like some twisted monster only brought out when you want to turn into a raging green fiend," Sonny said.

"First, my beast is a beautiful ebony." I flicked a finger up. "And second, the chemicals block me, not my anger."

"Are you sure about that?"

I bit back my response. Calling my brother names wouldn't solve anything.

"And..." Sonny's voice drifted off. He gazed outside, taking in the cloudy sky. Not a great day for flying.

The absence of my falcon's knowing shriek sank a pit in my chest. "And?"

He shrugged.

Well, crap. I'd only known Sonny a short time, but I'd learned his tells. He had something to say, and he knew it would hurt.

The words from my SRD mentor Donny trickled through my memory. *"You will be hurt, Carus, and maybe not in the physical sense."*

Sonny sighed. "Have you thought about what would've happened had Tristan lived?"

Heat flared up in my stomach, burning a path through my lungs. I swallowed it down. "Careful."

Sonny held his hand up. "I'm not saying he deserved to die, and I don't make this point lightly."

I growled.

"You showed me his letter. How long could he have resisted the call after you mated? Sure, he no longer craved his final resting place, but the call would've returned. It comes for all Weres and Shifters eventually, with or without mates. Had he lived and mated, he would've hurt you. And you wouldn't have recovered."

"He'll hurt you in the end," Angie's voice whispered in my mind. She'd tried to warn me. At the time, I thought she was just being a bitch.

"He wouldn't have wanted to hurt you, of course," Sonny continued. "But he would've realized the truth and walked away before mating, or he would've died after bonding, only to leave you to go crazy in a mate-less state of anguish."

Air abandoned my lungs. My stomach recoiled as if sucker punched in the gut. *Or we could've lived a long and happy life together.*

"I know his death hurts. I know this truth hurts as well. But it's nothing compared to what you would've gone through."

Had he lived.

My knuckles popped, and I clenched my teeth. The kettle whistled behind me. Sonny walked around my stiff body and turned it off. He poured the steaming water into the two mugs and plunked the tea bags in. The smell of spices floated through the air.

We stood side by side in silence—Sonny faced the counter, our drinks, and the window to the outside, while I faced the interior of the cabin. I tried to collect my thoughts. They scattered like cockroaches from the light.

"So you're saying I should let my anger for Christine go because she did me a fucking favour?"

A pause. "No. Absolutely not. Let go of your anger because it only hurts you right now. Christine's actions will come back on her."

I grumbled. Sometimes karma took too long.

"We could've been happy," I said.

"Tristan obviously loved you very much. He loved you enough to give you time and space, but he would've told you his age and the dangers of mating with him eventually. At least I'd like to believe he would've done the right thing."

I took a deep breath and swallowed my words. *Breathe. Just breathe.* Tristan's loving face flashed through my mind, his gaze tender when he watched me, when he told me he loved me. His feelings for me weren't a lie.

Sonny watched me for a moment before picking up one of the mugs from the counter. He handed it to me.

"Thanks."

He nodded and picked up the second mug.

"What about the Pharaoh?"

Sonny smiled into the fragrant steam lifting off the hot tea before leaning back into the counter. "He's thousands of years old. If his diabolical plans for world domination haven't worked yet, we have little to fear. Besides, the Pharaoh is not your problem, not your responsibility."

"But—"

"And even if this all rested on you, even if the Pharaoh's plans might actually succeed, we have time. The Pharaoh is ancient. From what I've heard, he's no different than any other Vampire and operates on a longer time scale than the rest of us."

For the sake of all British Columbians, I hoped he was right.

20

The cool wind caressed my face like a lover, as I tramped through the lush temperate rainforest of the North Coast. After travelling south in a power boat all day, Sonny and I rowed to a barren beach on what amounted to little more than a raft. Without a word, he'd handed me a backpack. Weighed down with supplies, I'd hefted the bag and turned my puzzlement on my brother. He'd been cryptic all day. It had been three months since I'd arrived on his doorstep, and although he didn't fill the silence with idle chitchat, Sonny was usually more adept at conversation than this. He wouldn't even tell me where we were going, only that *it was time*. Bloody soul-seers and their cryptic, mysterious ways.

Sonny pointed to the tree line. I replied with a blank look.

He shrugged and said, "You must go that way."

"For what?"

"To find yourself." So very cryptic.

Shifter girl is wasting daylight, Tank crooned in my head.

Maybe they just planned to leave me here and head back. Maybe Sonny had a lady friend coming over, and he wanted some privacy in his small cabin. Whatever his reasons, I now walked alone in a pristine forest with only the sounds of nature to keep me company. I had no idea of my location, although if my directional intelligence pinged right, I was near the southern tip of the Haida Gwaii.

A bald eagle screeched overhead.

Sonny? Tank?

The eagle remained mute.

I watched the powerful bird soar above. Even if it was Sonny or Tank, this journey was meant as a solo trip. *Great.*

The air was rich with a bouquet of fertile soil, ever-greens, and wet bark. The ocean, growing distant, but never far, sprinkled salt and moisture to cling on the leaves and my skin. Long sage-coloured lichen hung from old snarled branches.

I hiked through the forest, thick with dense moss and long ferns, and damp with dew. The flora encroached on the old, worn trail.

Well, may as well see where this leads.

The quiet curses directed at my soul-seer brother faded away to silent appreciation for my surroundings. As I continued to walk, the trail took a more distinct shape with white clamshells bordering the path. Half-fallen totem poles stared back at me, covered with moss and cracked with age.

I continued down the path to where the trees gave way to a remote beach. Facing south on a long isthmus, gentle waves broke against large boulders and rocks jutting out of the sea below. With each gust of wind, the ocean spray brushed my face like a cool caress.

Haida watchmen had protected and defended these shores for over fourteen-thousand years. Beside me, amid the looming spruce and overgrown grass, stood more totem poles, all facing the ocean as if guarding the land from unseen invaders. Aged by harsh elements, some had toppled over for nature to reclaim them.

I walked over the green blanket of moss to the nearest totem pole. With my hand centimetres from the broad wooden face of a bear, I hesitated. Would it be disrespectful to touch the old relic?

Reading one of Sonny's many books on the subject, I'd learned the Haida raised totem poles as a symbol for their family or clan, in honour of the dead, or to record supernatural encounters. Other reasons existed, too, but totem poles were never worshipped or used as talismans.

The eagle circling overhead screeched with encouragement. At least, I thought it did.

Maybe for once, I should turn off my brain and follow my heart instead.

Taking a deep breath, I closed my eyes, and focused inward. My body leaned forward. As my arms opened and slid around to hug the old wood, cool to the touch, my head rested against the totem's rough surface.

Something powerful and ancient tugged at my essence.

I gasped.

I tried to pull back, but invisible arms wrapped around me, cocooning me in warmth. The totem pole sucked the essence from my body. I spiralled out of control until an odd heat spread through me and I became one with someone else, something other, looking out at a vision.

Or a memory?

The soft patter of bare feet beats on the red path like a drum—thump, thump. The sound stirs my heart and the old songs fill my soul. Before, I whispered them, but now, I'm awake. I sing to her, this child, as she skips toward me, fluttering like an errant leaf in a light breeze.

The diminished forest is alive with her presence. The sun breaks through the canopy and warms her chilled bones, soothes her prickled skin. Each step feeds the rhythm. The wind whistles through the leaves and sings a sweet harmony. The birds join in, and an eagle watches.

When she reaches me, she wraps her tiny arms around my ancient skin. I sing louder, hoping she will hear, but she is young. She does not know the way yet. Her father calls out and she returns to him giggling, unaware of the life she has breathed into this forgotten place.

The forest diminishes in its strength, in its beauty. Children die from disease while others desecrate the land. My brothers and sisters fall to iron warriors, their voices cut from the old songs too soon. They crash to the ground— thump, thump. I sing louder, but the lost will not heed my voice. I want to shut my eyes to these horrors, but they're forever open, forever watching, and time slides by like a jumbled mess.

The land around me changes. The wind, no longer a friend, rips by me, cutting and cracking my once smooth skin. The birds use me for shelter and peck away at my heart, and the sun, once a welcome sight, hardens the land around me and fades my once brilliant colours.

The woman's visits lift my laden heart. She sits with me, an eagle on her shoulder, and I soak up her salty tears as they fall to the soft soil. No longer standing proud, I lean to one side. Everything is now on an angle, slanted and skewed, yet she looks into my eyes without fear. She starts to hum, catching the beat of the old songs without knowing what she does. She is hope. My heart beats for her—thump, thump.

She comes to me with her guide one last time. She is older now, wiser, her face cracked and wrinkled, like my own, bent with age, yet proud, like me. She knows the way now, like I do. She has passed on the story. She walks on the worn path and sings in her heart of hearts the songs of our people, the old songs. She will join me, soon, to look upon the future.

And we will sing together.

As quickly as it happened, the totem spat out my essence, flinging me back into my body.

I staggered. Taking a step away, I tried to slow each quickened breath.

What the hell was that?

My head spun. The woman had been a Shifter. Had

this been her village? The memory felt old. Older than possible. Totem poles only lasted a hundred years or so. This one couldn't date back earlier than the 1800s. Sonny's book had said the oldest standing totem pole on record was from 1835.

Yet... Yet the memory sung of the long passage of time. As if this totem pole carried the memories of the family from a time before its own creation.

I turned to the ocean and closed my eyes against the refreshing ocean spray. The woman's face seemed familiar. Her kind expression pulled at my mind, tickled my neurons.

Her eyes. Her dark knowing gaze... Grandmother?

Thump, thump.

My eyes popped open. My heart beat so hard it rattled my bones. I spun around. Sweat broke across my brow. No one was there, except the sightless, all-seeing eyes of the totem poles.

Thump, thump.

I ran.

21

Pumping my arms and legs as fast as possible, I ran through the forest. Twigs and branches snapped as I sped by them. My arms burned. A branch sliced my cheek.

Thump, thump.

I put my chin down and ran faster.

In a mossy bed, a lone totem pole stood majestically as sunlight filtered through the surrounding forest. I staggered to a stop. The air sparkled with mist and refracted light. Moist loam, and pine, with spruce flooded my senses. The cold, damp air clung to my skin as I walked toward the centre along a worn path, almost completely reclaimed by nature.

I approached this totem pole slowly. It appeared different than the rest, the style slightly off, the animals not as commonly depicted. At the bottom, an intricately carved wolf held up a woman. She looked supported and trapped at the same time, wedged between the wolf below and a mountain lion above. The feline's face sat beneath a bird of some sort.

I stepped closer, breath caught in my throat.

The bird perched on the mountain lion's head with its wings spread as if to take off in flight. Not the thunderbird—a more common totem—something else, something smaller. A falcon.

I swallowed the lump of air, the meaning of the three animals not lost on me. My first three feras. My heart. My soul.

I was the trapped woman. My fingers itched to touch her carved face, but froze an inch away.

Not prey, my mountain lion would've hissed. Predators didn't run away. Why was I scared of dead wood?

A screech sounded from above.

That didn't sound like Sonny.

I looked up. And gasped. Hundreds of birds flocked in the air, circling the clearing. Eagles, falcons, ravens, seagulls, owls, sparrows—too many types to name and identify. They continued to loop around, lower and lower, as if forming a vortex of flapping feathers around the totem pole.

The ground trembled. My pulse rate increased. The trees swayed. Brambles danced. Sweat trickled down my forehead. I took a step back and looked over my shoulder.

The trees surrounding the clearing continued to sway.

Crap. No escape. I was trapped.

I returned to the centre of the clearing and crouched low. Whatever came, I'd be ready. Where the heck was

Sonny? Was he one of the squawking pigeons above? As sweat coated my skin, I waited. And waited. No attack came.

Animals by the dozens—no, more than that—gathered at the edges of the clearing. Bears, wolves, coyotes, foxes, deer... Now an entire wildlife foundation commercial circled and enclosed the clearing, fencing me in with the strange, lone totem pole.

Thump, thump.

An eerie silence fell over the moss covered rainforest as my heart beat along with the thump, thump of the land. My breathing slowed. These animals weren't here to hunt or hurt me. Their presence offered something else. Support.

Warmth, like the one I experienced with the other totem pole, spread through my chest. As if my soul expanded with nuclear energy, my body vibrated to the very tips of my fingers and toes.

I walked forward, extended my finger, and touched the totem pole.

Nothing happened.

I sucked in a deep breath and tried again. Nope. Still nothing.

Now, repeatedly jabbing the totem pole on the wolf's nose, like a non-responding vending machine button, my stomach sank.

What the hell?

I turned and sank down to sit with my back resting against the structure.

What now?

Why were all these animals here? Their idea of entertainment? Watch the Carus make an ass of herself? The birds had stopped circling and now perched on surrounding branches along with some of the smaller non-flying animals. Hundreds of beady eyes watched as

I looked around.

The wind whispered, too faint. I leaned forward and strained to hear. Again, the wind carried a whisper of words, quiet at first. It grew louder. And louder. Until finally, I could make out the high-pitched wailing of ancestors blended with the sounds of the wind, ocean and land, and the constant beat of a thumping drum. As if my brain already spoke the language, the words translated within my mind.

I am you. You are me. We are one.

My breath caught. I gulped. The mantra my feras always recited to me before bonding, echoed in my head. Like parrots, it was their only reply when I asked them direct questions, like what they were, where they came from, why I had more than one of them, or why they were in my head unlike other feras. The beady eyes in the forest continued to blink and observe.

With a deep breath, I closed my eyes and reached out with my mind. *Can you hear me?*

I am you. You are me. We are one, the response immediate. So many voices joined the mantra. I winced and covered my ears. Like that would help.

My head thumped back against the old totem pole. So all these animals were new feras? Their energies pulled, expecting me to suck them in like I had the others.

Okay, I said to them. *Come to me.*

An eagle swooped from a nearby tree and dove straight at my chest. Her essence slammed into me. I sucked in a breath.

This wasn't right. I normally had to touch them for the bonding.

A saw-whet owl barrelled into me next. Her presence filled and expanded into my bones on contact.

I always had to reach out and actively touch them with my hand. Before—

Another animal crashed into me. Then another.

And another.

My blood raced. My breathing grew shallow and fast. My head pounded. Too many. My vision faded to black as pain lanced through each vein and rattled my bones. I drew inside myself, letting darkness spread through my body as if the tissue sucked it in like a sponge.

Donny's faraway words from a distant memory flittered through the void to reach me. *"Remember, Carus. When darkness descends on your soul, you're not alone."*

Images of those I cared for flashed through my mind. Donny, Ben, Stan, Mel, Wick...Tristan. With each face, with each remembered smile or cherished moment, the darkness withdrew, fading to the sunlight beating down on the clearing from above.

The beast pressed against the artificial barrier. One of her growls squeezed through. *Accept them.*

Instead of fighting the animals as they flowed into

me, I did as she said. Embracing each of the feras as one, they continued to stream into me as if I was a drain in a sink, or a portal to another realm.

A roar like the winds of a prairie storm, the spiralling of a cyclone, the destructive force of a tornado, picked up with the swirling wind. The feras kept coming. I dropped my head back, flung my arms wide and took them all as they thudded against my breast bone.

As each animal poured into my essence, my mind opened to a place I'd briefly glimpsed once before. A forest. Within the trees, my lost feras huddled together among the new ones as they arrived. My wolf's soulful gaze met mine. She howled.

I am you. You are me. We are one.

A tingle rippled through my body. Bones vibrated. My soul hummed. The barrier locking away my beast, now a pathetic film, crumbled away. My vision exploded. A sound, like a thunderous rumble from the maw of a Demon ripped through my throat as feras continued to stream into my essence.

Understanding smashed through my brain cells and the beast rose. The vision from the other totem pole haunted my mind.

Feras.

They weren't truly animals, they were guides that accompanied a person for life, both in the spiritual world and the physical. Shifters normally received one guardian spirit, housed in the body of an animal. As the Carus, I saw their true essence, and their place beyond the mortal realm.

That's why I can bring Sid over. That's why I can talk to all feras. That's why I can talk to any animal supe.

I was a portal.

The beast expanded. I didn't fight her. I opened my essence and accepted her potent energy as the last of the animals flooded my soul, flowed through my veins, and travelled to the other side.

The beast sank into my mind, rolled into a ball, and grew. Swelling to push against my skin. Her divine energy ran along my limbs before settling into my bones. No longer was she the beast, and I, Andy.

The beast is the Carus. The Carus is the beast. We are one.

I roared.

22

A glowing opaque stag sauntered into the clearing, the last animal, the last totem, the last piece to the complex puzzle my brain still struggled to comprehend. The stag shimmered before transforming into Feradea. Evidently, the Goddess of Beasts could take any form she wanted, regardless of gender. Her barely-there animal-skin outfit revealed plenty of bronzed flesh as it shone in the sunlight.

"I'm proud of you, daughter-mine," she said. "You have discovered the true purpose of being a Carus. You are the gatekeeper of totems—the guides for Shifters known as feras. They wait on the other side for new Shifters to be born and reach maturity, though some will choose to stay in the forest for you."

Without her naming which feras, I *knew* she referred to those I'd bonded to prior to today.

My wolf growled her agreement in my head. Warmth flooded my body from the sound of my long lost fera.

Though she no longer loped along my neurons, she somehow pushed her thoughts and voice through the barrier anyway.

My mountain lion's purr filled my chest, and my falcon popped into the air, ghost-gray, to perch on my shoulder. Her talons dug into my skin, and tears welled in my eyes. She'd always been in my head before, but now her soft feathers ruffled my cheek. I'd always wanted to feel her beside me.

Another stag sauntered into the clearing to stand beside the Goddess.

Feradea nodded at the regal animal. The wind pushed the Goddess's red and orange mane away from her angular face. "The stag represents more than another fera. He is my strength, my essence, and a symbol of my divinity, as he will be for you. This, daughter-of-my-daughter, is my gift to you."

The stag stepped forward and bent his soft muzzle to me. His doe-like gaze settled on mine, asking permission.

I reached out and stroked his soft face. At my touch, his presence shimmered and wavered until he, too, joined with me. Instead of sliding to the other side through the portal to join all the other feras, he remained within, and settled around my heart like a protective barrier. His presence grew warm and comforting, ballooning outward, until he swelled out of my body and reformed as a ghost-like fera to stand beside me.

My mouth dropped open.

The stag leaned down and nuzzled my face. The short, soft bristles of his fur tickled my cheek.

I turned to Feradea. "I don't understand."

The Goddess cocked her head to one side. "What is there to understand?"

"Does this mean I can only shift into the beast or stag now?" How would that work? All my feras had been female until now. Would I literally grow a pair?

Feradea's head dropped back, and her bell-like laughter rang out in the crisp air. "Silly child. You can shift into whatever you want. You are no longer restricted by the limitations of your feras."

Errr. I glanced at the stag, his presence warm and comforting.

"The stag will remain at your side. He will fade in and out as needed, and can form fully for others to see, but he is more than another fera. He is a conduit for your transformations and..." Feradea smiled.

"And?" Geez. Did I even want to know? My mind stretched as if it would burst with one more piece of information.

"As a manifestation of your power, he is a portal to the other realms. I hope you will visit me, daughter-mine."

My head recoiled. Physically whiplashed back as her words hit me. A portal? I cast a wary glance at the stag.

Feradea smiled. She dipped her chin in a silent goodbye.

"Wait!" I called out. My hand stretched before me.

She rose an eyebrow. "What now?"

"Does this mean I have to stalk pubescent Shifter teens to dispense feras?"

Feradea laughed. "No child. Their nature will call the correct fera to them. You simply guard the door and keep the feras company in exchange for immense power and a set of skills unique to only you."

Sounded like an unfair exchange, but I didn't plan on complaining. "Any advice?"

"*Shine, not burn.*" With her cryptic words, she disappeared without a puff of smoke or incantation, the space she occupied a second before now sat empty.

"Shine, not burn," I muttered. "What the heck am I going to do with that?"

An eagle screeched overhead and circled with another above the clearing.

Sonny? Tank? I mindspoke.

One of the eagle's faltered. Sonny's reply came a second later. *You can speak to my mind?*

Guess Tank didn't enlighten him. *Yeah, I'm badass.*

Tank cackled in my head.

Sonny snorted and veered to the east. *Well, get your badass back to the boat. Wick called the satellite phone. They found your friends.*

Finally!

I reached inside and called for an eagle. The new form flowed out fast. Bones condensed, flesh transformed, feathers sprouted. Within seconds, I pumped my broad wings and launched my regal form into the air to join my brother.

You've learned new tricks.

You have no idea, I replied.

Though bigger and more powerful than my pere-

J. C. MCKENZIE

grine falcon form, the eagle lacked the quick maneuvering skills I'd grown accustomed to for flying. A gust of wind caught my large wingspan and toppled me over.

I squawked and righted my path before veering into a tree.

Sonny and Tank chortled in my head.

Shifter girl learns to fly, Tank sang.

I ignored both of them and pumped my wings until I cleared the tree tops.

The other two screeched and careened through the air to join me. *Let's fly.*

My soul swelled as I shrieked in response. I peered down into the clearing below. The totem pole no longer stood in the centre. Just *poof*. Gone. The trees around where it had been seemed to close in, forever removing any traces the totem pole existed. Just a memory, a ghost, a whisper of what once was. My discarded clothes and backpack sat on the mossy floor below as the only evidence I'd been there.

Sonny swooped by and cut me off with a playful squawk. I shrieked back at him. We danced in the air flows together, brother and sister, along with Tank, truly united at last.

R ed, my fox fera, ran down the path like a neglected pet dog, as it led along a calm river to a small open area. Across Yakoun River, what remained of a fallen tree sadly poked out of the surrounding forest and lay along the river bank.

Tank soared above the trail, choosing to keep his distance from the "yapping overgrown rodent."

"What is this place?" And more importantly, why had Sonny stopped here instead of taking me directly to the airport? As beautiful as this path and forest were, it looked no different than the one we ran through every day. I could be sucking back caffeine right now.

Sonny sat down on a lone bench overlooking the river and the sad fallen tree. "This is where the Golden Spruce used to stand."

I frowned. Something pinged in my head. "I remember the story. Some crazy environmentalist cut it down, right?"

Sonny nodded and ran his hand along the park bench before pointing to the large green sign. I had been too busy taking in the nature to notice the sign. Had there been other signs or plaques along the way, too? Probably.

I'd definitely lost my edge as an assassin. Something about this place put me at ease, too at ease. Lucky for me, the SRD appeared to have either lost my trail or gave up on retrieving me.

I read the government sign: *"The Golden Spruce once stood across the Yakoun River from this viewpoint. A genetic deficiency gave the tree its golden colour and it featured prominently in Haida lore. The tree was felled in 1997 in a misdirected attempt to protest logging practices in the province."*

Sadness settled on my shoulders.

Sonny's voice interrupted my thoughts. "Our parents loved to come here. It was their favourite place." He pointed at a nearby tree. Someone had carved "Maggie + Tyler" in a heart into the rough bark.

Maggie and Tyler. Our parents.

I sucked in a breath. Sonny hadn't spoken of them much, and I hadn't asked. With so much emotional turmoil to deal with, I hadn't wanted to broach the subject, and Sonny must've silently agreed.

Sonny clenched his jaw and looked away.

Red zapped out of existence. Guess she understood the need for a private conversation, even if the nosey feras eavesdropped all the time.

We do no such thing, Tank huffed.

Hah! Just proved my point.

Tank paused before squawking in my head. *You set me up. You thought that at me.*

Shush, featherhead. I want to hear what Sonny has to say. This is important.

I don't have to put up with this, Tank muttered. He didn't, but that's not why he left. Without explaining his true reasons, I *knew* Sonny's fera flew away to give us privacy, too.

Sonny swallowed and turned to me, the exchange between Tank and me providing him enough time to collect his thoughts. "They used to come here, even before we were born, to run among the trees. Said they felt the spirit of the tree running beside them, and felt one with the forest."

"Spirit?"

"*Kiidk'yaas*, the child who became the Golden Spruce."

I tilted my head.

Sonny smiled in that annoying, yet knowing, way of his. "It's not my story to tell. When you return, we'll visit the storytellers and you can hear it from one of them."

"You sound so certain I'll come back." Of course, I would, but we hadn't talked about it.

Sonny nodded. "I have your mate's truck. You'll be back."

"For the last time, he's not my mate." My mate had died.

My wolf snuck into my mind and howled her disagreement.

I winced.

Sonny shrugged. "If you say so."

We shared a smile, and I returned my gaze to the lonely stump across the river. "Who were they? Our parents? Tristan said they were killed because they were Shifters with a prominent position."

Sonny's smile dropped. "They were."

I sat down beside him and waited. His body radiated warmth. The wind ran across the river and brought more pine and spruce laden air to us. It brushed our cheeks and ran through our hair, tangling the long strands of mine with Sonny's.

My brother reached up, but instead of untangling our hair, he delicately collected the strands and started to braid them together as he spoke. "When the viruses and natural disasters swept the world, our parents helped lead the official outing of the Shifters. They did a pretty good job at educating the public, giving norms reassurance, and stemming the flow of hatred. After their deaths, the Shifter Shankings resumed in earnest."

Our hair, now braided together, lay between us.

Each ink-black strand blending in with the next.

"So they were the leaders of the Shifters?" I'd never heard of such a thing, and I certainly wasn't "princess" material.

Sonny tugged on our mutual braid. "No. More like a representative. Well, Mom was, anyway. Dad just acted as her man-candy accessory because he hated how her position put her in danger. He wanted to protect her."

Sonny let go of the braid. The constant trickle of wind through the trees and gravity worked to unwind it.

The sounds of the enchanted forest took over during Sonny's silence. He thumbed his leather wristband and looked across the sparkling water.

Sonny's last words echoed in my mind. Our mother's job led to her death, and our father's plan to protect her ultimately failed. They'd been killed in their own home by the very man I mourned. Not Tristan's fault. He had no choice but to follow his now-deceased master's orders, but it had taken a lot of soul-searching to get over it and redirect my anger on the correct target. The Master Vampire Ethan wielded Tristan as his weapon of choice.

My stomach twisted into a complicated knot.

Our hair unraveled, and Sonny stood. He brushed off his pants and held his hand out to me. "Come. Let's get you to that flight. We'd better get you some coffee, too. You look twitchy."

Rat bastard. He totally nailed it.

I grasped his hand, and he hauled me off the bench. Without hesitation, I stepped close and hugged him. Hard. With my face burrowed in his chest against his puffy jacket, I inhaled his pine and sea scent. A calming balm flowed through my body. His arms folded around me and squeezed. Sonny bent his head forward and his long hair fell across my face as a warm, fragrant curtain.

"I'm going to miss you," I said.

"*Háws dáng hl kingsaang.*" His breath brushed against my ear and he used one hand to stroke my hair.

"What does that mean?"

"I'll see you again."

24

Mel cast me a furtive glance as we drove along the highway toward Wick's place in Kits. Despite her god-awful driving skills, she wouldn't let anyone else pick me up.

"What?" I asked, after the millionth time.

"Nothing." She shrugged and pretended to watch the road more attentively. She didn't fool me. If it weren't for her fast Were reflexes, her driving would resemble a Monster Truck rally, and we would've died five minutes out of the airport.

"Come on, Mel. You're furrowing your brows and risking wrinkles. Spit it out."

"What's your brother like?" she asked instead.

My turn to shrug. "He's my brother. We've been separated for eighty years, almost my entire life." I drummed my fingers along the door frame. "But I have this feeling. I just know I can always go to him." My eyes stung. I shifted my weight in the seat and turned to look out the window.

"Is he hot?"

"Ew. He's my *brother*. And you're mated."

"Yeah, I know. I'm asking for *all the single ladies*." She tried singing the last part.

I winced. "Yeah, he's attractive."

"The girls would love to meet him." She giggled, and her cheeks flushed.

I grumbled. What girls? True, I hadn't met Mel's coworkers or *all* of the unmated females in Wick's pack, but there weren't many. After meeting Christine, my motivation to connect with more women disappeared a long time ago.

"So he's building a resort?" Mel asked.

"It will be pretty amazing when it's done." Although his plans looked beautiful, I couldn't envision Sonny excelling with the business side of running a tourist lodge—too much of a recluse. I'd swallowed my concerns. This project meant a lot to him and the community. He'd have tons of help.

Mel smiled and took the off-ramp.

I slapped my hand out to avoid smacking my head against the window. My breath caught. "Jesus!"

Mel's brows dug in more. "Are you planning to go back, after...?"

"After I mow down every motherfucker in my way to get Ben and the boys?" My blood boiled at the thought. My wolf snuck into my thoughts and growled.

Her lips twisted. "Such language."

"Ugh." I scowled. "Not you, too."

She chuckled and made another turn. Without slowing down. My stomach rolled.

"Well, are you?" she asked.

"I can't exactly go back to my place, can I? Where else would I go?" I tapped my fingers along the arm rest.

"What about your job with the Vancouver Police Department?"

My skin grew cold and my breath hitched. I looked out the window at the hordes of vehicles. "Well, that's probably finished, but even if it wasn't, I don't know if I'd go back. Tristan made sure I'd never have to work again if I didn't want to." I paused. "I might get bored, though. The VPD offers some entertainment."

Mel smiled. "You could have both."

"I could." Maybe.

Silence swamped the inside of Mel's white SUV. "Mel?"

She sighed and her tense shoulders dropped down. "Wick is planning to step down as Alpha."

"What? Why?"

"He can't accept another mate and he's trying to move on. Ryan has agreed to wait until after the revenge tour to challenge him."

I gulped. My stomach flipped, and a weird buzzing sensation consumed my mind. "To the death?"

"Of course not," Mel said. "Our pack isn't like that."

"But he'll be a lone wolf." Sometimes, that was worse than death.

"He'll be okay." Her voice wavered.

Well, what did I expect? An unmated Alpha always created a potential weakness in the pack. Normally this wasn't an issue, as long as a mate was a possibility, but Wick's wolf wouldn't accept anyone else and I'd chosen someone else. I'd also grieved the loss of Tristan extensively in front of Wick, pushed him away when he tried to comfort me, and flung insults at him. He said he'd move on. I knew he planned to move on. I wanted him happy, and that meant he'd have to move on.

My mouth developed a bitter taste from the repetitive thought of "moving on." Really, I didn't know how to feel about this news.

My wolf popped into my head again and growled.

When I flinched, she disappeared.

Be honest, the stag whispered in my ear. I jumped and turned around, but the stag hadn't appeared.

Mel glanced at me, eyebrows furrowed. "I barely swerved that time."

Be honest? I clenched my jaw and squeezed my fists. I'd never stopped loving Wick. Not really. But now... Now it was too late. I'd ruined everything. Not just my relationship with Wick, but myself as well.

Tristan's death had occurred over five months ago. He'd been gone longer than our entire relationship. Although it hurt to think of him, and the loss of what we might have had, my soul had spent a lot of time mending on the Haida Gwaii. My brother's presence and love, combined with the silent strength and freedom of the surrounding nature, had helped immensely. My mind had replayed Sonny's sage words about letting go over and over, until it healed the gaping wound from losing Tristan.

Enough to accept a new mate? Maybe. But I was too late—entirely my fault, too.

Mel cleared her throat.

"I'm processing," I said, voice catching.

She glanced at me. "He hasn't stepped down yet, and even if he does there's still a chance for the two of you."

"Mel..."

"Don't." She shook her head. "Don't lie to me. We're too good of friends for that crap. I know why you chose Tristan, but I also know you never truly let go of Wick."

I sucked in a breath. How could she sound so sure?

"You would've mated with Tristan already if you had," she answered, as if hearing my unspoken question.

I shifted in my seat again and stared at my hands. Images of intimate moments with Tristan flashed through my mind, particularly one instance where I'd bitten him, hard, nearly claiming him as mine. Almost. Something had held me back. At the time, I'd explained my inaction as fear of commitment after my experience with Dylan.

Though very dead by my own hands, having a past featuring a sadistic, abusive ex who claimed to be my mate and tried to force a bond on me made my reluctance to jump into any mate bond understandable.

Now? Now, I wasn't sure I could lie to myself like that and believe it.

"And—" Mel bit her lip and pretended to shoulder check.

"No point in pulling punches now." Even if they were poorly formed.

"And I always thought you forgave him too easily."

She didn't need to elaborate. I'd told her how Tristan had killed my biological parents when I was a baby. "He was under Ethan's control, and it's not like I remember the incident or my birth parents."

"But you always wondered about them, and what your life would have been like. I know you loved your adoptive parents, but Tristan's actions, even if directed by Ethan, robbed you of your intended childhood."

"It wasn't easy to forgive him, Mel."

"No, but it was easier than forgiving Wick."

I squeezed my eyes shut. The car swerved again as Mel changed lanes. Or at least that's what I hoped had happened. "Wick acted on Lucien's orders when we were together. Well, sort of. It's still very vivid."

"And it triggered memories of Dylan and the pack."

My eyes popped open, and I watched my friend. She still bit her lip. Anger no longer flared at the mention of Dylan and his fucked-up Werewolf pack. The pain he'd inflicted and the nightmares of my time under his control no longer plagued me at night. Tristan had helped me heal from that part of my brutal past.

"But I always thought there was more to it," Mel continued.

The honking horns, swearing, and screeching tires faded to a background hum as I waited for Mel's next words. Hovering like some starving seagull waiting to swoop down on a dropped French fry.

Mel's blue gaze flicked to me and she released her lip. "I know you loved Tristan, and part of you always will, but I don't think you ever cared for him as deeply as you do Wick. It explains why you were such an irrational head case when Christine threw herself at him, why Wick's betrayal cut you so much deeper, and why you let him go."

Because I love him, whole-heartedly and unequivocally.

My wolf chose this moment to pop into my head again and howl. Loudly.

Tension flowed from my muscles as the truth moved in. I already knew I loved Wick, but now I had to face Mel's words and accept them. No more running. No more pretending. Big girl panty time.

Mel said it was still possible to win back Wick's heart, but what if she was wrong? A lump grew in my throat. "Dammit, Mel. I've made a mess of things. I'm a mess."

She reached out and grasped my nearest hand. "You're human."

I laughed. I'd already told her about my experience in the clearing with Feradea.

"Well, mostly." She turned to wink at me. "By the way, I don't think—"

A car cut in from the inside lane. "Look out!" I screeched.

Mel dropped my hand, gripped the wheel, and swerved. The motion flung my body into the interior side of the door. My head whipped against the frame. Pain lanced out from my right temple and shoulder.

The vehicle settled. Mel regained control and composure. *Maybe I shouldn't have left Wick's truck with Sonny and driven back instead.*

Mel pushed the window button down. When it opened, she thrust her hand out to give the other driver an inappropriate gesture. The cold air rushing into the SUV flipped her big blonde hair in all directions and her laughter filled the interior.

I laughed along. "God, I've missed you, woman."

A Norse God opened the door to his home for us. His smile didn't reach his intense gaze, and his posture remained stiff.

Mel, a sub in his pack, shifted her weight from foot to foot.

Great. Whatever she sensed through the pack bond put her on edge.

"Mel. Andy. Trip okay?" he asked as he moved to the side to let us in. His gaze quickly scanned our bodies as if checking for injuries. His gaze lingered on me before snapping away.

"Just swell." *If you count three more hair-raising near misses on the road and the emotional turmoil bubbling in my gut.* I moved past Wick and tried to shut my senses against the rosemary and sugar scent licking off his skin.

Mel mumbled something polite behind me, and we shuffled into Wick's beautiful home.

"*Just swell* wouldn't be the words I'd choose to describe Mel's driving," Wick commented.

"Hey!" she protested.

"Well, we survived. So it was a successful trip." I clarified.

Mel grumbled as we walked into the large, open plan living room. Naturally lit with bay windows, the calm neutral taupe of the walls, dark espresso furnishings and crisp white trim, embedded with Wick's rosemary and sugar scent, brought back a flood of memories. Some bad, some good, some incredibly naughty. My cheeks flushed as images of Wick and me on the couch resurfaced.

The majority of Wick's pack waited in the living room, among them stood Steve, Ryan, John, Jess, and Mel's mate Danny. Stan, Veronika, and Lucus had also travelled in to join us. No Sid. Apparently, the need for a Demon hadn't arrived yet.

I waved a silent hello to everyone before Stan enveloped me in a large hug. My eyes stung as I returned his squeeze.

"Hey partner," I whispered.

"Hey." He sniffed and pulled back. Were his eyes red? "Getting too sissy around here without your cursing."

I laughed.

"I resent that," Steve called out. "I added at least three new slurs to my vocabulary." His emerald gaze twinkled. His casual demeanour often clashed with his role as a pack enforcer. Stan said something rude to Steve, but I ignored it, pulled back my shoulders to face the group.

Everyone stood tensely, their gazes flicking between me and Wick. Why would he ever consider stepping down as an Alpha? He was their leader and they needed him. If he went lone wolf, he might end up feral and then the SRD would get called in and...

No.

Is that what Wick wanted?

Death by SRD agent?

My stag chose this moment to appear, full force, not ghost-like. Everyone in the room gasped. A few wolves growled.

Fight for him, he said, before nuzzling my face. He blinked out and disappeared.

"What the hell is that?" Ryan growled, his freckled cheeks flushing to match his flaming red hair.

"My new fera."

"A deer?" John's voice sounded incredulous. "A goddamn herbivore is going to lead us into battle?"

"I'd spit that mule out for dinner," Ryan said.

I pulled the beast, and let her form flow through my limbs. I halted the shift before I ripped through my clothes, but the majority of the beast features pushed through. Including the horns.

I focused my feral gaze on a frozen John. The divine energy of the beast rolled over the crowd.

Stan narrowed his gaze.

"No," my deep beast voice rumbled. "You have the

power of a Carus, the progeny of Feradea with the skills of the divine."

John blanched. The dark tone of his skin somehow paled, and sweet sweat broke across his brow. My beast swelled, pushing forward, demanding domination. The seams of my shirt groaned from strain. Something ripped. Instead of going with the change, I pushed the beast back and flipped my hair away from my now-human face. A quick survey of my clothing revealed small tears in the seams under the arms. I shrugged. *Still good.*

"I know there's history here," I addressed the group. "But I came to kick some ass. Keep your shit opinions of me to yourself and if you're not going to help..." I paused to give Ryan a pointed look.

He snarled.

"Then stay the fuck out of my way."

Silence settled over the group like a prickly wool blanket.

Jess cleared her throat. Her spiky hair tipped blue today. "But a deer?"

"He's a stag, actually, and he was a gift from Feradea."

"The goddess of animals and the hunt?" Jess asked in a hushed whisper. Her tone implied disbelief. "You spoke to her?"

I turned to the shewolf and smiled wide. "I've spoken to her more than once."

"That's so cool," she said.

The Weres in the room stiffened, smelling the truth of my words. Mel beamed and practically vibrated beside her mate. If we stood closer, she'd probably try to high-five me. With terrible form.

The Witches exchanged a look, and Lucus rose from the oversized armchair he'd perched on. "You've come into your own, Andy. A fully-realized Carus. Congratulations."

I nodded. Images of the day in the clearing and meeting with Feradea flickered through my mind and warmed my entire body. The Weres unfroze and started mumbling among themselves. I didn't catch what they said, I didn't try.

Lucus's head shone almost as brightly as his teeth. "We'll have a chance now."

"Against the Elders?"

He shook his head. "They no longer have the boys."

"What?" My sharp tone drew everyone's attention. Stan walked over to place a hand on my shoulder. Veronika leaned forward. "The Elders gave the Witch coven to the Pharaoh in exchange for immunity from whatever plans the Pharaoh has for the Lower Mainland."

"How can they do that?" My voice rose an octave. The willingness of the Werewolf pack to help me made more sense now. Before it had been Wick's desire to help me, but now that I was safe from the SRD, the pack really had no interest or connection with the Witch coven. The Pharaoh on the other hand...

Lucus and Veronika exchanged another look.

Veronika answered my question. "The Elders justified the trade as a reasonable penance for the coven for their part in Bola's massacres. The Pharaoh is supposed to release them after a year of servitude."

"The Elders will pay for this." My fists clenched and each knuckle popped.

"Andy..." Stan started.

I tried to shrug off his hand, but he clamped down. "The Elders are fucking twats, but they made our job easier," Stan said. He grimaced, or possibly tried to smile, his teeth like slats of a crooked picket fence.

His statement got my attention. The tension flowed from my muscles and I turned to my friend. "Huh?"

"Instead of going against the Elders *and* the Pharaoh, both formidable foes, you only have one target now," Stan said.

"One target instead of two," Wick agreed, breaking his silence since insulting Mel's driving.

"Why should I let the Elders get away with Witch trafficking?" I asked.

Lucus cleared his throat. "It's not actually illegal, and some would argue Ben and his coven deserved it."

I grumbled. Maybe Matt, Patty, and Christopher, but not Ben. The Witches he mentored had snuck around behind his back and when they realized their mistake, they'd hid it from him.

"Andy?" Mel asked.

"Yeah?"

"The Pharaoh?"

"Fucking dead," I spat.

The room relaxed and some of the wolves nodded.

Time to plan.

25

With my hand on the doorknob, I froze. Rustling in the hallway told me I wasn't the only one who couldn't sleep. The scents trickling in told me Wick and Mel were both up, and from their forced tones, they weren't happy with each other.

I pressed my ear to the door and pulled the beast close to listen in. Her hearing trumped any of my feras, and probably surpassed the wolves as well. The Were-proof door no longer provided an adequate block for sound. Not like it prevented Weres from hearing beyond the door if they were close enough, but it had acted as a barrier to my once inferior Shifter hearing.

"You're an idiot," Mel hissed.

Wick paused. His next words came out dangerously low. "Excuse me?"

Mel didn't answer right away. Probably quivering with fear. Speaking to her Alpha like this went against every instinct in her Werewolf body. Facing his rage would be terrifying.

"She let you go because she loved you. She never stopped. It's plain to anyone who looks," Mel whispered.

"Not to me."

"You need to fight for her. Claim her."

"I tried." His tone hardened. "I tried and she threw it in my face."

Mel sucked in a breath in time with mine. "She was grieving. Give her a chance."

"How many?"

"What?"

"How many chances should I give her? I'm tired of chasing. Of waiting. I'm moving on. If she wants to love a ghost or run away, fine."

Mel groaned. "If you hadn't noticed, she's not running away. She's at the end of the hall, behind that door. In your house. It's you who's preparing to run away."

I recoiled at the mention of the door I hid behind. Warmth rushed to heat my cheeks. I shouldn't eavesdrop on this conversation, but a flock of flamingoes on steroids couldn't drag me away.

Mel grunted, and her footsteps stomped away.

"Mel?" Wick called out in a hushed tone.

She stopped.

"I haven't stepped down yet. You'll not speak to me like that again." His voice remained hard.

"Of course, Alpha. Please accept my apologies." She walked away. A door shut in the distance.

Wick swore.

My cheeks heated again. My skin grew clammy. I'd never heard Mel talk that way. Certainly not to an Alpha. She'd rather go belly up and bare her soft neck.

I remained frozen at my door. Mel had walked away, but Wick hadn't moved. Did he stand in the hallway, staring at the very door I leaned against? If I moved now, he'd know I was up.

Maybe this was a chance to talk to him.

What would I say? That the ache in my chest wasn't just from losing Tristan, but from losing him, too?

How could I have predicted Lucien's demise, Wick's freedom, and Tristan's death? Hindsight was always twenty-twenty. I thought I'd saved Wick and myself from pain and hurt. Instead, I caused more.

How could I have asked Wick to endure the torture Lucien would've no doubt enacted to control me? How could I have expected him to suffer, even if he'd been willing?

I took the high road once and crashed. Should I take it again and let Wick find happiness without me or should I—

"Andy?" Wick's deep rumble vibrated through the door.

I jumped and stumbled back. Frozen, I stared at the door, too lost in my own head to hear Wick's approach.

"Andy. I can hear you breathing."

Not to mention my graceful startle-response.

Reflexes? Check.

Of course, he heard me through a Were-proof door at

that distance. They weren't completely sound-proofed and as an Alpha, Wick's senses were even more heightened than the rest of his pack.

Dumb, Andy. Real dumb.

Red chose this moment, of all times, to wink into existence and run around my feet. I'd already accused her of acting like a hyped-up Chihuahua once. Obviously, she didn't get the message.

Wick, Wick, Wick, she chanted.

Shoo!

Red shot me what could only be described as a grin before disappearing.

I sighed and opened the door. Wick's large presence filled the doorway. His sleep tussled hair stuck out, and his rumpled T-shirt and boxers clung to his muscled body. I ripped my gaze away from Wick's chest and focused on his narrowed gaze.

"I couldn't sleep," I said. I wanted to bolt, but I locked my knees and tensed my muscles instead. Dangit. I wouldn't buckle. Not prey. Not submissive.

The beast rumbled approval.

Wick's jaw clenched. "How much did you hear?"

"Enough."

His hands folded into fists.

Claim him. The stag's voice echoed through my mind.

Wick nodded and turned to go.

"Mel was right," I blurted.

Wick froze, half-turned away.

My heart raced in my chest, and sweat dripped down

my back. My feet itched to run. *Crap.* Maybe I should've kept my mouth shut.

Wick slowly turned to me. His gaze still narrowed, his eyebrows furrowed. "What?"

"I never stopped," I mumbled to my feet. So much for not cowing to his dominance.

Wick sucked in a breath.

I gripped the door and forced my chin up to meet Wick's gaze. He'd clamped his lips shut, but his look smouldered.

Maybe I should bolt. Dive out the open window of my room, shift to falcon, and fly away. My wolf howled.

Wick stepped forward. His warm hands slid up my bare arms. The contact zinged my nerves in a million directions. Hope ballooned in my chest.

Startled, I looked up. Wick's hands gripped my shoulders and pulled me closer. I staggered forward.

"You never stopped what?" Wick demanded. His fingers dug into my skin, and his angry gaze bore into mine.

"Loving you," I whispered.

Wick pushed me away and I stumbled back. My breath lodged in my throat. The warmth in my chest fled as ice trickled up my spine. What the hell?

"Fuck, Andy!" He ran a hand through his hair.

Umm... What should I say now? I hadn't thought that far. Stupid stag. Where was that soft-nosed, antler-head now?

"You've never said those words to me, before." A

bitter laugh. "And now? You choose now to say them?" His gaze flashed wolf yellow. "Now?"

"I—"

"I, what?" he stormed.

"I'm a mess, Wick," I hissed back. "Haven't you noticed? I'm a fucking mess, and I've made a shit storm of everything. I know that. I have to live with that." I thumped my chest. "I thought I made the right choice, for everyone. I couldn't stand to see you hurt, and tortured, because of me, so I let you go."

I shoved him back. He didn't move.

"Don't you get it? I loved you so much, I let you go."

Wick growled.

"I had no way of knowing your wolf wouldn't accept another. No way of telling the future—"

Wick's lips crushed against mine. My next line melted into his warm tongue claiming my mouth. Molten lava flowed through my veins as his delicious scent wrapped around me. My fingers ached to run over every inch of his hard body. Wick's mouth moved over mine with delectable pressure and need. My stomach fluttered as my thoughts spun off their tracks to get lost forever. Time slowed to an exquisite pace where every cell tingled with awareness and begged to be tasted, and then—

Nothing.

Wick pulled back without warning. His gaze searching.

Too soon. The kiss, the contact, the connection... He

ended it too quickly, too abruptly. My whole body reeled from the unexpected loss of contact.

"But let me guess." Wick's mouth curled down. "You need time and space."

"What?" I sputtered, still swaying from his kiss.

"You always push me away." Wick took a step back. "I understood your reasons. I tried to be patient and let you heal, but another man stole you from me instead. I have my own interests to protect. I meant what I said on the Haida Gwaii. I've been without a mate for almost two hundred years. I can go another hundred or so. I'm not waiting for you to be ready, Andy. Mating be damned." He spun around and stalked back to his room.

"No! Wick, I—"

His door shut on any protest I could muster.

My mouth opened and closed. My mind reeled.

What had I done?

My stag flittered back into existence.

Fight for him.

Shush, you...you...herbivore.

The beast rumbled through my essence, shaking with my breaking heart. I'd professed my love to Tristan too late, and we never had a chance at a happily-ever-after. I didn't want the opportunity for love to slip by again. But I finally put my feelings out there, and Wick shot me down. He had every right to, every reason, but it didn't make the deep wound hurt any less.

I gently shut the door and walked my heavy limbs back to bed. The soft duvet did little to assuage the cold seeping through my body. Wick had refused me, and the sad part of me understood. The other part locked itself in denial, and a small itsy bitsy part, hated how every other Were who'd stayed the night at Wick's place overheard our conversation and witnessed my humiliation.

WIND RAN ALONG MY LONG NIGHTGOWN LIKE soft caressing tendrils. The dark forest loomed around me as I waited in a clearing by a fast flowing river.

Having experienced this artificial forest in a dream before, I knew immediately what lurked beyond the mist-shrouded bank.

Sid.

As I walked to the end of the water, the mist cleared to reveal the Seducer Demon waiting patiently on the other side, this time fully clothed. No "big gun" swinging to and fro.

Huh.

I wondered when I'd see the Demon again. Although there'd been more than a few full moons since my escape from the SRD, he hadn't used the bond to pull through to the mortal realm. Maybe he couldn't until I fully broke the effects of SomaX on my beast.

"Carus," his deep voice greeted me.

"Hey, Sid." I yanked down on my sheer nightie. "How about more realistic clothing?

Instantly, my body lost the dated outfit and became clad in form-fitting fighting leather.

"Not exactly realistic." I frowned. I hated leather pants, they always made my legs and butt sweat and ridiculously hard to peel off after that. But they made my ass look great and they were good for washing off blood and guts.

"When I think of you, little Carus, this is how I see you."

"As a ball-busting dominatrix?"

He shook his head. "Badass."

I sputtered. Not sure how to take a compliment from this guy, I narrowed my eyes at him. "What are you playing at? You promised no sex mojo."

Sid sighed and held his hands out to his sides. "I can't help it if you want to jump my bones because of a compliment, Carus. I merely wished to praise you."

I grumbled and crossed my arms. The leather outfit creaked.

"I wish to discuss the next full moon."

"Why haven't you used me as an anchor after my release? Did the SomaX prevent you?"

He shook his head again. "No. After you escaped the magical confines of the prison cell, I could've used my bond with you to pull across at any time."

"Too busy eye groping Veronika?"

Sid's lips compressed, and something dark flashed across his gaze.

Oops! Touched a nerve there.

"I left you alone these past months because the

anchor business is hard on you. Not fully in touch with your abilities, I didn't want to risk hurting you more."

"Huh." I shut my gaping mouth and stared at the Demon.

"How is your health, Carus? I sense you've reconnected with your divine nature, and it's stronger now."

"Yeah, I'm full badass, now," I mumbled.

He shifted his weight and glanced around. Silence stretched over the dream world as I waited for him to speak, too shaken by his changed demeanour to make any snide comments.

I scratched my head. "Thank you for getting me out of the lab. I would've gone certifiable in there."

"More than you already are?"

"You know what I mean."

"I do." His chin dipped down in a nod. "And you're welcome."

"How'd you get the rescue team together?"

His white teeth flashed and contrasted with his olive skin. "I cashed in a favour and it allowed me access to Lucus. Once in contact with Veronika's brother, it was a simple matter of rallying the troops." He paused. "Or rather, willing participants."

A fuzzy feeling spread through my chest at the thought of Wick and Stan risking their lives to rescue me. As for Clint and Allan, well, they had their own agendas, but I didn't despise them anymore.

"What was the favour?" I asked.

Sid tsked at me. "I collect favours easily, but I never

kiss and tell. I'm a Seducer Demon, little one, not a gossip."

I rolled my eyes.

Sid hesitated. "Would it be okay with you if I used our bond on the next new moon?" he asked.

Asked.

The big, bad, Seducer Demon *asked* permission. My jaw hit the dream world's floor.

Sid's lips curled up, and he snarled at me.

"Yes," I heard myself saying. "Yes, it would be okay."

Sid nodded. Before he disappeared and the dream world faded, his words whispered in my mind. "Thank you."

26

I bent my head toward the mug and hid my face in the aromatic steam lifting off the caffeinated surface. I'd waited until others arrived or got up before I slunk downstairs to show my face. Not only reeling from Wick's rejection, I mauled over Sid's odd behaviour from the night before.

Mel had wordlessly handed me a supersized mug filled with coffee. Her blue gaze soft, and her half-smile sympathetic. The Wereleopards phoned with more information, and Olly was on his way over.

I avoided Wick, and he appeared to have the same game plan. Though he sat, staunchly silent, two feet away, the emotional distance spanned like a dark abyss between us.

What more could I do? I hadn't asked for more time. Hell, I wasn't sure I wanted or needed it. But if I acted now, I needed to be sure. I couldn't play with Wick's heart. Assuming he still wanted me.

My thoughts faltered. That kiss.

His searing tongue twisting with mine to claim my mouth as his hard body pressed into me...

That kiss said he still wanted me.

I drummed my fingers along my mug. If Wick hadn't pushed me away, would I have done exactly what he accused me of? Another long drag of caffeinated air, followed by a deep sip of heaven.

No.

The answer shocked me. Although I still hurt from the losing Tristan and grieved his death, I had time to heal—first as a rampaging beast hell-bent on destruction, then in the lab as a chemically-curbed shell, and last, and more importantly, on the Haida Gwaii as myself with my brother's help.

No. I didn't need more time or space. I glanced at Wick. His mouth remained clamped shut in a firm, thin line, and he refused to look at me.

I'd already loved and lost. I refused to let another chance at happiness escape. Would Wick believe me? Maybe I should tell him and find out.

I breathed out and let the tension slide off my shoulders. *Wick.*

Wick tensed. His fingers gripped his mug tightly.

He didn't reply to my mind speech.

I—

Wick leapt out of his seat, coffee sloshing over the sides of his mug. He ignored the liquid dripping down his hand and placed the cup on the kitchen counter.

"I'm going for a walk." Wick's strong voice shattered

the uncomfortable moratorium on speaking and drew my attention away from the window. "If the Wereleopards arrive while I'm out, start the planning without me."

My stomach dropped, and my eyes stung.

Everyone's gaze turned to me, but I ignored them. How could I meet the sympathy in Mel's expression, or the smugness in Ryan's?

"Enjoy the weather. It looks nice out there." If I could smack my face with my palm right now, I would. Instead, I gripped my coffee mug and moved away to look out the bay windows. Dog walkers, joggers, and people in general milled around outside, completely oblivious to the pain whirling inside me like a tornado.

Everyone else inside remained silent and frozen.

Wick's footsteps grew fainter and the door closed on his exit. I didn't breathe the entire time. My stomach kept trying to tie itself in knots, and my heart convulsed, the beat echoing as if in an empty chamber.

Wanting to have Wick now, after I screwed everything up, was selfish. I saw that now. I'd hurt him. He deserved happiness, or at least the freedom to pursue it,

I sighed again, and Mel walked up to stand beside me.

"He'll change his mind," she whispered.

"Doubt it," I mumbled. "Whatever. We have an evil Vampire empire to destroy."

A knock on the door, and the citrus and sunshine scents of the Wereleopards punctuated my statement.

WICK'S WOLVES, THE WERELEOPARDS, THE
Witches, Stan, and I convened in various places around
Wick's supersized dining table. Hordes of paper lay scattered across the dark surface, along with tablets, laptops,
and smart phones. The scents of everyone in the room
swirled together in a heady mixture, sprinkled with frustration and apprehension.

I kept Sid's visit to myself. It wouldn't change any of
our plans at the moment, and frankly my dreams were no
one's business.

The door shut softly as our planning group bent over
the table dissecting building plans and surveillance
reports. The quiet click sent a shiver down my spine
along with a cold prickling wave. Wick was back. His
rosemary and sugar scent barrelled down the hall ahead
of him. He approached the table.

"Nice walk?" Steve asked. Though he spoke to his
Alpha, his emerald gaze trained on me. Before Steve refocused on the maps, he winked at me.

"Refreshing." Wick's gaze stayed as far from mine as
possible.

No one else seemed to have a problem looking at me.

The group parted to allow Wick space, and he rested
both hands on the table. "Where are we?"

The Wereleopards brought a lot of intel to the table,

quite literally, thanks to Kayne Security Solutions, but we still needed a way into the Pharaoh's lair without going against the entire horde. We might stand a chance, but Vampires weren't honourable fighters. They'd likely kill my Witch boys before we reached them.

Wick's eyebrows furrowed. His neck bunched as Olly filled him in. "So we still need a stealthy way in."

Everyone nodded.

Stan drummed his fingers along the table. "Why doesn't Andy just infiltrate the building like she did with the KK warehouse? Slither through a vent and use the air ducts to gain entry?"

Wick growled.

We jumped.

"No," Wick said.

"Why not?" Stan folded his arms across his chest. "She's more than capable."

Wick nodded. "That method will land her in the lion's den without any backup. She can't take on the Pharaoh and save Ben at the same time."

"Maybe I could take on the Pharaoh after getting you guys in somehow, and you use the distraction to get the boys out," I piped up.

Wick's mouth compressed. He still avoided my gaze. "Absolutely not."

"They might've installed external surveillance prior to vacating the KK Warehouse," Steve said. He tapped his chin. "They might've studied the footage. If so, they'll know about Andy's skills. There might be a nasty surprise waiting for her the next time she tries to slither around air ducts to gain access to someone's building."

"Exactly," Wick huffed.

Silence settled over the group as the wheels in everyone's heads clanked around. My thoughts focused on the KK Warehouse Stan mentioned. Like a little breadcrumb, I followed the memory down a sequence of events.

"Something's not right." I rifled through the surveillance pictures.

"What do you mean?" Stan asked.

Everyone turned to me except Wick. He kept his gaze trained on the reports.

"When we raided the Pharaoh's drug operations—almost half a year ago, geez—they knew we were coming. Now we know Tucker works for the Pharaoh, and his phone and office tapping probably gave him the information he needed to tip off the Pharaoh about our plans to take down his drug operation, but..."

"But?" Ryan snapped.

"Who bugged Lucien's horde? The SRD found out about the blood bond Lucien forced on me from recordings, but no one ever discovered the source. That couldn't have been Tucker, and Lucien said he grilled his entire horde and inner circle, including Wick." Prickles raced up my spine. Connecting the dots sent my stomach in a knot. "So who's the leak? According to Lucien, the recording came from an area not easily accessible by general visitors, which means whoever planted the bugs had to have access to someone in Lucien's inner circle. And that person sent the evidence directly to the SRD and Tucker."

John growled. "What are you trying to say?"

"There could be someone in this pack with ties to the SRD. Hell, maybe even the Pharaoh. We don't know how deep the corruption at the SRD goes."

Ryan and John growled and pushed away from the table. Olly and Angie exchanged a smug glance. The Witches twitched but didn't say anything.

"You have some nerve, lady," Ryan seethed. "We save you, we house you, we help you, and you turn around and point fingers at us?"

"Whoa!" I held my hands up. "I mean no disrespect. I'm certainly not saying it's you or anyone at this table. But it is a possibility, and after the VPD raid experience, wouldn't you want to be sure? It won't hurt to be extra cautious."

Wick growled.

I tensed and turned to him slowly. Surprise, he wasn't looking at me.

"She's right," he said. "A mole exists somewhere and the most reasonable explanation is our pack, since Lucien questioned his entire horde. Although I was the only member of the pack to enter that room, a bug could've been planted on me or my clothes."

"It's an easy problem to solve," I said. The Werewolves stiffened.

Before anyone else had a chance to growl or snap at me, I explained. "We can all sense a lie, either through smell or spell." Well, almost everyone could. I winced and turned to Stan.

He gave an exasperated sigh and waved at me to continue.

"One by one, answer this question: do you work for the Pharaoh or the SRD?"

Wick's molten brown gaze met mine. I tensed but refused to bolt. When he didn't look away, I raised my eyebrow. He didn't need to answer the question, he'd already been interrogated by Lucien, but once he made eye contact, he couldn't look away first. Alphas.

He smirked. "No. I don't work for the Pharaoh or SRD. I did not plant the bug, and I will not communicate the information from our planning to any other group in any way."

Well, he went above and beyond. His gaze bore a hole right through me, and my muscles itched to squirm in my seat. He'd enjoy that though. I broke the staring contest and turned to John. He grunted and repeated Wick's more thorough statement.

One by one, everyone around the table repeated Wick's words. Even the Witches, the Wereleopards, and Stan, none of whom were on the suspect list.

Not one single liar.

"Well, that clears everyone here," I said.

"Still leaves the question of who was involved," Steve said.

"Maybe we're not looking at this quite right. Who would jeopardize the pack to rat out Andy to the SRD?" Stan asked.

"Christine," Wick, John, and Ryan answered in unison without hesitation.

Of course!

John and Ryan's lips curled in mutual grimaces.

Wick looked like he sucked on bitter apples.

"The question is." Stan broke the silence. "Did Christine act as a jealous, scorned woman, as an agent for the SRD, or as a mole for the Pharaoh?"

A grin spread across my face. "Why don't we catch her and find out?"

27

Apparently, stick insects, aka Christine, were adept at hiding. Honestly, the only thing I thought that woman excelled in was resting bitch face and spending a stupid amount of money on designer clothing.

Wary glances avoided my frothy glare as I searched for something, anything, in the faces around the table. After a week of hunting, we were no closer to finding Christine or the boys than we had been before.

I looked around the table while my brain attempted to compute a new course of action. The Wereleopards and Vampires sat this meeting out. Until we had all our ducks in a row, they weren't really needed anyway.

"Well," I said. "There goes that plan. At least for six days."

Wick's head snapped up. "Six days?" He tapped his fingers on the table top. "What happens on the new moon?"

"I'm a Demon anchor, remember? Sid will help. I won't give him a choice about it." For once, Sid's impending visit didn't send nervous pee signals from my brain. If he showed up as planned, I may as well make it worth my while.

Wick recoiled at my Demon anchor reminder. His chest rumbled with a low growl. Surely, he remembered the circumstances of how I became an anchor. Lucien's doing, but Wick's hands held me down so Sid the Seducer got what he wanted. My blood. It had been the final straw for me and what ultimately led me to choose Tristan over Wick. None of it was Wick's fault.

The other pack members shifted in their seats.

"If Veronika's locator spell was blocked, what can the Demon do?" Wick snarled.

Veronika and Lucus ended up using a contact within the Elders' compound to discover the fate of my friends, not magic. We assumed Ben and the boys were held in the mansion the Pharaoh claimed in Shaughnessy, but we had no confirmation.

I rolled my eyes at Wick's comment.

Wick's gaze flashed wolf yellow.

Witches and Demons had as much in common as Vampires and Werewolves, but I wouldn't point that out just yet. "Sid can do lots."

Stan snorted.

"Not like that." I shoved him.

Stan chortled into his beer before taking another swig. The wolves and Witches looked less impressed. Actually, I had no clue what Sid could do to help our circumstances, but I'd momentarily tapped out my idea bank.

While we twiddled our proverbial thumbs, Christine, the Pharaoh, and Tucker continued to skip along...

"Tucker," I hissed.

The Werewolves turned to me in unison.

"Let's put Christine on the back burner for now. We can't confirm she's a traitor until we interrogate her, but even if she is, she's not a key player." Not in our plan to get the boys back, anyway. She still ranked number one on my revenge hit list. After all, she was responsible for Tristan's death.

John tapped his foot. Ryan gave me a pointed glare to get on with it.

Geez. Tough crowd. "Tucker works for the Pharaoh, and he's too arrogant and stubborn to know when to run and hide."

"You need to get information from him *before* you kill him," Wick's tone disapproved.

My smile grew. "Oh, I don't plan to let him die anytime soon."

TUCKER SLIPPED INTO HIS CAR AFTER TURNING his nose up at the guards who escorted him out of the house. The air rustled under my eagle wings as I circled above, hopefully too high for any magical detection.

Nicely settled at the northwest corner of Davie and Nicola, in the West End area, the grand Victorian estate home embodied everything a classic haunted mansion should. It also seemed familiar. Like I'd eaten pasta there, once.

Crawling with supes, the home left little doubt as to who owned the property now.

The Pharaoh.

With a stone exterior, stained glass accents, and lavish garden space, this home looked like an out-of-place relic in the otherwise bustling area. Beautiful, but on the smallish side of things when it came to power-thirsty world-dominating Vampires. Why would the Pharaoh choose this location? Certainly, larger mansions existed on North Van or Marine Drive to appease his ego.

This location wasn't the massive complex we'd focused on during our planning. In fact, this building wasn't listed as an asset of the Pharaoh's at all. He must've had it under someone else's name. One factor working in our favour was the vastness of the Pharaoh's empire. He had so many properties and interests within and outside the Lower Mainland he had to spread his army of loyal followers thin.

Now that we knew the physical location of this mansion, a call to Kayne Security would result in more building plans and information on their security system. It also left glaring questions: Did the Vampires hold Ben, Matt, Patty, and Christopher at this location or another? Were they being held together or in separate places? If they were at this house, together, who else lurked in the shadows to greet us? They had someone shielding the boys, which meant at least one powerful Witch in the Pharaoh's employ. Hell, maybe he ordered Ben's coven to cloak themselves. We couldn't count on the boys to help us liberate them.

We needed Tucker for information.

Thankfully, his meeting had been short, and from the smug look on Tucker's bland face, also sweet. More questions. What had the Pharaoh offered him? Eternal life? Five hundred adoring virgins? Popularity?

A personality?

A screech ripped through my throat. I tried to swallow it, failed, and squawked into the night. *Dammit!*

I pumped my wings and flew higher into the darkness, veering toward Tucker's home. Hopefully, no one detected that.

The flight to Tucker's modest two-story house in West Vancouver took little time, and I beat ATF home, perching on a nearby roof with a good vantage point. Wick and John roamed among the trees of the nearby park in wolf form, while Ryan, Steve, Lucus, and Veronika sat in a van.

I have an address of another Pharaoh house, I sent Wick.

Good, he grunted. *Phase two?*

Absolutely. I'd looked forward to this part all night.

Time to curb stomp ATF.

Delight bubbled up from my bird chest; I clamped my beak shut on the threatening screech. I wouldn't make the same mistake twice.

Geez. And I thought the falcon was a squawker. I had no idea.

Two cars pulled into Tucker's driveway

I gulped. Neither vehicle belonged to ATF. My muscles tensed. I clenched my beak harder until it hurt, and dug my talons into the soft wood of the roof's trimming.

Randall Tucker, ATF's father and the Director of the SRD, stepped out of the first sleek black sedan in full, crisp business attire. He gently tugged at his sleeves and buttoned the top button of his jacket. Three large men exited the same vehicle, followed by four more from the second car.

Dear ole daddy planned to visit his useless progeny, and he'd brought seven bodyguards. Surely, he didn't worry about ATF harming him. Why the entourage, then? Or did he always have them?

I'd never met Randall, but from all accounts, he was as norm as his son. The guards represented unknowns. Were they human?

I peered closer. At the moment, they appeared like norms, sluggish when compared to a Vampire, and utterly lacking grace. But that meant nothing nowadays. With a history rife with persecution, most supes possessed at least some rudimentary skills at masking their true natures.

Movement from one caught my eye. He stepped around the vehicle a little too smoothly. Shifter? Were? Vampire? Too bad eagles sucked at smelling things out.

We have company, I told Wick.

How many?

Eight. One norm, seven unknown, I reported.

Change the plan?

Common sense said yes. We needed to sit back and revaluate. Certainly get more information on the guards or wait for them to leave.

Y—

Tucker's car pulled up and squashed my answer to Wick. Fuck sitting back. This useless sac was going down tonight.

The guards moved with Randall as he came forward to clasp ATF's hand, bro-style, and pull him in for a hug. As they walked, their business suits moved suspiciously tight around the guards' hips.

I leaned forward, eagle eyes straining.

A flash of metal. My breath caught, and I swallowed another screech. At least one of the guards had a firearm. Safe to assume they packed some heat. Another guard betrayed his otherness when he moved to survey the yard.

They're carrying, I told Wick. *At least two are supes.*

Your call, replied Wick.

He might not trust his emotions around me, but he trusted my judgement for tactical assaults. My chest constricted a little as I continued to watch the men move to the house. Wick had John with him in wolf form. The others still waited in a van down the street. That made seven supes, including me, against nine.

Good odds.

We go in. Have the Witches spell the guns first, I told Wick. I'd been shot in the ass too many times not to give the weapons the respect they deserved. Sure, the spell wouldn't last long, but we didn't need a lot of time to disarm seven guards.

Got it. Wait for my signal.

While Wick communicated with his pack, I launched in the air and angled toward the house. Tucker and Tucker Senior strutted into the two-story home with their brat pack of douchebags following close behind.

Before landing in the glow of street lights, I shifted to a crow and perched on the edge of the roof. The wind curled around me and rustled my black feathers. Dark shapes moved in the night.

I tensed.

Two crows appeared in the glow of light to land on each side of me.

Piss off, I sent them.

The birds cocked their little heads and blinked their beady eyes at me. Not Shifters or feras, just regular pests. Gah!

They croaked a greeting and shuffled closer, wedging me between their little feathery bodies. One nudged my side with her wing, the other nestled his head down into his puffed-out feathers.

Surrounded by crows, I squawked into the night. Their beady gazes once again turned to mine. I croaked again. They snapped their beaks shut and launched into the air. One cawed back at me. She sounded pissy.

We're in place. Everything okay?

I detected humour in Wick's tone. Had he witnessed the crows trying to befriend me?

Just an attempted murder, I replied.

Wick snorted in my mind but didn't comment.

Yup, he'd seen it all.

What's the plan? he asked.

Front door?

A little obvious?

I hopped along the roof ledge. *Tucker's a norm. With the guns immobilized, it will take little to overpower the guards.*

The others?

Have the Witches stay outside with a phone. Leave Ryan and Steve in human form. You and John can come through the windows or the front door if there are any problems.

Wick growled.

What?

I hate breaking through windows.

Afraid of a little paper cut?

He snarled in my head again. *No. I'm afraid of ramming the stupid stuff with my head only to find out the hard way it's Were-proof.*

Crows couldn't smile, but on the inside I did. The image of Wick head-butting a window only to get knocked on his ass sent warmth flowing through my tiny bird body.

Steve will knock on the door. You and Ryan follow, Wick said.

I bristled. *But—*

My pack. Besides, no norm in their right mind would open the door to you in beast form, and ringing the bell naked would... His voice trailed off.

I let out a rambling mix of caws and clicks into the night. He had a point. *Let's go.*

When Ryan and Steve walked into the light, I launched off the roof and settled on the ground. Luckily, Tucker had his blinds closed.

Having already received his orders from Wick, Steve walked up the front steps and rang the bell. Ryan stood to the side, opposite me, out of sight from the entrance. The air around them clouded with rosemary and crayons. They were just as excited as I was to take Tucker down.

With a deep breath, I focused inward and embraced the beast. The dark energy ran fast and ready. Feathers fell, bones cracked and stretched, and rage poured into my veins as I stretched my long limbs and unfurled my wings.

In beast form, I resembled something between a dragon and human with hard obsidian scales running along my back and legs. The impenetrable scales gave way to my face and the soft black fur coating my stomach and chest. Large, black wings with almost translucent webbing instead of feathers spread out and a long, spaded tail swished around my feet.

I caught my reflection in the window. Surrounded by straight black hair and two short horns, my dragon-slit eyes took in my vaguely familiar features before turning my attention back to the attack plan.

The door creaked open. A guard grumbled, "What do you want?"

Steve stepped in. A swish of fabric. A bone snap. A grunt. One body down. The soft thudding of strikes and blocks. A muffled cry. A second body down.

I rounded the corner and moved quickly to enter the house. Steve stood in the entranceway over the two guards.

Wow. I'd seen Steve in action before, but I always forgot how ruthless and efficient he was as an enforcer. The guards never stood a chance. I followed Ryan and stepped over the bodies. Norms, from their smell.

Another, less pleasant smell, wafted down the hall— asparagus laced urine and cooked shrimp. My body recoiled. My nose hairs shrivelled. Werehyena. *Ugh.*

Steve turned to me and tapped his nose.

Of course, I smelled that! I mindspoke to him. He smirked and waved us forward.

Before his head got disconnected from his body, the late Master Vampire Ethan had loved using a sick, perverted Werehyena called Mark as his lead interrogator. Was there a connection?

Footsteps slapped against the hardwood up ahead. Three Werehyenas rounded the corner, weapons drawn. Their fingers squeezed the triggers as their stench barrelled down the hall.

Click, click.

I liked having Witches on my side. Nice to avoid getting shot for once. Bullet-dodging wasn't in my Carus skill-set.

The men glanced down at their guns. Gazes widened. Jaws clenched. They crashed into us with a raging thump. Weres had faster reflexes and more power than Shifters, but as the Carus, I possessed unique skills. Besides, as the MMA fighter Conor McGregor once said, "Precision beats power, and timing beats speed."

We crushed them. Sidestepping the brunt of their attack, using arms and legs to deflect their blows, we bobbed and weaved out of the way and countered with deadly strikes. I ripped the head off the Werehyena sporting a greasy blond manbun.

Rage thrummed through my veins as sweat pebbled along my nose and blood spatter dripped down my body. The man's face reminded me too much of Mark, the sadistic Werehyena who'd tortured me. Another sick addition to team Ethan who'd died along with his master.

Five guards down, two to go, plus the Tuckers. Steve rounded the corner, then Ryan. I followed, and stopped short. Waiting for us in the large, opulent living room, as if tea was served and we were late, the men stood in a curved line, crossing their arms across their chests in stiff suits.

I gently pushed Ryan and Steve to the side as I approached the group.

"Mighty bold." Randall Tucker's voice flowed like smooth liqueur. I hated him instantly. Tall and lean with a hint of a soft midsection, Randall shared similar features to his son, his hair slightly darker, and his hazel eyes duller. His expensive watch and cologne did little to mask his contempt and arrogance. I guess the apple didn't fall far from the tree in this family.

"Mighty stupid," ATF sneered. He snapped his

fingers like a bad villain, and the two Werehyena thugs beside him stepped forward. Their AK47s trained on us, and their muscles tensed as they braced to pull the triggers. Amateurs. You don't tense to take a shot.

A memory of Mark's twisted face as he hovered over my prone body slapped through my mind. I shuddered. Mark was dead. Dylan was dead. Ethan was dead. I killed them. And the rest would die soon enough.

No one appeared intimidated to face the big, bad Carus. I was supposed to be the most powerful Shifter currently in existence, and not a drop of sweet sweat dripped from their pores. Instead, the scent of steel and iron barrelled through the room, along with a tinge of fresh crayons. Not only were these men prepared and determined to cut us down, but some of them enjoyed the idea. Fuckers.

Click, click.

ATF's smug smile faltered.

"Mighty stupid," I agreed and lunged forward. Ryan and Steve followed as we took down the remaining guards with quick efficiency. Their bodies slapped against the shiny hardwood floor, now streaked with blood.

When I straightened, a stiff ATF glared back at me. Randall tugged on his sleeves, his expression bored. Bored?

"Enough of this," Randall said, seething. He took two lunging steps toward me and raised his hand.

To what? Bitch smack a beast? I barred my fangs in a toothy smile.

Before he could land his weak blow, Steve snaked

between us and caught his arm. The enforcer tensed to retaliate, but a low growl vibrated through the room from the front door. Two large Werewolves slunk into the room and circled around to stand on the other side of Tucker Senior. Wick and John.

Randall's actions confirmed the thought bouncing around in my brain since we entered the living room. He was no mastermind. No devious enemy. No plotter of mass destruction; instead, just another stupid puppet for the Pharaoh to manipulate and control.

Steve slowly, but firmly bent Randall's hand away from me until it cracked. Randall bellowed out in pain, and fell to his knees.

Overkill, much? I told them all. *I had that.*

"It's the principal," Steve snarled.

Okay... Maybe I'd grown so immune to Tucker's douche-baggery, I expected pitiful slights whenever and wherever possible. Or was there some other reason Steve's protectiveness had amped up a notch or two?

The last time he'd played the over-protective mamma bear was when...

I shook my head. Wick removed his mate claim over me a long time ago. Steve was acting out of friendship or working out of some ancient war ethic manual I knew nothing about. *Thou shall not strike thy victor.*

ATF remained frozen under the direct, menacing stare of Ryan. He wasn't going anywhere. Good. We needed him in one piece for information.

"Andrea McNeilly," Randall spat. "You've turned out to be quite a thorn in the Pharaoh's side. I should've known Maggie and Tyler's progeny would try to ruin our plans."

I faltered. The names of my biological parents sent a chill running along my spine.

ATF swivelled his head quickly to his father, his gaze wide. Guess *Daddy* didn't believe in honest, open communication between loved ones. Had Randal known all along? Or had the Pharaoh told him after I became a *thorn in his side*? Randall couldn't possibly have lived when my parents ran around making life miserable for the Pharaoh.

"How do you know who my biological parents were?" I asked.

Randall sneered. "Please, who do you think Ethan worked for? When his lapcat servant started following you around like a love-sick kitten, it took little effort to track Tristan's movements. Imagine our surprise, and dismay, to discover you're the daughter of that Shifter-bitch activist. The Pharaoh thought he got rid of her meddling eighty years ago."

I growled, deep and low. Beast fury flashed hot and raced through my veins. So a connection between Ethan and the Pharaoh existed. He was another puppet, and the Werehyenas, the link.

"Why would the Pharaoh care about a Shifter couple trying to keep the peace?"

Randall barked out a laugh. "The Pharaoh doesn't want anyone to get along beside those under his control."

The pieces clanked into place. My parents fighting to maintain peace between Shifters and humans, and the proposed Demon-Vampire alliance both failed because of the Pharaoh's actions. He wanted everyone else weak because it made his power more impressive by comparison, and prompted the most vulnerable to seek protection from him. Once he granted protection, his control and power base grew. A self-perpetuating evil cycle.

"If the Pharaoh hadn't tried to manipulate events and position you on our side," Randall continued. "You would've ended up in the lab long before now."

I stepped forward and gripped both sides of Randall's ruddy face and squeezed. Steve dropped Randall's broken arm and stepped away. Wick growled encouragement. The others remained motionless.

I pressed harder, and Randall's cheeks squished until his lips bubbled out. "You need me alive," he wheezed through fish-lips.

"Wrong," I snarled. "I need one Tucker alive."

Randall stiffened. His salty, sickly sweet sweat permeated the air. Finally. His gaze shifted to his shuffling, pathetic son. If he planned to say goodbye, he never took the opportunity. Nor did he beg. Too proud.

I snapped his neck in one swift motion. His body sagged to the floor and slumped against the bodies of the guards. Emptiness met Randall's glazed stare. In a master game of chess, he simply represented another evil pawn knocked out of my way to get the king. No guilt or feelings of sadness plagued my mind. Randall got what he deserved. Memories of another SRD agent's fate played in my mind. Agent Nagato died a painful death due to Randall's orders. The crime scene had reeked of cruelty.

Fera loss was the worst way for a Shifter to die, and they'd killed Nagato's fera not only to slowly watch Nagato die, but to torture him as he drew his final, painful, breaths. His only crime? A hard working SRD employee.

Randall and Tucker did not deserve mercy or pity.

They deserved retribution.

"No!" ATF bellowed behind me somewhere. He fell to the ground with a sob.

Wick stepped up beside me, still in wolf form. *The Witches are bringing the van around.*

Good.

You okay? He growled in my head.

My wolf preened from the attention. *One down, a handful more to go.*

Wick pressed his large, furry body against my legs. Not sure why his chose now to do so, but the warmth of him beside me calmed the raging beast. He moved with me when I took a deep breath and knelt beside Tucker. The agent sniffled and swiped at his tears and snot running down his face. His body tensed as my shadow fell over his face.

"What do you want?" he whispered.

"Remember what I promised in the lab?" The memory resurfaced in my beast brain like sweet nectar. *I'm going to get out of here. And when I do, I'm going to slaughter the fuck out of all of you. Every single person remotely responsible for Tristan's death will feel my wrath, suffer my claws, and scream as my teeth rip into them.*

His hazel gaze widened.

"I always keep my promises."

28

Once again, Team Andy stood around a large planning table with the Werewolf pack, the Witches, Stan, and the Wereleopards. This time, Allan and Clint joined us. And this time, we used Kayne Security Systems headquarters as a meeting place.

The simple-styled business building with reflective windows and four stories of office space housed Tristan's security empire. The profitable company offered personal and business solutions for safety and security of people, information, possessions, and property—everything and anything for a pretty little price tag.

When we arrived, we walked through the ultramodern lobby, tracked by security cameras. Suzy, the ocelot Shifter receptionist with graying brown hair and kind eyes, greeted us. Skipping the lower floors used for offices, weapons, and training, we made our way to the third floor that housed the IT department and security programs.

Returning to this place brought back memories. The short elevator ride had always been exquisite torture, trapped in a small confined space with Tristan's enchanting smell, but too short a ride to do much about it. Though the sweet memories plagued the edges of my mind, I found them more bittersweet than sharp. The thoughts brought a smile to my face instead.

Olly, completely ignorant of my walk down memory lane, rolled out floor plans and brought up schematics on the flat screens. "Fifteen thirty-one Davie Street is one of Vancouver's oldest buildings. Also known as Gabriola House, the building was constructed in 1900 for the industrialist Benjamin Tingley Rogers."

"Why is that name familiar?" I asked.

"Rogers Sugar. Benjamin was called the Sugar King and he was the founder of B.C. Sugar and its refinery."

Huh.

Olly brought up some old pictures on a nearby monitor. "The house was built with green sandstone quarried from Gabriola Island—hence the name—and it's still considered one of the most lavish heritage homes in the area once known as Blueblood Alley. There have been numerous renovations over the years, converting the home to an apartment building and different restaurants, but after reviewing the building plans submitted to the city, we feel the overall layout of the house is still relatively unaltered. This is good news."

I straightened from the floor plans and snapped my fingers. "That's why it looked familiar. It was a restaurant. I've probably sat in one of the rooms."

"Stuffing your face with cannoli, no doubt," Wick said. He obviously knew me well. When I looked up, he held my gaze, irises flashing wolf yellow, before looking back down at the plans.

Olly grunted. "It recently sold to a developer for over ten million dollars. He plans to remodel the building into condos."

"Figures," Wick spat.

"You're a developer," I pointed out.

"Not one who tears down historical sites."

"There's more," Olly interjected, sounding a bit annoyed by our banter.

"Sorry. Proceed," I said.

"The property used to span the entire block with horse stables, greenhouses, and work sheds. But here's where it gets interesting."

Thank Feradea for an interesting part. So far, I could've found a textbook with more flair than Olly's reconnaissance. Not that it was bad, just not exactly helpful. I didn't care about the age of the old building, what kind of decorations it sported or where the builder sourced the stones. How did I get in and out without dying?

"The house is rumoured to have tunnels linking Gabriola House with another old building. Maxine's Beauty School at twelve fifteen Bidwell allegedly ran a brothel in the basement."

Stan snorted and used air quotes. "Allegedly."

I elbowed him in the gut. "Maybe that's our way in."

"Unlikely. The beauty school was torn down in 2012 to develop condominiums." Wick growled.

"Relax," Olly smirked. "The Bidwell building wasn't as lavish or historical as Gabriola House. Any tunnel that may or may not have existed to Gabriola House would've been removed or boarded up when the condominiums were built. Looking at the building specs and comparing it with the expense claim for materials, my guess is the Bidwell end of the tunnel is now filled with concrete."

"Well, if it had a brothel in the basement, at least we know the purpose of the tunnel," Stan muttered.

"Tunnels, as in plural," Olly continued, shooting Stan a dark look. "And not just for the Gabriola House inhabitants to run to the brothel for a quickie, there's a lot of rum-running anecdotes connected with the location, too. More than likely they used the tunnels for bootlegging during Prohibition."

I nodded, but so far he'd only mentioned a tunnel to the whore house. The silence in the room grew as everyone mulled over what little information we had.

"Tunnels?" I prompted.

"There're also rumours of a tunnel running to English Bay, but if it still exists it's probably boarded up and concealed with magic."

"Anything else?" Stan asked.

"Yes. Lots of sightings of apparitions."

Stan grumbled.

I shot him a look. "You're standing between the progeny of a goddess and a Werewolf Alpha, but the idea of ghosts makes you uneasy?"

He shrugged. "You ever seen a ghost?"

I pressed my lips together. A couple of times. When I was with Dylan's pack. I didn't like to remember that part of my life.

Wick's gaze flicked between me and the cop. "Go on, Olly."

"Some customers report seeing cutlery float in the air, and there's one account of an older gentlemen freaking out a painter, but the most consistent sighting is of a young man. He's been encountered several times."

"How old was Rogers when he died?" Stan looked up from his notepad. Old cop couldn't break the habit if he tried.

"Fifty-two."

"Probably not him then. Is the ghost hostile?" I asked.

"By all accounts, no. Just curious, and a little sad." He drummed his fingers along the top of the boardroom table. "Has the spineless SRD asshat given you anything?"

I liked Olly for a reason. My smile broadened. "Not really. He did confirm the Witches went into Gabriola House and never left as far as he knew. He doesn't have a code, but he's expected to visit with his dad and guards tomorrow night."

"You believe him? Not intentionally leaving anything out?"

The Werewolves laughed.

"Swore we wouldn't get anything from him. He'd rather die. Two strikes to the gut later, and he pissed himself." Steve tapped his truth-scenting nose. "Five minutes in, he spilled everything and didn't lie once."

"The way I see it," Wick interjected. "We have two options."

His smouldering gaze met mine and held me captive with his intensity. As an Alpha, he wouldn't break the eye contact, it showed weakness, but as my weakness, I couldn't look away. My skin warmed under his attention, and my mind reeled to remember what he'd been saying.

Someone cleared their throat. "The two options?" Olly asked.

"Force our way in, or use magical cloaking and Tucker," Wick said, his voice breaking the spell he'd cast over me.

I mulled over Wick's words. "Either way, we'll be under attack as soon as we step into the home. If the Pharaoh is anywhere near as paranoid as Lucien was, he will have some sort of magic-stripping spell put in place. But with the first option, we alert them to our presence right away and risk more casualties. My vote is for the Tucker method."

"He's a snivelling brat." Clint's lips curled, as he spoke for the first time. "He'll give away our presence in seconds."

Allan shook his head. "If Lucus and Veronika can cloak us to look and smell like Tucker's guards, then I'm sure they can cloak two of us to resemble the Tucker twats."

I beamed at Allan. The Witches nodded. Lucus's laugh sounded suspiciously like a cackle.

"Who's going to play those two?" Stan asked.

I raised my hand like an eager six-year-old. "I call dibs on ATF." When they stared at me blankly, I explained. "Agent Tucker Fucker."

They blinked in unison.

"Richard Tucker," I clarified.

Stan shook his head. Whatever comment he wanted to make, he bit it back.

"I'll be your daddy," Wick winked.

Everyone laughed, except Stan and me. My wolf loved his words, of course.

My cop partner narrowed his eyes.

"Um..." I glanced away from Wick's teasing smile. My cheeks heated. What the hell? He said he wasn't interested. I'd avoided him because I tried to give him what he wanted. What if I'd been wrong?

29

We'd taken more than one vehicle over to Kayne Security Solutions, and for whatever reason, I found myself sitting shotgun in Wick's work truck with no chaperone. His rosemary and sugar scent filled the cab and soaked into my skin. I shifted in my seat, very aware of his proximity. He might sit less than two feet away, but the distance felt insurmountable. Too much lay between us.

Despite this, my fingers itched to reach out and touch him. My lips quivered to press against his and re-enact the kiss we'd shared over a week ago.

We drove in silence. Wick staring straight ahead, while I attempted to follow suit, but continuously snuck sideway glances at the vibrating Werewolf Alpha.

When we pulled up Wick's driveway, he shoved the gear in park and turned off the truck. He pocketed the keys, but instead of moving to exit the vehicle, he gripped the wheel while I stared at him.

"What the hell was that?" I blurted.

"What?"

"Back there?"

He shrugged. "I don't know what you mean."

"*I'll be your daddy.*" I tried to imitate his deep, husky voice and failed miserably.

Wick smiled. Either at my attempt to mock him, or the memory, but I couldn't tell which.

"Why are you flirting with me?" I held my breath and waited for his answer.

"Do you like it?"

"No..." My lie stunk up the truck.

He raised an eyebrow at me.

"Yes..." My pulse hammered through my body.

He leaned in. "Then why does it upset you?"

I gulped. "It confuses me."

Wickedness flashed across his gaze, but the twinkling quickly faded, replaced with something colder and darker. He sat back. "Now you know how I feel."

What the hell? "You're intentionally trying to hurt me by teasing? The Wick I knew would never be so cruel."

Wick's lips flattened. "I'm not trying to be cruel. I'm just—" He clenched his jaw and looked out the side window. His grip tightened on the steering wheel.

"You're just what?"

"Conflicted." He turned back to glare at me. "Okay?"

My heart lodged in my throat. I swallowed before answering. "Okay, that's fair."

We sat in silence as I mulled over his words. This didn't mean Wick had forgotten or forgiven me for, well, everything, but maybe I could mend this bridge, preferably without grovelling. Not that I didn't deserve to grovel, it just wasn't the way to Wick's heart.

Wick ran his hand through his hair. "I'm struggling to stick to my game plan when you're near."

"What exactly is your plan?"

"Ignore you and take down the Pharaoh."

My skin grew clammy. His uncertainty stabbed at my chest. "Maybe change the game?"

His gaze softened and he reached out to stroke my cheek. Before his fingers touched me, though, he dropped his hand and looked away. "The very thought of my actions teasing you, gives me hope." He breathed in deep. "When I know I should have none."

"Wick—"

I reached out. He shrugged my hand away and popped the door open. "It will be easier once this is all over. Then you will go home, I will leave the pack and I'll have a chance to move on."

He hopped out of the truck and shut the door on my protest. *Dang it!* I needed to corner that Alpha and hash this out. After the revenge mission was over, I'd do exactly that. Now that I knew Wick still wanted me, neither his "conflicted" heart, nor a wild pack of rabid Weremonkeys could keep me away.

Mine! The beast rumbled, deep in my core.

Ours.

30

With a boring as paper norm scent clinging artificially to my skin, I tugged at my suit and flashed Daddy-Dearest a large smile. "Randall" grinned back. Wick's toothy smile didn't fit Randall's face or personality. It looked all kinds of wrong, but I liked how I could see Wick, even through a thick cloaking spell.

A glance around confirmed everyone else's preoccupation with their own fake personalities and new wardrobes.

I sidled up to Wick-Randall, putting an overly-feminine sway to my hips. "Looking good, *Daddy*."

Wick looked up from fixing his tie, and his gaze widened.

I walked my fingers up his chest. His fake norm scent tickled my nose and infuriated the beast, but I knew the Alpha lurked under the magical surface. "I think I've been a little naughty."

Wick barked out a laugh. He glanced at the others, before leaning down. "I'll just have to put you over my knee and give you a spanking, then."

"Now I've seen it all." Steve's voice, directly to my left made me jump.

Wick straightened and stepped away from me. He adjusted his suit and pretended to whistle innocently.

"I think I puked a little in my mouth," Stan grunted. "You're supposed to be father and son. Please don't do that again."

With ATF's entourage, we planned to enter the Pharaoh's house with nine people in total. With Wick and I acting as the Tuckers, that left seven Werehyenas —Allan, Clint, Ryan, Steve, John, Stan, and Lucus. The aforementioned Witch had refused to allow Veronika to come. Instead, he left her at home to babysit ATF. When I voiced concern, he'd waved me off. "He's not going anywhere, and she'll get revenge her own way."

When I'd peeked over Lucus's shoulder at a caged ATF, the agent met my gaze and whispered, "Please kill me." I'd snarled in unison with Veronika. He deserved whatever she dished him.

Shaking my head at the memory, I focused on the here and now. Once in, we'd leave the door open for the others. The rest of Wick's pack and Allan's horde waited a safe distance away for our signal to enter Gabriola House.

Steve wrinkled his Werehyena nose. "I smell like piss."

"How's that any different than usual?" Ryan bumped his shoulder.

"Fuck off," Steve said without heat. He brushed down his clothes again. A few months ago, in a Bola inspired rage, the two had been at each other's throats, literally. Steve wanted to kill Ryan because he'd made a comment about the size of his junk, unwarranted, and Ryan tried to squeeze the life out of Steve because he made a comment about how I'd used his attraction for me as a means of escape.

I still felt bad about that.

Ryan viewed me as a lesser being than the mud on his boots.

"Let's do this." I shoved both of them forward. "Look guardly."

The Werewolves snarled and growled at me, some in play like Steve, some not-so-jokingly, like Ryan. They had to know they far-exceeded the Werehyenas we'd taken out, but they acted like I'd mortally offended them, or something. Or were they playing with me? Hard to tell with Werewolves sometimes. The guards turned stiff and moved to surround me and Wick-Randall as we climbed into the vehicles. We were kilometres away from Gabriola House, but I guess the wolves were getting into character.

"Tsk, tsk." Wick shook his head. "Riling up the help is so beneath you."

"Not at all. If I'm Richard Tucker, it's in character." I straightened my tie. "Expect excessive douche-baggery from this point forward."

Ryan turned around from the driver's seat and sneered at me. "How's that any different than usual?"

I barked out a laugh. My chest warmed. He'd used the same line on me as he had with Steve. Aww, how sweet.

"Fuck off." And just like Steve, I said it without heat.

Ryan grunted. Steve turned to me from the front passenger seat and winked.

Guess Ryan was on the path to forgiveness. Or at least tolerance.

THE DRIVE WENT SMOOTHLY CONSIDERING Vancouver traffic generally sucked no matter the time of day. I refrained from playing with Wick. Flirting in the middle of a mission never boded well. Not only did it feel wrong with him in a Randall façade, but I didn't want to make Ryan and Steve sick. Plus, I got the sense Wick didn't trust me. He didn't trust my feelings and he didn't trust his reactions to me. I needed to fix that first.

We pulled up the street to Gabriola House, parked, and climbed out of the car. The other vehicle, full of our fake guards pulled up beside us. As a group, we headed toward the entrance. The Gabriola sandstone slabs loomed down as we closed in on the house, passing the sprinklers.

"You're late," a Werehyena guard with a big nose and

greasy hair spat at our approach. His well-tailored suit did little to hide his soiled personality. The stench of hyena flooded my nose. Riding in the car with Ryan and Steve cloaked in the thick odour had been bad enough, but now, with the real deal looming down at us while four other guards joined him, my nose hairs shrieked in horror and curled up to hide.

Wick-Randall tugged his sleeves down and twisted his lips in a sneer. "I don't take orders from you, mutt."

Hah! Wick totally nailed Randall's condescending tone.

I smiled smugly at the guard.

He grumbled and swivelled on his foot. The other guards nodded and followed. *Yes!* They bought it. Then again, acting like an asshole wasn't too hard for any supe. Call it a defence mechanism against anti-supe vigilantes, years of persecution and general hatred.

We followed the real Werehyenas up the front steps and into the house. As soon as we stepped over the threshold, my skin tickled then stung, as if I'd decided to lightly bathe in acid. Wick's appearance wavered beside me. His Randall persona fell away as if washed off by an invisible shower. He met my gaze and nodded. We'd have to act quickly, now. The stripping of our disguises probably triggered a silent alarm somewhere.

"What the—" The greasy guard had no chance to finish his sentence. My fist in his face stopped his words.

I stepped to the side, wrapped my arm around his neck, and with my new position behind his back, snapped his neck.

Geez, been doing a lot of that lately. One trick pony.

My beast chuffed and preened. Her satisfaction with our actions grew like a warm bubble in my core.

Wick, Ryan, Steve, and John moved out and took down the other guards, swiftly, smoothly, and more importantly, quietly.

"Well..." I looked down at five very-dead guards. "That was easy."

"Let's move." Wick nodded toward the interior and broke into a slow jog as we moved to follow.

After we passed an ornate terra cotta fireplace, a grand staircase greeted us. The elaborately decorated walls stared back as we climbed the steps, no doubt holding their own memories from the passing years.

A door clicked in the distance. Deep voices called out, the language unfamiliar. The house shook. The sound of something large, like stone or concrete, rumbled. Wick threw open the study door, and we stumbled in to find a team of Werehyenas standing guard. Along with the lingering smell of dirt and dampness, the old as fuck scent of dried leaves wavered, growing fainter. I peered around the guards as we lunged forward to attack. No Pharaoh. He'd slipped out somehow. And no other Vampires. The few he kept with him at all times as guards must've gone with him.

A fist glanced off my jaw. I stepped to the side a split second too late. Another hit my gut, hard. I fought the instinct to double over and cry for my mamma. Instead, I called for the beast. She rose fast and hard, relishing in the grunts of pain and spurts of blood from the surrounding fight. My bones ached and snapped as they stretched. I grew from my normal five-foot-ten frame to over eight feet.

The Werehyena who'd hit me stepped back to stand with the others who surrounded me, eyes wide. I stretched my arms and wings, and *roared*.

Gabriola House shook as fire raced through my veins.

No one else had shifted. Weres took too long to complete the transformation process, and it left them vulnerable. Instead, they stayed in human form to fight. At least they had been fighting. Now the real Werehyenas stood frozen as they watched my transition, gazes wary. Team Andy moved swiftly to take them out. I grinned and let a growl vibrate deep from my chest. The sound triggered the Werehyenas, and they moved. I jumped into the fray and took out as many of the enemy as I could.

Minutes later, I stood, sweat-free, in the middle of the study surrounded by dead, dying, or knocked out Werehyenas. Team Andy suffered no casualties.

"That was fun," I rumbled, my beast voice much deeper than my human one.

Stan frowned at me. As the only norm in the group, he'd been the most vulnerable, but a quick glance and sniff, he appeared unscathed. He held his gun loosely at his side, finger off the trigger. Gunpowder lifted from his skin and surrounded him like an invisible cloud.

That's right. I'd heard a shot or two. He must've squeezed off a couple of rounds.

Stan's gaze travelled up and down to take in my beast

form. He looked away quickly and shuddered. "Still not used to seeing you like that."

"Like what? Awesome?"

He barked a laughed and turned back to me. "Intimidating."

"Please, like I didn't scare you before."

Stan grunted. "Not like this. Besides, hard to be scared of a scrawny nitwit who's been shot in the butt... twice."

Wick growled. He didn't know about the last time I'd been shot. Gauging from his flashing gaze and stiff posture, he wasn't too pleased to learn of it now.

"Not by me," Stan snarled at him.

I laughed. I couldn't help it. The sound bellowed out of my throat before I could gulp it down. The sight of my middle-aged, balding, beer-bellied norm friend staring down a virile, giant Werewolf Alpha while looking indignant at the same time cracked my funny bone.

"Hate to break this hi-lar-ious moment," Steve interjected. "But the Pharaoh?"

"Gone." I straightened and cleared my throat. "Must've been a silent alarm triggered by the entrance's magic-stripping spell. He left this room before we entered."

"How the fuck is that possible?" Ryan kicked an unconscious Werehyena.

"Vampire speed?"

Wick shook his head and moved around the room.

"We would've at least seen a blur or caught his scent as he passed us."

"There's only one entrance into this room," John pointed out.

Or was there? "Olly mentioned tunnels."

"Do you know where they are?" Ryan turned to me, eyebrow raised, head tilted with attitude.

At least he spoke to me. "No, but—"

...I do...

I turned and froze. The ghost of a young man stood beside my stag with his hand gently draped across the animal's back.

31

Cigar smoke and men's cologne, with the sweet edge of sugar, drifted from the wavering white and blue image of a young, attractive man. With dark hair combed from a side part and a stylish moustache, the man wore a coat with covered buttons and matching waistcoat. A floppy bow tie matched his dark trousers. He stood casually with one hand holding a cigarette while the other arm remained draped over my fera.

That makes no sense.

This house was built in 1900, and good ole Benji didn't die until 1918, at a much older age than the ghost standing before us.

Unless...

Unless this ghost was of an earlier, younger version of the Sugar King, one of him in his prime, instead of middle aged. Maybe his ghost held on to what little vanity remained.

Wick slowly walked to stand beside me. His hand drifted to the small of my back. The warmth of his touch radiated out and sank in to heat my blood as his rosemary scent curled possessively around me. I smiled down at him. Odd to stand over such a giant man in this form. The height difference didn't seem to bother him any.

"Mr. Rogers?" my beast voice rumbled.

As soon as I spoke, my stag disappeared—no longer interested in this show, or he figured his job was done. The pretty grass-eater probably didn't want to get his hooves wet with blood. Typical herbivore behaviour.

...Benjamin...

The sugary cigar scent grew stronger as the image wavered. Wick's chest rumbled, and his fingertips pressed harder into my scales, like he wanted to rip me away or hold me back. He did neither, but his hand remained planted on my body, the pressure oddly reassuring.

I stepped forward and ignored Wick's vibrating apprehension. "You said you know where the entrance to the tunnels is?"

... Yes...

He wavered again and flickered. A brief clip of sound, like the static of a radio, gave the only warning before the ghost vanished. His scent disappeared.

I froze.

Rogers reformed a foot away from me. His cigar scent flooded my senses as if he dropped a ghostly stink bomb at my feet.

...Follow me...

I jumped to the side. My spine tingled as if a troop of

miniature monkeys dug their claws into the tender flesh and climbed to my shoulders. A shudder racked my body, and my fur stood on end, like a giant puffed-up cat. I flicked out my wings before resettling them tight against my back. Luckily, Wick had moved out of the way.

...Hurry...

"I'll follow. Why do we need to hurry?"

...Not much time...

"Okay," I nodded. Who was I to argue with a ghost about ghost stuff?

...The desk...a button...

Wick stalked over to the large business desk, more solid than the exterior of present-day houses. He dragged his hand underneath. His body tensed. He looked up.

Click.

We all jumped as the back of the fireplace rumbled and the solid barrier slid to the side. The dank smell of an old house spread across the room, along with the dissipating aroma of the Pharaoh.

...Quickly...

Instead of walking, the spectre of the Sugar King flickered with a zap of radio static before reappearing in the tunnel behind the fireplace.

We ducked under the large, ornate mantel and moved into the small landing on the other side. The platform led to a spiralling staircase. Like those found in a castle turret, the old stone steps dropped to unknown depths below, leaving just enough height for me to remain in beast form as long as I stooped. The fireplace door slid shut behind us and darkness engulfed the staircase.

Good thing for animalistic night vision.

"Fuck," Stan grumbled. His clothing rustled.

The stale smells cloaked us as the unknown waited below. My beast growled as my scales rippled. *Not liking this.*

"None of us *like* this, kitten," Allan grumbled somewhere behind me, responding to the thought he plucked from my head. Allan might feed off our fear, but as a control freak, the idea of following a ghost into the unknown probably had him hanging out on the edge with the rest of us.

Benjamin flickered away and reappeared lower down, his ghostly blue-gray form providing a little light in the otherwise dark area.

Stan clicked on his flashlight and led the way down the stairs.

"Stan…" Why the heck would a norm lead this brat pack? The rest of us could see fine in the dark. The Weres benefitted from night vision like myself, and Lucus had already generated a little glowing ball of magic.

"Fuck off, Andy, I'm not bringing up the rear," Stan grumbled as we continued to move.

"Why the hell not?" It would be safer for him back there.

"The last thing I need in this life is to follow a spot-light on your ass."

Clint barked a laugh, and the others had the nerve to chuckle. I chose to take the mature path and let the comment slide. I'd cuff him later when no one watched. Since entering Gabriola House, the rooms had been perfectly heated, probably updated decades ago to comply with city regulations, but each time the Sugar King reappeared, farther down the stairwell, the temperature dropped.

We reached the bottom of the stairs. Stan opened the door at the base and moved into a dark tunnel. With the walls roughly boarded up with old wood, and the flooring unevenly patched with large slabs of stone, the smell of dirt, mould, and dampness surrounded us. The faint aroma of the Pharaoh mingled in the air and teased us like a gentle reminder of our mission.

Each time Benjamin flashed to a new location with the radio static, his scent disappeared, then come back, full force, to almost knock me on my ass.

...This way... The whisper of the Sugar King's voice trickled down the corridor as he reappeared to the left of a fork in the path.

My skin rippled, and my tail swished like an annoyed cat. Although the ghost of Benjamin Tingley Rogers didn't appear antagonistic, his presence set my teeth on edge. Each flicker, waver, zap of sound, and the whispering voice ping-ponging down the corridor sent shivers racing through my veins.

Why would a ghost trouble me so much? I was part divine with beastly skills and supernatural strength. Fear often defied logic. Besides, I couldn't kick a ghost if he pissed me off.

The Sugar King relocated faster and faster until we moved in an all-out run down the dark corridors. Finally, an old rickety door confronted us at the end of the tunnel. The cry of seagulls broke through the silence surrounding us. A soft sea breeze blew through the cracks and water gently lapped at a shore nearby.

The ghost of the Sugar King stood by the door, his face solemn, his hands folded in front.

"Thank you," I said.

He stared unblinking. He didn't acknowledge my words. Instead, he zapped out of existence.

A shudder ran up my body. I tensed and waited, but the spectre didn't reappear.

Wick slipped his warm hand to the small of my back again, running his fingers along my scales. "That was creepy."

"Let's get out of here." Stan yanked on the door. It wouldn't budge.

Steve walked up and gently placed his hand on Stan's shoulder.

The veteran cop shot him a dark glare but after a few seconds, relinquished his position in front of the door.

Steve yanked the door open on the first try.

Stan grumbled.

We poured out of the dark tunnel, which looked like a large storm drain. It led to a beach. A few yards away stood the infamous bathhouse. I'd recognize this old, landmark building anywhere. I strolled past it countless times every summer. English Bay, then. Olly's reports on the tunnels had been correct.

A motorboat sped away in the distance, making its way toward West Point Grey.

Wick stood beside me and watched the boat. His

mouth flattened into a thin line and his muscles bunched as he tensed. "Looks like the Pharaoh got away."

"Can you get a boat quickly?"

He peered up at me. "The rest of the pack is still waiting at the entrance of Gabriola House."

Allan sauntered up to us, cell phone in hand. "I'll have one here in fifteen minutes."

"Good." I crouched low and allowed the new seagull form to flow over me, wiping out the beast form. Now condensed in a vulnerable pest of a bird, I gathered my strength and launched into the air. With my wings spread out wide, I caught the gentle breeze and flapped hard to gain altitude.

I'll follow them by air and keep you posted, I told Wick.

You're going to have to haul seagull ass to catch up.

My indignant squawk pierced the night, only to blend in with the rest of the water fowl. As I put distance between me and the shore, Wick's chuckle floated through my mind and warmed my soul.

THE POWERBOAT DIDN'T STOP AT JERICHO beach. It didn't approach the opposite shore at all. Instead, it veered around the point. I followed from a safe distance above, beating my wings frantically to keep up.

Maybe I should've chosen a different form.

No. No one would think twice about a seagull in this area. An eagle or hawk, however, might draw attention.

Still, my energy waned with little progress, and the motorboat grew smaller and smaller in the distance.

Fuck this. My seagull screeched. I reached inward and wrenched out the familiar peregrine falcon form, the one I'd held in my heart since the tender age of fourteen, and shifted. My body dropped, free falling toward the dark water below. The streamline form slid through my cells. Harmonious delight danced along my bones. I spread my wings and caught the wind, relishing the feel of flying in the falcon's form again. Warmth flooded my body despite the cool night air.

Falcon.

I'd missed her.

Instantly, I picked up speed. With an average horizontal speed somewhere around eighty kilometres per hour, I could push it to over one-hundred if needed.

Tonight, I drove my little bird body to the max. And I loved every second.

As one of the fastest birds in existence, it took little time to catch up to the boat, now navigating its way up the Fraser River.

Where the heck were they going?

I didn't dare get closer. They'd spot me, and a hovering peregrine, unlike a seagull, was not normal.

When the boat slowed near Mission, I shifted back to the seagull form. With night set in, the moon dropping to the horizon, and my high altitude, confidence bolstered my move. I dropped down toward the water, soaring close to the surface. The operator of the boat ahead maneuvered carefully along the river.

My little bird body pulsed with energy. A dark vessel loomed amongst a graveyard of ships near the shrouded shore of Mission.

What is this place?

32

The wind funnelling down Fraser River caressed my face and hair as I stood in human form on the small motorboat. Thankfully, one of Allan's minions had included a housecoat with the powerboat package, so the night air couldn't cut too harshly at my naked skin.

After determining the location of the Pharaoh, I'd fallen back to rejoin Team Andy. The rest of the pack, Wereleopards, and Vampires travelled in vans toward the Pharaoh's dark and icky new hideaway.

Wick stood beside me, the heat emanating from his solid body licked my skin and offered comfort.

My wolf popped into my head and gave my brain a nudge.

Wick reached out and slid his arm across my shoulders, pulling me in for a side-hug. "We'll get him."

Did he say that for me or himself?

"Your brow is furrowed," he pointed out.

"I'm not worried about success."

"Then what's bothering you?"

What bothered me? Every time he got close, he remembered how much I'd hurt him and he'd pull away? That I'll never fix the divide between us? I sighed. Now was not the time to get into the emotional stuff. After all this ended, I'd sit this Alpha down and dish out my heart out and serve it on a platter for him. "I can't decide between ending everything quickly, so there's no chance for escape, or...not."

Wick nodded, but his gaze grew distant until he eventually looked away. He released me, and his arm dropped back to his side.

Idiot, my wolf growled.

As our small boat drifted closer to the abandoned BC Ferry, my breath caught. The Queen of Sidney was once a regal vessel responsible for shipping hundreds of passengers to and from the Lower Mainland on a daily basis. I'd been on her many times. Now, her derelict and deteriorated form sat moored off the Fraser River shoreline, striking an apocalyptic pose. Green slime and black sludge dripped down her bow. She must've haunted Mission's waters for years.

We pulled up to the starboard side of the vessel. A few guards loped along her decks, some with Vampire grace, unaware of our presence, thanks to Lucus's cloaking spell.

We need the ladder down, Wick's smouldering gaze met mine.

Leave it to me.

Concentrating inward, I called the form of a small gecko. My blood cooled as my body shrank and compacted. Fabric fell away and hit the floor, the heavy folds of the housecoat pooling around me. My feet stuck to the deck of the motorboat. Movement cast a shadow over my small body. I froze.

Wick crouched down, large and looming.

Hide, the essence of the gecko demanded. I gulped and refused to move. Though small, and incredibly vulnerable, I was amongst allies. I wouldn't feel the crush of a boot tonight.

At least, not on purpose.

Give me a boost? I asked Wick.

He held his hand open, palm up against the boat's deck. I clambered on. The heat of his hand seared the bottoms of my adhesive toe-pads.

I could melt right into him.

Gah! If I didn't know any better, I'd swear geckoes were invertebrates. *Focus!*

My little body shook as the cold air slipped by, too cold for a regular gecko, but tolerable for me. At least for a short while. The wind stung my unblinking eyes. My tongue darted out to lick them.

Ew! Did I just lick my own eyeballs?

My gecko essence cackled as Wick lifted me to the ferry.

I scurried to the edge of his fingertips and reached out to latch onto the side of the ship. I'd never used this form before, but geckoes rocked at climbing vertical things, so it had to be a good choice. The animal essence flowed through my body and took over the command centre for movement. With digital hyperextension, my feet spread out and stuck to the cool surface of the vessel.

The bottom of gecko toe pads had hair-like setae—projections used to increase the surface area of the feet and, therefore, the force of attraction between my body and the surface I climbed on. Of course, my gecko essence didn't tell me this, my subscription to *Random Animal Facts Monthly* did.

With movement I didn't know possible, I peeled my toes off from the tip inward. Secreted lipids lubricated the setae, and I detached my foot for the next step. With the repeated combination of peeling and adhering, I scurried up the side of the large ship, slow at first, then moving faster as I got the hang of it.

My little gecko body grew cold from the old metal and biting air. As soon as I reached the first deck, I shifted to human and threw the nearest ladder down the side. A guard whistled up ahead and rounded the corner.

Crap! We didn't want early detection.

I quickly shifted to a snake and undulated into the shadows for the protection of darkness. When the guard passed my hiding spot, I shifted again, this time to beast form. My ears rang, my vision wavered. Lurching forward, I slipped my arms around the surprised guard—a norm—and snapped his neck before he could utter a sound. My heart beat like a drummer on crack, erratic and crazy.

Still dizzy from the quick, successive shifts, I grabbed

the guard's clothes and hauled him into the shadows behind a storage compartment.

The team climbed over the side of the deck and crowded the section. Wick motioned at his packmates, silently commanding them in one direction, while Allan and Clint went another. Stan and Lucus silently nodded at each other and took the stairs to move to the upper levels.

Looks like we're going down. Wick winked at me. Before we could move toward the staircase, another guard stepped out from the depths below. His eyes widened as his gaze landed on us.

My muscles tensed.

Wick froze.

The guard drew his firearm, and a shot rang out in the silent night.

33

The guard's blood sprayed across my face, neck and chest as I ripped his throat out with my sharp, beast talons. His body sagged. Before he hit the deck, I spun and ran back to a limp Wick, lying sprawled in a small puddle of blood, about thirty feet away.

My beast rage had taken over my body, acting so fast, the guard had no chance to shoot another round.

I slid to Wick's side, my long ebony arms gently picking Wick up enough to turn him and cradle him in my lap. Without thought, my body changed back into my weak vulnerable human form, no longer having the energy to maintain something as fierce as the beast. Pain lanced through my veins. My throat tightened. Images of holding a dying Tristan flashed through my memory.

So much blood.

Not again.

My heart pumped so hard, my hearing became over-whelmed with the thudding sound.

Please, no. Not again. I finally know what I want.

Who I want.

The colour continued to drain from Wick's face. I clutched him closer, taking in his rosemary and sugar scent with shaky breaths. Warm blood trickled down my arms.

Please, Feradea. I'll do anything. Just give me the time to tell him how I truly feel.

The wind whipped around us, flinging my hair in front of my face while my heart stopped and my breath lodged in my throat. Time stood almost perfectly still, like each second passing painfully stabbed at my soul with excruciating accuracy.

Wick grimaced, and his eyes fluttered open. I breathed out and pulled back.

His body's self-healing pushed the bullet from the wound in his chest. The deformed bullet dropped to the metallic deck with a clang. The blood on Wick's shirt stopped spreading, and now the wound knitted together before my eyes. The shot had been too far to his right to hit Wick's heart. A lung, maybe, but with Were healing, and only one bullet hole, he'd survive a punctured lung.

I released a deep sigh. My shoulders dropped. *Oh thank you, Feradea! He'll live.*

Wick growled. "I hate getting shot."

"Tell me about it." My voice sounded thin, even to me. But I knew what he meant. I'd been shot three times in the last year. At least Wick had Were healing on his side. Seeing him vulnerable and injured like that made awful flashes from my past resurface.

Wick's smouldering gaze locked on mine. My thoughts halted. His gaze flicked down quickly to take in my naked body, and flashed yellow. His nose flared. "Worried?"

Wick stood and pulled me up with him. His hard body close and warm.

"I thought...I thought I lost you." *Again.*

Wick hesitated. Something soft streaked through his expression before hardening. He pushed my hand away and turned to walk away. "You keep me at arm's length. Why would you care now?"

My belly knotted. No amount of wishing could turn back time and erase Wick's pain or prevent this distrust from cloaking his fierce heart. My vision wavered. My muscles tightened.

Oh, to hell with waiting until this mission was over. "I never said I needed more time or space."

Wick froze.

"I'm not keeping you at arm's length. Not anymore. You keep pushing me away in fear I'm going to bolt or lead you on. And you have good reason to think that, I know, but you put words in my mouth I never intended to say."

"What?" He stepped forward and gripped my arms. His fingertips dug in and his chocolate gaze flashed yellow, again.

"If recent events have taught me anything, it's to cherish the time we have. Not to let chances at happiness slip by." I slid my shaky hand up to cup his face. "I'm not going anywhere."

Wick squeezed his eyes shut, but he didn't let me go.

"I know I hurt you. I'm truly sorry for that." I took a deep breath. "But you don't need to wait for me. I'm ready now."

A loud boom shook the vessel, and we staggered to the side. An alarm blared—the kind that sounded for the passengers to abandon ship. My sensitive ears throbbed from the high-pitched wailing. The boat rocked.

"The boys." I turned to run, breaking free of Wick's hold.

His hand clamped on my arm and spun me toward him. His other hand gripped the back of my neck and hauled me closer. His hot mouth claimed mine. Strong arms encased me. My heart beat heavy against my ribcage as I kissed Wick back, matching his haste, desperation and passion.

Finally. My wolf howled in my head. Her energy reached out to caress Wick.

He lifted me in his strong arms, his muscles bunching as his tongue twisted with mine and sent heat pooling low in my belly. I wrapped my legs around his waist and clung to his tall, solid frame. My nerves tingled, yearning for more of his touch. He slammed me against the nearest wall and pressed his hips hard against mine. Fire raced through my veins as he stroked my tongue with his own, his hand still clutching my neck possessively.

Gunshots sounded toward the stern. We froze,

Wick's tongue still in my mouth, his free hand gripping my naked breast.

Wick gave my lip a nip before withdrawing. I dropped my legs and settled on shaky limbs. My body reeled from unfulfilled promises, and shivered from the loss of Wick's warmth.

"You better shift to your beast form now." His gaze burned as it travelled down my naked body. "But we're not done, here. When we get home, we will finish this."

34

We ran down the nearest corridor. Tarnished and corroded by rust, the surfaces were muddied by filth and dirt, the floor stained with grime. The alarm no longer blared with deafening intensity. Eerie silence settled on the vessel, punctured only by the slapping of our feet against the wet thinly-carpeted floor and the occasional groan and creak of the ship. We rounded a corner and almost crashed into Stan and Lucus.

Lucus held his finger to his lips and tilted his head toward a nearby stairwell. Ben and his coven must be that way. We nodded and followed at a brisk jog.

Gunfire sounded again, somewhere above us. Must be the other half of Team Andy making a ruckus and providing a much needed distraction. Hopefully, they were okay.

They're all right, Wick whispered in my head as his hand settled on the small of my back and pushed me forward. He picked up his pace and passed me to join Lucus. He leaned down to ask the Witch something quietly. My pulse thudded in my ears as I continued to keep pace and prevented me from hearing the conversation.

Something gnawed at my senses. Kind of like another fera wanting to bond, but different. Darker. Creepier. The hairs on my arms and neck stood up, and ice crept through me. I slowed, but the energy continued to taunt my neurons. I stopped running. The team ahead rounded the corner at the base of the stairs.

Andy? Wick asked.

Go ahead. Find the boys.

Wick growled, but I ignored him and turned to climb the stairs. Floor after floor, I kept climbing, following the juicy tendril as it led me somewhere. I hoped it was the Pharaoh. Let the guys save the Witches. I wanted to sink my fangs and talons into an ancient Vampire tonight.

Sweat dripped from my face as my skin grew cold and clammy. Where the hell was the rest of the team? The other half of Team Andy? Surely, I would've passed them by now, or at least scented them.

My limbs screamed as I continued to keep the hard pace. Soft light trickled through the closed double doors at the end of the hall. My heart skipped a beat. The paneling and ornate door handles gave away the importance of who, or what, lurked on the other side.

The boat shook again.

Someone called out on the deck below. I didn't recognize the voice.

The trickle of voices floated down the hall, along with the Pharaoh's scent. Different than the usual Vampire perfume of death and blood, this ancient supe smelled old, like dried leaves from the end of a hot summer before the rains started.

I threw open the double doors. The dim light from two lamps illuminated a lone figure in the middle of the room. The doors closed behind me with a thud of finality.

The Pharaoh turned around.

My breath caught. Though I'd seen the Master Vampire before, his appearance was no less startling.

With a long slender neck, elongated face, high cheekbones and a sharp chin, the Pharaoh's face had a harsh, alien-like appearance. Large, angled brown eyes, full lips, and delicate arms and fingers on his tall, willowy frame made him appear delicate. Yet, I'd never use delicate to describe this supernatural being.

The ancient Vampire radiated strength so powerful it hung heavy in the air.

"Andrea McNeilly. What a pain you turned out to be." His deep voice contradicted his weak frame and vibrated the air.

"Pharaoh." I inclined my head. No point in listing all the reasons he'd been more than a pain to me.

"Please, call me Tancheres." He flicked his wrist like revealing his true name was of no importance. It wasn't, really. I already knew it, having researched the Pharaoh extensively after discovering his connection with the KK drug.

"Tancheres." I took a step toward the Vampire. He didn't move—not in a frozen with fear way, but in an I-couldn't-care-less way. "Or do you prefer Djedkare Isesi?"

The Pharaoh's full lips twitched and his eyes sparkled. "You've done your research."

"One thing I never understood."

He bowed his head, feet still firmly planted and unmoving as I continued to approach.

"Why didn't you just squash us all when we had no idea of your plans?"

The Pharaoh tilted his head back and laughed. The deep, unsettling sound didn't fit the frail, odd form standing before me. "With any kind of coup, you need to identify all the key players first. Otherwise, you risk an uprising. Revolution is like an infection. To prevent a future rebellion, I needed to identify and *squash* every person involved. In the beginning, too many unknowns existed, including you. Had Lucien played you better, he'd have the Werewolves, the Carus, *and* the Wereleopards under his thumb. Instead, he lost it all." He flicked his wrist again, the gesture so similar to Lucien's.

Would he appreciate the comparison?

"Every significant member must be eradicated." The Pharaoh's deep growl of a voice continued. "Or like a disease, unrest will fester and flare up again, and again. A premature coup would've inevitably led to a revolt. Much better to identify all the pieces first and then pick them off like a strategic game."

He may as well have said a direct attack was uncouth and beneath him. Not sure if I agreed with his logic, but then again, I'd never attempted to take down a Vampire empire, much less succeeded at it.

"Of course, you weren't meant to survive this long. I'm not particularly pleased with my minion's failures."

Christine. Who else could he mean? He had to refer to the female Werewolf who'd tried to kill me three times, and instead, succeeded in murdering Tristan. Had she always worked for the Pharaoh? Or did he use her hatred for me to convert her to his side? My knuckles popped as I took another step closer, only a few feet from striking distance.

I clenched my fists and smiled wide, knowing my beast fangs would gleam in the dull light. "Well, in about two seconds you'll wish you'd chosen a different *minion* for the job. Let's do this."

I drew my hands up to fight.

Instead of tensing, or preparing, or the preferred cowering in fear, the Pharaoh remained relaxed and aloof. He made no move to run or to attack, instead, he tilted his head and his gaze twinkled.

I let my hands fall to my sides, and frowned. Sure, I wasn't a centuries-upon-centuries old Vampire, but surely I merited a little caution, maybe a pinch of fear? A dollop of respect?

"Silly child. I'm far too old to get dragged into scraps with mortal weaklings." He snapped his fingers.

A sense of déjà vu swept over me. Images of Lucien snapping his fingers that fateful night so long ago—the night that revealed Clint's survival and my impending servitude. The night that set all of this crap in motion.

Clint didn't step out of the shadows, though. He was downstairs somewhere.

Instead, a large Demon stepped into the soft light. Obscured with his own magic, I hadn't seen or smelled him until now. One of his many parlour tricks. He relaxed his control on his scent, and it barrelled forward, almost knocking me over.

The walls and room flooded with demonic almond, yet the scent had been twisted with something cruel. The essence of blood and steel seeped from his pores. With the head of a feral dog, and the body of a nine-foot professional weight lifter, the Demon stretched his black feathered wings out, the only beautiful thing about him. His canine jaw gaped open, fangs dripping thick, putrid saliva. Dead and black, with no discernible pupil or iris, his gaze held unbound malice as it met mine.

Bola.

35

The sound of water lapping against the ship echoed through the room. The decrepit boat swayed, and the dim light flickered as I took in Bola's smug expression.

Should I gut him or rip out his throat? Fast or slow?

"I believe you know one another." The Pharaoh turned to Bola. "I've held up my end of the bargain."

The Demon's soulless gaze glistened. He flicked a vial toward the ancient Vampire. The Pharaoh snatched it from the air and smiled.

My eyes narrowed. What the hell was that?

Bola stepped forward, teeth gnashing, dog grin widening.

My muscles tensed.

"Finally." His low voice rumbled. "Some alone time."

I glanced over to...Goddammit! The Pharaoh used his Vampire super speed to escape. Again. I needed to pin the tail on that donkey.

Bola crept forward, arms wide, as if "Come give me a hug" would be his next line.

I snarled.

"I like this look on you, Carus."

"You're going to find it a bit harder to fight me."

"Please. You're only half-divine, not even, your blood diluted over generations." He flexed and his body appeared to swell as his chest puffed out. "I'm *full* Demon."

"Full asshole." But the curse fell flat when describing this netherworld entity standing in front of me with his puffed chest and gnashing jaws.

Bola lunged at me, arms outstretched, straining for my neck. He always went for the jugular. About as subtle as a drunk frat boy. I slipped his attack and countered with a strike to his ribs.

Bola grunted but spun quickly to face me again.

Body shots were so under appreciated.

Again, Bola leapt forward, powerful arms lashing out in a frenzied, but precise attack. With beast-fast reflexes and power, I blocked, dodged, weaved, and slipped past the majority of his attack. My talons shredded his skin.

Bola was stronger. But I was faster.

We continued exchanging blows. Sweat dripped off my fur and ran down my scaly spine. I snuck more shots in than Bola. I should be winning. But with less power, the damage wasn't enough.

I growled.

Bola smiled and renewed his attack.

Could I wear him down? My spine tingled, and my

skin grew clammy even though adrenaline raced through my body.

The boat shook. We staggered to the side as the vessel lurched, and a low groan vibrated through the metal.

A wolf howled.

Wick.

My head snapped toward the exit. My breathing stopped, air trapped in my throat. What happened? Was he all right?

Focus!

I turned to Bola. Too late. His fist met my face, flush with my cheek and jaw. White stars burst into my vision. The room moved around me. My knees buckled. Instead of stepping forward, I staggered to the side.

Another shot to the head.

I keeled over. The back of my head slapped against the hard floor. Without a moment of reprieve, Bola crushed me under his body weight. His snarling face so close, multiple faces swirled around in my reeling vision. Rank smelling saliva dripped from his fangs and splattered against my cheeks.

Crap! Had he been right? Did all my Carus skills count for nothing when against a full Demon? Fear pecked away at my brain as sweat dripped off my heaving body.

Bola wrapped his hands around my neck. His fingers dug into my flesh. I thrashed around and tried to fight his hold.

What the hell was I going to do? He was too strong, his advantage, too great.

Stag! I called.

Bola squeezed and black dots speckled my vision.

The air shimmered as the stag appeared ghost white to my left.

"I'm going to rip Sid's pitiful mark away from your soul and stamp a claim on you so hard it will never wash away."

My breath caught. Bola's pressure increased. Heat flooded my face. I stretched my arm out, straining to reach the stag. My fingers fumbled, millimetres away from his soft schnoz.

Closer.

Stag bumped his muzzle closer. My fingertips sank into the supple bristles on his snout. My vision wavered, the speckling of black dots so thick, little sight remained.

"I never understood why Sid didn't fully claim you with sex to complete the anchor bond. His mistake. His loss."

Sid wasn't a complete asshole, that was why. His interest in me never lay between my legs, not really. I closed my eyes and reached into my mind, pulling the stag with me.

A portal, Feradea had said.

Come visit me, she'd said.

Okay, Stag, I whispered. *Let's go visit G'ma.*

I pulled the stag's energy into my own. Power washed through my body, like a giant tidal wave, before whiplashing back, drawing the beast force from my essence as the sheer energy licked my skin. A deep thrum filled the room as the air spiralled around us. The streams kept circling into a thunderous vortex until a portal formed in the centre. My body lit on fire, consuming, burning.

Feradea's advice trickled through my memory.

Shine, not burn.

Instead of letting the potent energy consume me, I pushed it outward. The heat burst through my pores, radiating out as white light.

Bola froze.

His hands around my neck slackened.

The blood ballooning in my head drained away.

Sweat matted my fur. My vision cleared.

Bola looked up. His gaze widened as he took in the formation of the portal above my head. His throat moved as he swallowed.

His nice, vulnerable neck.

With beast reflexes, I thrust my hand up, sharp talons first, and drove them into the soft, exposed tissue of Bola's neck.

He gagged. Blood spurted.

Bola's dark soulless gaze dropped to mine as the portal consumed us.

"Surprise." I pushed my long talons deeper. Warm, thick flowing blood ran down my arm.

My body became weightless. Time stopped. Frozen in a state of suspension, I held the panicked gaze of Bola as his blood continued to spurt and spray from his wound, and splatter against my face.

Slowly, the blinding white glare of the area surrounding us gave way to the lush green of a healthy, old-growth forest. Pine and spruce curled around me, and a natural flowing spring lined with fragrant flowers trickled in the distance.

Bola continued to gurgle. He grabbed at my hand, the one with talons still embedded in his throat, feeling the dying ebb of his pulsing blood. I batted his weak attempts away with my free hand.

A twig nearby snapped. Bola stiffened.

I looked over, first taking in the bare feet, then the shapely tanned legs leading to a barely-there leather outfit.

Feradea.

Her mouth twitched. "Well met, daughter-mine. I see you brought me a gift." I slammed the talons of my free hand into the side of Bola's neck and sliced, increasing the damage and blood flow. His body jerked and writhed as his Demon nature attempted to heal the damage.

I turned to Feradea. "Help me get him to the Demon Realm."

Her face scrunched up, and she examined her nails. "You don't want to go there."

Bola gurgled and bucked.

"Yes, I do! I want this fucker destroyed. If he dies here, he'll just pop up again." My chest constricted. I was so close.

Bola's blood flow decreased, and Bola's soulless gaze drew distant.

Feradea's expression relaxed. "I understand. Fear not, daughter mine. The realm of the divine and demons are essentially the same. His death here is final."

Tension flowed from my muscles, and a smile spread across my face as the life leeched away from Bola—from the entity whose face once plagued so many of my nightmares.

Dead.

He was finally dead.

Warmth expanded in my chest as his body sagged against mine. I pushed him off and stood beside Feradea. Unlike a Demon death on Earth, his body didn't quickly disintegrate.

The Goddess reached down and tore Bola's head from his body in one swift motion

"Wha—?"

She turned to me, with Bola's lifeless, decapitated head dripping blood in her hands, and winked. "Your gift to me."

36

As soon as the mouldy, rodent infested room with slime covered walls fully materialized, I let the stag go. The room still swayed a little, as if I'd taken a few shots too many of cinnamon whiskey on ladies' night, but as a Carus, I would recover from my fight with Bola sooner than later. After confirming with Feradea for the umpteenth time death in the domain of the divine meant no resurrection in the nether realm, and Bola was truly, forever gone, never to return, never to torment me again, I promised to visit and said my good-byes. She'd laughed, clearly amused at mortal haste. Bola might be dead, but Wick had howled with rage, the boys hadn't been found yet, and the Pharaoh was on the run, again. Rat bastard.

The old desk and the lamps providing the dim light solidified and merged into concrete images.

"Where the fuck did you go!" A deep, raw voice growled behind me.

I spun around to face the entrance. The room continued to spin. Weakened, naked, and in my human form, nausea rolled up my throat. I gulped.

Wick stood naked in the centre of the room. Werewolf yellow eyes bore into mine with a smouldering heat. The intensity so potent, his Alpha power rolled over me like a wave of lava.

My wolf whined, wanting to go belly-up.

Wick's body heaved with deep breaths, his skin splattered with dried blood. Grease and more blood streaked his Norse god-like face, slashing across with the severe angle of his brows.

Why was he frowning at me? He looked like he survived a landmine.

I sniffed.

Only a little of the blood was his.

My shoulders dropped, and I let out a long breath.

"You disappeared," he whispered.

I shook my head. And winced. The room swayed again. I took a step to the side.

Wick hurried forward to reach me. "I came in time to see you disappear with that...that animal. He was on top of you." Wick shuddered. He knew all about my painful past and the role Bola had in it—the rape and torture. Bola's death had been too quick.

Strong hands gripped my arms and pulled me in for a hug. He wrapped me into a naked cocoon made of his warmth, his strong arms borderline crushing.

"Are you okay?" he whispered into my ear. His light breath fanned my hair, and tickled my neck.

"Bola's gone."

Wick growled. "At least you're not hurt."

Much. "No. Bola's gone, gone. As in dead. I killed that motherfucker in the divine realm, and he's never coming back."

An image of his black soulless gaze glazing over as the blood, spurting and oozing out of his neck, ran along my arms flashed across my vision. The matching part of my mind, the dark place, dripping with pain, shame, and all the other unsavoury feelings that resurfaced with any thoughts of my time in Dylan's pack settled. As if instead of waiting like a coiled spring to pounce given any chance or flicker of a memory, Bola's death squashed the potency of the past. An invisible weight lifted from my shoulders. Free. The fear of Bola returning dissipated. The lurking possibility, gone. I was truly free of him. Forever.

Wick squeezed me and burrowed his face in the crook of my neck. He ran his nose along the soft, vulnerable skin. The not-so-distant memory of his heated kiss tingled on my lips, spreading heat through my body for more.

Musky coconut spiralled out from my skin.

A low rumble from Wick's chest vibrated against my body. His hands relaxed their grip and slid down my naked back. Now, very aware of our lack of clothing, I yearned for his hands to continue travelling along my skin, for his mouth to take mine as his body claimed me.

Someone cleared their throat.

I jumped back. "Oh god! The boys."

Wick straightened and chuckled. Instead of speaking, his lips twitched and he stepped to the side.

In dirty rags for clothes, four young male Witches used the enforcers from Wick's pack for support. Stan and Lucus peered in from outside the door. One of the Witches in the centre looked up. Underneath plain blond hair, browner from grime, a soft gaze met mine. I'd know that adorable puppy-face anywhere.

"Ben!" I crashed into my friend and wrapped my arms around him. He hugged me back as my senses took in details. No blood of theirs had been spilled recently, no scent of pain. Just dirt. A lot of dirt, and sweat, and... grime...like months and months without a shower and proper facilities grime.

I wrenched back, my face twisting. "Ugh, no offence, Ben, but you—"

"We all stink!" Patty exclaimed, seconds before he lunged in from the side and hugged me as well. His greasy black hair slid along the bare skin of my arms.

"Group hug!" Matthew joined in from the other side, his green eyes sparkling underneath a mop of sandy hair.

Over Ben's shoulder, Stan's smile broadened. He enjoyed this.

"Yeah." An unfamiliar voice spoke behind me, deep and rugged, like we met on a hiking path in the middle of nowhere. "I'm good."

I looked over my shoulder, half expecting to find a man dressed in plaid wielding an axe. Christopher. He always reminded me of a gruff logger. Well, he got his voice back, and it matched his appearance, but there'd been a hefty cost. Bola had used his body to enact horrific deeds, events that put the Witches in this very mess.

"Witch, I goddamn saved your life. You better take a step in, and join, or I'll finish what I started months ago." Namely, killing him. I'd been close. Only love for the other Witches had stayed my hand.

Christopher tensed, his gaze searching. I maintained my death stare.

Christopher shrugged and stepped forward, tentatively wrapping his arms around the whole group.

"Thank you," he whispered into my ear.

I do not like watching four young men grope you, Wick huffed. *You're still naked.*

It's a group hug.

It's over.

I laughed and twisted to meet his wolf yellow stare. It was positively murderous. Burnt cinnamon spiralled off his body, and he clenched his fists.

The Witches followed my gaze. Almost as one, they tensed before breaking away. Patty leaped three feet, sideways, like a deranged leprechaun.

Stan's gaze twinkled as he handed me his shirt. He still wore a white tank, but it did little to hide his pasty skin and beer belly.

"Thanks." I gently plucked the shirt from his hands and pulled it on. It smelled of Stan—soap and leather— but the shirt covered my hoohoo, and that's all that mattered.

Wick continued to growl low, probably not impressed I wrapped myself in another man's scent.

I rolled my eyes at the vibrating Werewolf Alpha. *Relax.*

I will not. We have unfinished business, Andy.

That'll have to wait.

I'm not waiting while you belt out old songs into carrots and beer bottles with four lunatic Witches, Wick growled.

My hands flew to my hips and I glowered at him. *Our...stuff...will have to wait until we kill the Pharaoh.*

His mouth formed a perfect O, and he had the decency to look chagrined. He rubbed the stubble on his chin with his fist. *We could just let him go.*

I shook my head. The motion too quick, my vision swam. I staggered to the side. Wick stepped forward. I waved him off.

His gaze narrowed, and his lips flattened into a grim line.

He's too powerful, he'll just rebuild, I said.

The gazes of the others in the room ping ponged between us, probably guessing a silent battle waged, but having no idea of the outcome.

You can't even stand up straight. Let me take you home. Let me...

I smirked. The heat in Wick's gaze left little doubt to what he wanted me to let him do. *No, Wick. We need to take him down. Now. Besides, someone told me to identify and squash every person involved, or like a disease, they'll just fester and flare up again, and again.*

Who the heck said that?

The Pharaoh.

Wick grunted.

Our spectators snapped their attention to Wick, brows raised.

"What are you two lovebirds fighting about, now?" Allan sauntered into the room, all swagger, no urgency, hands clasped behind his back like he'd taken a leisurely stroll among the peasants on the boardwalk. Clint entered the room after him with a cheese-eating grin, his swords, dripping with blood, grasped loosely at his sides. At least the immortal had avoided dying-not-dying this time.

I turned my death stare to the Vampire. "We need to find the Pharaoh." *And gut him.*

"Oh?" Allan said, suspiciously coy. "This Pharaoh?"

With swift Vampire reflexes, he held up a decapitated head from behind his back. The glazed-over almond-shaped gaze met mine.

My jaw dropped.

37

The rage circling in my body, calling for the Pharaoh's death, continued to race around with nowhere else to go. My shoulders slumped. "Are you fucking kidding me?"

I stared at the remains of the most ancient Vampire I'd ever met. Young Vampires disintegrated to ash almost immediately. As an older Vampire, the Pharaoh's head would take days to deteriorate.

Something pinged in my brain, like an errant thought leading to something important, something missed, but as I groped to grab the dangling thread, it slipped away. Lost.

I mentally shrugged. Who the heck cared? Allan killed the Pharaoh.

How? How was this possible? Allan wasn't powerful enough to take him out. Right?

"How... How..." I shut my mouth and glowered at the smirking Vampire. The tension tightly coiled in my body bloomed outward and drained through my veins. Gone. I'd been so intent on killing this son-of-a-bitch, and now? Robbed. I felt robbed, and empty, and a little relieved. I would've needed a giant horseshoe up my ass to defeat Bola *and* an ancient Vampire on the same night.

Allan tossed the head at my feet. It bounced off the metal floor with a sickening slick and hollow sound before coming to rest against my bare toes, the flesh cold and sticky.

Ew. I shuffled a half-step back. Sure, I used to deliver death to unsavoury supes, but I never fondled their amputated body parts. I got in and got out without getting dead...or covered with decomposing Vampire slime. Yuck.

"Your face is priceless, Carus." Allan adjusted his sleeves. "Like a fish sucking air."

Clint chuckled and muttered something about me and sucking something under his breath.

Gross.

Wick growled and stepped forward.

Clint held his hands up in mock surrender. "Oh, come on. I was joking."

Alan shot Clint a dark look, and the human servant thankfully shut his mouth.

"You're right, Carus." Allan turned back to me. "I lack the strength, age, and power to take out the Pharaoh in a one-on-one battle, but I never planned to fight the Pharaoh honourably. I caught your thoughts and from there, I tracked the Pharaoh's mind. Luck placed me in the right location. As he ran to escape you, he quite literally ran into my blade."

Huh. Never pegged Allan as a lucky bastard, but geez. "Well, that was..."

"Easy?" Wick finished for me.

I feel like we should have a button to press or something.

Wick caught my thought, and his smile grew.

The Pharaoh's death had been too quick after a significant build up. Adrenaline still raced through my body, screaming for a fight where an opponent no longer existed.

"Um, guys?" Steve said. "We should get these Witches home. I don't think they've been dining on five course meals."

John supported Patty as the Witch sagged against him. The Werewolf's face scrunched up. "And they really do stink."

Allan nodded. "Well, Carus, it looks like you achieved your goals. The Pharaoh is dead, and if I'm reading your mind correctly, so is Bola. Well done. There's nothing left to do here."

"Except kill Tucker. Loose end and all."

"Yeah, uh... About that." Lucus pulled on his shirt collar.

I snapped my attention to him and watched his cheeks flush. "About *what*?"

"Veronika might be working out some of her, uh, healing process with Tucker."

Stomach acid rose up my throat. Geez, it's like they

banded together in a private meeting beforehand and thought of ways to trigger my gag reflex. "That's...ew."

"No." Lucus waved his hands and shook his head. "Not like that."

"Like what, then?" I narrowed my gaze at the Witch, now sweating profusely.

"She planned to pull Sid over from the other side. They had a deal. I don't think...I don't think Tucker will be alive by the time we return."

I opened my mouth.

"She has just as much right to revenge as you do, you know. It's not all about Andy McNeilly." His tone increased an octave. "You don't know... You don't know what he put her through. What he did..." Lucus's hands trembled, as if one wrong word or move, and he'd blast me to another realm.

He was right. I didn't know what ATF did to Veronika. I didn't need to. Two brain cells could make an accurate conclusion. I stepped forward, ignored his flinch and twitchy hands, and laid a hand on his tense shoulders.

"I can guess. He was a sick fuck." A greedy, sick fuck with an overinflated ego. Tucker had only been an irritating nuisance to me. He'd been a torturer to Veronika. She deserved this vengeance more than me.

Lucus straightened. His gaze searched mine, and seeing no malice, his shoulders dropped under my hand, and his muscles relaxed. "She promised to make him suffer."

My lips twisted. "Good."

erewolves, Witches, and Stan milled around Wick's large living room, clasping hands, slapping backs, and clinking beer bottles before downing the amber fluid. The Wereleopards, Allan, and Clint had gone home, opting out of the after-party.

The mysterious vial Bola had tossed the Pharaoh in exchange for luring me to him contained KK, or something like it. Maybe a perfected version. Fuck that. We didn't want to risk it getting into the wrong hands, and without debate, Allan had crushed it under his boot on the ferry deck while the rest of us watched. Now, with the majority of our enemies taken care of, everyone wanted to relax and celebrate.

Wick had handed me a shirt and a pair of his sweats without a word as soon as we got back, silently demanding I cloak my body in his scent. Amused glances and knowing smirks from the others darted my way.

Stan had his shirt back and with a beer in his hand, mingled with everyone else as they rejoiced in our victory. Everyone acted like they were completely unaware of the tension building between me and Wick. How could they miss it? The tension tugged at my soul so hard it felt as though it would rip from my chest to plaster itself against Wick's body.

My falcon popped into my head and shrieked. I winced. She sent images of pecking the party guests and chasing them out the door.

Wick stood in the midst of the celebration, muscles taut, surrounded by an invisible cloud of burnt sugar and cinnamon.

My heart hammered in my chest, knowing full well what drove Wick's agitation. He'd planned to finish our discussion when we got home.

Well, here we were. At his home. And surrounded by meddling Witches, a nosy cop, and Wick's entire enforcement team from the pack.

My wolf paced, waiting, anticipating.

Cold shivers spread across my pebbled skin. I clutched my beer as if it would calm my nerves. Did I want to back out? Run away?

Wick's heated gaze met mine across the room, smouldering the airwaves, burning my retinas, claiming my mind before spreading through my body as if he sprawled naked beside me instead of standing twelve feet away.

My mountain lion perked up and purred. Her support somehow finalized a decision I'd already made. I smiled. My cat grinned and disappeared to the other side.

"Everybody out." Wick's voice, though quiet, held a steely command.

Guess he had enough of waiting, too.

I gulped down the rest of my beer and gently placed it on the coffee table beside me as everyone straightened and snapped their attention to Wick.

Taking in his tense posture, scent, and trained gaze on me, understanding spread across their expressions. Mel giggled, grabbed Dan's hand and practically skipped out of the house. The others shuffled behind them, some smiling, and some frowning.

Except Stan.

He hesitated and turned to me. "Andy?"

Wick growled deep and low.

Stan stiffened, but held his ground, his hand drifting to his sidearm. "You going to be okay?"

I certainly hope so. Not trusting my voice, I nodded my head.

Stan grunted and stalked out of the house, muttering about bat-shit crazy supes along the way.

"Andy." Whiskey and cream vibrated the room. He stood still, muscles tense, gaze Werewolf gold.

"Wick." The corners of my lips curled up.

"I don't have much control left. If you plan to back out or push me away, or you're not sure you can go through with this, you need to leave. Now."

I had no plans to ever let this man go again. I knew

his worth, always had, and now I'd pay any price to have him, consequences be damned.

Instead of replying, I pulled my borrowed shirt over my head and flung it across the room. The cold air hit my bare skin and goosebumps pebbled along my arms.

Wick closed his eyes and clenched his fists. "I don't think... I won't, can't, be gentle."

Hell yes. I was in no mood for slow and sweet. There would be time for that later. I pulled my jogging pants down and let them drop to the floor by my feet. Wick's scent ballooned up from the discarded clothes.

Wick's yellow gaze popped open. His nose flared. His chest rumbled with a deep growl. He pulled off his shirt. The soft whisper of fabric landing on the floor fanned the ache growing between my thighs. His strong chest and abs caught the light, and my mouth watered.

"If you stay, I will claim you," he warned. His gaze swept over my naked body from three feet away and sent warmth rolling through me.

I stepped out of the pants pooled around my ankles and used a foot to flick them away. With my feet shoulder width apart and hands relaxed at my side, I waited, naked and vulnerable. I wouldn't run from this man, this Alpha who'd shown me patience, understanding and vulnerability when it went against his nature. Wick had also shown strength, leadership and power. The dichotomy of his actions—how such a formidable figure could bend to show what ignorant people considered weakness—made my pulse race.

Wick's gaze remained trained on me, unsmiling,

unyielding, holding on to his humanity as his wolf pushed for control. His wild lupine energy rushed forward and licked my skin. The animal nature within me rose to meet Wick's wolf energy as it spiralled out and wrapped around me.

"Your eyes." Wick frowned.

My eyes prickled telling me they'd shifted, but Wick had seen this before. Heck, he'd seen all of me before. But tonight was different. Tonight was special. My skin tingled with the promise in Wick's gaze.

"What about them?" I croaked, my voice well-passed sultry. I'd rather do something else with my mouth. Wick's body bordered on perfection. I'd seen it many times, touched it, licked it, but never experienced the full potency like I planned to tonight. Over six-and-a-half feet tall, with broad shoulders, his chiseled abs led down to... his pants, with a definite bulge. My memory replaced the clothes with vivid recollections of the uncensored version of what lay beneath. I licked my lips.

"They're Werewolf yellow," he explained.

Huh? I ripped my gaze from his ready body, and scrambled to recall what we'd been talking about. What was yellow? The sun? What the hell... *Oh, that's right.* My eyes. Guess my chameleon nature could pick and choose without any direction.

Right now, the choices of my nature could go fly a kite. My mind preferred to think about positional choices.

Wick's zipper broke the tense silence following his words. He pulled his pants down. The dull thud of his belt against the cold floor sounded as a starting gun for my breathing. He'd been commando like me, and his sizeable erection jutted out.

And still, he remained infuriatingly out of reach, three feet away.

"What are you waiting for?" I asked.

Wick's jaw clenched. "For you to bolt."

"I'm not run—"

Wick was on me before I finished the sentence. His powerful body slammed into mine. His hot mouth claiming as his wolf energy swirled to merge with mine. Strong arms circled me as we fell to the floor. Weightlessness flowed over my mind as time seemed to slow down. Wick pushed inside before I hit the hard wood floor. His arms protecting me from the brunt of the impact.

The heavy weight of Wick's body pressed me into the cold wood as his searing warmth pulsed inside and his wet tongue tasted my mouth.

He flexed his hips and pushed deeper.

"You feel so good," he mumbled into my mouth. The heat of him filled the emptiness inside. My body sent shooting shivers across every cell in response, anticipating what was to come. As incredible as this moment was, every inch of me yearned for him to move. With slow precision, he withdrew, his gaze boring into mine, daring me to look away, to break this connection building between us.

Another moment of stillness settled over us, like the moment right after jumping off a cliff before gravity takes hold and hurls your body toward the waiting sea. And just like that, Wick slammed back in with a groan.

With my arms wrapped around his muscled torso, I rose to move with him, and feed the searing ache in my core. He dragged a hand down to cup my ass and pull me closer, spreading my legs wider. The hard wood beneath us warmed as my body slapped into it with each thrust. Nerve endings stirred and tingled. My breathing quickened, growing shallow and fast. Wick's tongue drove into my mouth in time with his hips.

The room around us faded away, time slowed to the point it no longer existed. Nothing existed but this moment between us.

He slowed his pace, pushed deep, and changed his rhythm, his hips grinding in a spiral, sending shockwaves of pleasure through me. His hard body moved over mine, encasing me in warmth and muscle.

Wick's intense gaze trained on my face. His full lips parted and the tips of his partially shifted canines jutted out, as he continued to stoke the searing heat building inside me.

Sweat broke across his brow and his strong arms tensed as his hold on me tightened. I rocked to match his rhythm, slow and deep, then quick and shallow. His skin seared mine with every touch. As my heart beat in tune with Wick's, it expanded, pushing against my bones and tissues, as if it wanted to get outside my body and touch Wick, or merge with him.

The exquisite ache continued to build. When he leaned down to trail hot kisses along my body, and changed to a shallow scooping motion, a guttural sound escaped my mouth, more animal than human.

"I need more," he groaned.

I braced against the floor as he drove into me while holding me in place with his strong arms. His hands drifted down to rub against me. The move shot pleasure through my veins like a lightning bolt. My lips parted. My animal rose up to entwine with Wick's wolf. His lupine energy dove inside, invading my core with each pump of his hips. The energy expanded, all consuming until I couldn't tell where I ended and Wick began.

Wick's hoarse breath caressing the soft skin on my neck drowned out the slapping of our bodies. Sweat broke out across my skin. He gripped my hips so hard, his fingertips dug in. The expanding heat in my chest continued to press against my skin, as if I'd burst if I didn't let it out to claim Wick.

The beast joined the intense energy and spread out. My eyes and gums tingled. Blood pooled in my mouth as fangs descended.

Wick looked up from the breast his hot mouth claimed. Blazing yellow irises bore into me, as if he saw the scorching power expanding and demanding release. He snaked his hand to grip the back of my neck and pulled me in for another dizzying kiss. His tongue twisted and swirled with mine, tasting, consuming, claiming. When the pressure built to an unbearable level, I pulled back.

Wick licked the blood off his lips, and his challenging gaze met mine.

My animal nature leached into my fiery veins and melted my bones. My body throbbed, my core ached. As the pleasure reached its peak, I sank my fangs into the tender flesh of his neck. The orgasm broke in waves over my senses. I moaned into his skin as the pleasure rippled through my body, and Wick's blood coated my tongue, delicious and sweet.

Wick's wolf howled inside my mind. The beast growled. Wick shook as my animals claimed him. His muscles tensed, yet he continued to stroke, thrusting again and again with his powerful hips.

Mine. All mine.

With retracted fangs, my head snapped back. Blood dripped down my chin. Wick's blood. My mate.

I *roared*.

Wick's rhythm faltered, and he leaned forward. Dragging his nose against the skin of my neck, he brushed my hair to the side. Tingles raced down my body. Long fangs pierced my neck, penetrating, as the wolf energy claimed me. He thrust one last time before he shuddered.

A second orgasm slammed through my body.

Unexpected, but not unwelcome, it vibrated my bones. I cried out as my body bucked against Wick's. He kept me pinned down, his fangs embedded in my flesh as he pulsed inside me.

When I settled, and my breathing calmed, Wick lathed the trickling blood on my neck.

"Mine," he growled.

The sensitive flesh where he'd bitten my neck throbbed in response.

"Yours," I agreed.

I ground against Wick and rocked out the lingering tendrils of the most potent orgasm of my life. The constriction around my heart released, as if sunken barbs retracted and let go. My chest expanded with warmth and freedom. I smiled into Wick's neck as all tension flowed from my body and my muscles grew limp.

He leaned forward and rested his sweaty forehead against my breast. More warmth spread across my chest as Wick pulled me closer, his strong arms shaking as he encased me. Our animals sank into each other, and Wick's contentment hummed through my veins.

I *felt* him. He existed inside my body, my mind, my heart. He was inside my soul.

"And you're inside mine." The tips of his lips twitched. Blood from his bite had smeared across his face.

The beast's low voice rumbled, *I am you, you are me, we are one.*

Wick stiffened. "What the hell was that?"

"My beast. She likes you."

Wick chuckled and relaxed as he rubbed his scratchy cheek against mine. He kissed his bite mark. Tendrils of pleasure danced along my neurons from the contact.

Distant, as if he fenced them on the other side, multiple wolf energies howled and milled around. The pack. Their energies hummed through my bond with Wick.

His arms tightened around me briefly before he

ducked down to kiss a nipple. "You're officially invited to join the Lower Mainland Werewolf Pack."

I laughed, and Wick's chest rumbled.

"You're not leaving the pack?"

"Not anymore. I have a mate."

"Will Ryan be pissed. He was going to challenge you."

Wick chuckled. "Ryan will be relieved. He only agreed to challenge me out of love and respect."

"Then I accept." There'd be a ritual later, but now was not the time to think about the pack, or anything else other than the man with me right now.

Wick twitched against the sensitive skin of my thigh, the tension returning to his body, and a hungry look replaced his content gaze.

"Already?" I trailed my finger down his back to his ass, and gripped the corded muscle.

He chuckled in response. "We're not done here."

Wick's wolf howled inside my mind.

"I can go slower this time. Gentler." He pulled me up so I straddled him.

I hung my arms around his neck to hold him close. "Please don't."

Wick's bare chest rumbled, and rubbed against my breasts. Delightful tingles zipped along my nipples. Definitely not done here.

W ick spent the rest of the night proving he was a considerate lover, and he could, in fact, be gentle. He put my needs above his own, and, well, it was a good thing no one had remained in the house. The sounds that man made me make...

Fresh cut grass and the aftermath of musky coconut swirled around Wick's bedroom, evidence of our happiness. We lay wrapped around each other in Wick's supersized bed, the sheets in disarray, our hair wild and crazy, and if my content smile looked anything like Wick's, we both wore large, ridiculous grins.

"You don't mind hearing my thoughts in your head?" Wick asked out loud.

I didn't catch everything going through his impressive brain, but I caught the powerful ones, the emotional ones, the ones that turned my limbs to goo. My heart swelled, as if doubled in size with the mate bond. It beat in tune with Wick's. "Not at all. I'm used to hearing voices in my head. You?"

Wick's chest rumbled, and he nuzzled the soft skin on my neck, the bridge of his nose running along the scars of his mark. My body trembled. My nipples pinged.

"I'm used to housing the angsty emotions of a whole pack of delinquents in my head. I'm good." He paused and ran his hand along my naked skin. "I love you, Andy. I always have."

I smiled as the truth of his words wound around me in an invisible hug. "I love you, too."

Wick leaned in and kissed me. His hands continued to stroke, and potent need rose again.

The air in the room rushed over my body, as if someone opened a door into the room quickly. I pushed away from Wick, but the bedroom door remained closed.

Like the air above hot pavement in the summer, the space at the foot of the bed shimmered. Before I could react with something more effective than "Uhhh," Sid appeared with Veronika clinging to his side.

I bolted upright in bed, pulling the sheet with me. Wick jumped up. His menacing growl rumbled from his chest. With a flashing yellow gaze, he fought the change. Hair grew and his skin darkened. My bones ached, itching to shift with him. Unease, both his and mine, coiled inside my chest.

Sid and Veronika remained still. Thankfully, instead of his normal naked state—if you called that normal—the Demon wore stylish form-fitting jeans and an old school reggae shirt. Veronika had also dressed casual in jeans and a purple T-shirt.

What the hell?

"Bad time for a social call," I said.

Veronika blushed and looked away from Wick, still vibrating with anger, poised to attack, and still very much naked. My gaze travelled down his glorious body and every inch of skin I had kissed, licked and sucked the night before.

Burnt cinnamon shrouded the space between us and ruined my fantasies.

Sid's lips curled into a sneer as his gaze snapped between the two of us. "I suspected as much. Be grateful I waited as long as I did."

My eyes narrowed. "If you fed..."

He held his hand up. "Please, Carus. Now that you're mated, you're one of the few entities I cannot feed from. Instead of looking like a fat, juicy steak, you're about as appealing as a salad."

Did he just call me fat?

And juicy, Wick snarled in my head.

I laughed. I hadn't meant to project that thought. Everyone turned to stare at me, gazes wide, as if I finally lost it. Maybe I had.

"Is Tucker dead?" I sighed and dropped back against the headboard. Impending doom seemed unlikely.

Wick remained tense, ready to pounce and rend at the slightest provocation. The part of my body reserved for him and the bond shuddered.

"Most painfully." Veronika glanced up. Her gaze

turned cold and her body tensed. "He begged for death in the end."

"Good." My limbs tingled with warmth. Looking at Veronika, and the tremors racking through her petite frame, she needed to exact her revenge, her way. "Is that why you are here?"

"I came to wish you congratulations," Sid said.

"Could've waited," Wick seethed.

"Remember who I am, Wolf." Sid turned his dark Demon gaze on the Alpha. "My anchor is no more. Instead of smiting her, I am here to wish her well."

He squeezed Veronika to him. They exchanged a soft look, and a small smile touched Veronika's lips.

Well, that's an interesting development. A lot of what Sid just said and did was interesting.

I sat up. The constricted heart from last night, the release of the talons once sunk into muscle, made sense now. The freedom I'd felt had been the removal of Sid's claim on me. "You released your mark?" My voice came out more incredulous than intended.

Wick relaxed, following my thoughts. He shot me a grin. We were free. Free of Lucien, free of Sid, free of my nightmares, finally free to make our own decisions with only the intense bond between us.

Sid laughed. "I did no such thing, little one. You did the one and only thing that could remove the mark."

Mating.

Tristan's words from an eon ago floated through my mind: *There's no room for a third person in a mate bond.*

I smacked my forehead. It was so obvious, so ridiculously simple. The mating bond had pushed out all other marks and claims.

"Could mating have removed Lucien's mark as well?"

Sid nodded.

"Could it have prevented him from controlling Wick?"

Sid hesitated. "Not fully. He didn't have a bond with Wick. Lucien controlled Wick by controlling his wolf. However, as his mate, you'd have equal sway over the animal, and the power to prevent Wick from harming you or others."

Anger vibrated through my bones. Stomach acid bubbled up my throat as my gut twisted. If only we had known. We could've prevented so much heartache. If I had jumped in and embraced the mating call when I first heard it, instead of running from Wick in fear, I could've avoided so much death and pain.

Tristan would still be alive.

My limbs shook. Tears welled up, but I blinked them away.

Wick climbed on the bed and gathered me in his strong arms. His heartbeat echoed in my chest. "Shhhh. We had no way of knowing."

Sid grunted somewhere near us. "You can't live your life dwelling on what could've been, little one."

Sid, the poetic Demon, again.

"Congratulations on your mating," he continued. "When you're both decent, meet us in the living room. We have news on your missing pack member. Former pack member, that is."

I lifted my head away from my mark on Wick's fragrant neck and met the Demon's twinkling gaze.

Former pack member? Who the hell—

My muscles quivered, and my pulse sped as heat flushed through my body.

Christine.

40

Wind laden with pine and ocean curled around me as I sank my talons into the tree limb and pulled my head down into warm, black feathers. Waiting in raven form, I watched the Grouse Mountain Resort as Allan's Vampires waited close at hand for a call to action. Wick and his pack roamed the forest from a safe distance nearby. His presence still thrummed like a warm pulsating blanket in my chest. The reassuring love bolstered my confidence and put the beast at ease.

Of all the methods to discover Christine's location, online purchases of designer clothing had not been considered high priority. Heck, it hadn't been on my list. She demonstrated unexpected intelligence and used someone else's name and credit card. She had the clothes delivered to the resort instead of her actual address, but she hadn't anticipated Kayne Security Solution's ability to hack into the online retailer, nor the ingenuity and diligence of cross checking. They'd gone into all her favourite sites and ruled out the other non-residential deliveries.

When Wick and I both neglected to answer our cell phones—hello? Busy mating—Olly contacted Lucus with the information, which led to the awkward morning-after house call from the sex Demon and Veronika.

After cursory surveillance of Grouse Mountain revealed lurking Vampires from the Pharaoh's now disbanded horde, confirmation of Christine's whereabouts seemed certain.

That left the simple task of waiting for her to show up to collect a pair of bedazzled jeans and a burgundy scoop neck sweater.

It wasn't Christine.

With the smooth and fast movement of his tall, lanky body, clad in black camo, he screamed Vampire. It made no difference. We knew they lurked around the area like parasitic ants scurrying around an ant hill. We didn't know the location of their base, or the entrance to their lair. They had to be in an abandoned mine, or cave somewhere. That was the only thing that didn't fit in this whole equation.

Christine in a mine shaft. I couldn't *picture* it.

Unease trickled along my small bird spine as I launched from the branch with a hearty croak and followed the Vampire from above, swerving and maneuvering around the trees and their branches.

Vampires moved fast, but this one didn't move at top

speed, and I didn't need to stay directly on top of him, just close enough to see where he went.

There!

He ducked around a large boulder a few kilometres east of the Grouse Grind and disappeared. I flapped my wings and perched on a nearby branch. With a few hops and branch jumping, I positioned myself in front of a dark entrance. It looked like an old cave converted into a structured tunnel with wooden supports. A Vampire stood sentry to the right of the entrance. A branch snapped below, and I watched another Vampire move in. Definitely concentrated in this area.

Gotcha.

FROM A BIRD'S EYE VIEW, THE ATTACK WAS breathtaking, in a seamless tactical assault way. Allan's Vampires and Wick's pack moved with swift efficiency. The speeding shadows of Vampires flowed through the forest, flanked by wolves, taking out the Pharaoh's team with little difficulty. Their pace never faltered, and the second line took over as others dropped back to finish the job. Decades of working together, though not by choice, resulted in this beautiful display of teamwork.

I pumped my wings and moved forward to sit and watch the entrance. It would take little to get past the measly guard. I leaned forward.

Don't you dare go in without me, Wick growled in my head.

Dang that mate bond. He'd read my intent.

I rocked back on my perch and settled. *You only lectured me fifty million times before we left.*

You're exaggerating, and obviously the lectures didn't work. You're still thinking about it. Let our team go in first. We'll leave Christine for you.

I'm freaking part goddess. I'm not weak.

You're my mate! He growled. *Let me do this for you.*

He had a point. As Christine's Alpha, the kill technically belonged as much to him as it did to me. Not only had she tried to kill me more than once, and when I was under Wick's roof, but she'd evaded Wick's orders and needlessly jeopardized the pack by siding with the Pharaoh.

Wick would snap her neck in a second, but even with her tally sheet of wrongdoings, Wick hated violence against women, and he knew my need for vengeance trumped his need to assert Alpha discipline.

Just...just wait, he huffed, breath light as he raced through the woods. With the mate bond, his concern and worry coated my tongue, and sent physical pain running along my bones, as he drew closer and closer. *We're almost there.*

Fine.

The Vampires and Werewolves burst through the forest. The guard's cry cut off as Allan snapped his neck. The team continued to move with fluid grace into the cave's entrance. A large, menacing black wolf, with a white tipped snout, mitts and boots, splattered with Vampire blood, paused at the base of trees and peered up at me. Wick.

Mate, he growled.

Warmth flooded my body, and I floated down from the branch, shifting to wolf before I reached the ground. The familiar form rippled through my bones, light and dark gray fur replaced black feathers. As one of my first feras, the wolf form felt like home, and now, with the mate bond, it was more than that, something potent and indescribable, yet undeniably awesome.

Run with me. Wick stepped forward and butted his head against mine. His wolf dwarfed mine, in strength and size, but his presence beside me, with our energies flowing, brushing and moving past each other as they entangled and meshed along the mate bond, sent over-whelming love racing through me.

I nipped his jaw and took off down the tunnel, with Wick and his—our—pack running close behind. Wet dirt, mould and moss cloaked the air in the entranceway as my paws sank into the open ground.

The deeper we moved into the tunnels, the darker, colder and drier they became. We slowed and came to a stop when we reached the tunnel's main room. Dust, churned up from our run, settled around us. The large chamber had been converted into an underground lair with surveillance camera feeds, and more hallways running off the main room, and farther into the mountain.

Christine stood stiff among the Pharaoh's truly-dead

and dying Vampires. In aiding us tonight, Allan ensured the eradication of the Pharaoh's horde and any imminent threats to his seat of power.

The Vampires and Wick's wolves surrounded Christine but didn't make a move. They didn't dare. Blood splattered her grim face, perfectly coifed hair and flashy designer clothes. Her hands balled into fists at her side.

As we entered, her chin lifted and she pushed her shoulders back. She sucked in a breath and her gaze glittered when it met Wick's.

Christine, he spoke to her using his Alpha power. *You've been sentenced to death.*

She jerked her head away.

I won't carry out the sentence.

She looked up, eyes wide, with something like hope playing at her expression. Clean, lavender-tainted air flowed from her. She looked around until her gaze snagged on mine. Her brows dropped.

The hope washed away, replaced by something else. Something bitter and dark. She squeezed her eyes shut, as if to process my presence and what it meant. Sweet sweat lifted off her fragrantly-moisturized skin, and her muscles tensed. Finally, she opened her eyes, cold gaze meeting mine.

"Figured," she spat.

I shifted to human and stood to approach her, not caring who saw me naked, or how cold the air was against my skin. For added effect, I continued the shift and embraced the true form of my beast. Now over eight feet tall, wings folded tightly against my back to allow more room, and rage racing through my veins, I closed the distance to Tristan's murderer.

The air spiralling out from the hallway to the right smelled wrong. A few moans and cries, more animal than human, trickled up to the main room. I hesitated.

"What's that?"

Allan spoke, "My team is still moving through the labyrinth of tunnels in the mountain. Seems there's a prison section housing the few super supes that survived the KK transformation." The drug Bola and the Pharaoh had worked on elicited extreme supernatural abilities from roughly one percent of norms who dabbled with the drug. The rest either got high or died, but those weren't the results the Pharaoh cared about.

I turned to Christine. "Why are they caged?"

"They refused to carry out the Pharaoh's bidding."

I snorted. "All that effort to make an unbeatable army."

"And the transformed norms are spineless turds," Christine finished, not quite using the words I would have.

"And you're their guard?"

Christine sneered. "All that work I did for the Pharaoh, only to be reduced to some prison guard in a dirty, uncultured cave."

I paused and searched within. Nope. No feelings of sympathy surfaced for Christine.

Sonny's words echoed in my mind. *You need to let it go.*

The anger I held toward Christine washed away. Not

forgiving, certainly not forgetting, but letting her power over me go. She couldn't hurt me now, nor could my anger. I had to make sure she couldn't hurt anyone else.

Wick pawed the dirt.

Christine lifted her chin. "Aren't you going to fight me fairly?"

I laughed. She'd already used that line to pressure me into fighting her in my wolf form, a severely disadvantageous move for me, and I'd still beaten her in the dominance fight. Instead of answering, I snatched a sword from a nearby Vampire, stepped forward, beast-quick, and skewered her heart with the sharp point of the blade. I left the sword buried in her chest and took a step back.

Her gaze widened as blood soaked through her shirt. She coughed, sputtering blood along her lips, before her gaze lost focus. Her body dropped to the floor and sprawled amongst her former allies in a bloody heap. Even Were healing couldn't mend a pierced heart. I pulled the blade free and returned it to the nameless Vampire, his gaze fixed on the blood coating the shiny metal. He licked his lips.

My shoulders drew up, now completely weightless. No longer burdened by unwanted bonds or unfulfilled promises. With the final piece of my revenge carried out, my steps fell lighter on the dirt packed ground. If I didn't know any better, I'd worry I could float away.

I brushed my hands and turned to Wick, his mouth open in a lazy Werewolf grin. I reached for the wolf. Another scent, faint, but present, trickled up from another hallway.

I froze. Tasting the air with long successive breaths, followed by short ones. Blood and death. "No way."

"What is it?" Allan grumbled, no longer granted free access to my mind. Another awesome perk of the mate bond we'd discovered.

"Can't you smell it?" Blood and death, with the signature scent that used to remind me of Italian good looks and ridiculously flashy designer shoes. Unease prickled at my skin.

He shook his head. The Vampires shuffled their feet, and the wolves tensed.

"Lucien."

41

The air burned as I raced down the hall, closely followed by Werewolves and the Vampires. Luckily, Allan had no desire to relinquish his control over the Lower Mainland Vampire horde now that he had it, and we hadn't brought Clint. We all knew he was a big softy as far as his former master was concerned. All of Lucien's inner circle had died with him, or appeared to. With his scent present in this place, albeit weak, nothing remained certain.

Allan hadn't joked when he said this place was a labyrinth. The halls and tunnels crisscrossed and continued deep into Grouse Mountain. I paused at some junctions to sniff out the right path.

The trail of stench grew stronger. I put my head down and raced faster, past rows of cages with freakish-looking super supes cowering in corners.

There!

The tunnel veered sharply to the right. When I

turned, I stopped at the sight greeting me. The tunnel opened into a small room. In the centre, Lucien hung on a beam, crucifix-style. Or at least, what used to be Lucien.

Severely emaciated, his body consisted of shrivelling, ash-coloured skin clinging to bones, like someone took a vacuum-packing machine to him and sucked out all the flesh and blood. One of his arms had been amputated, and a long, rusty metal bar had been inserted in its place to string him up. Lab equipment lined the room.

The air shuffled through the tunnels in sporadic gusts. The rustling fabric and slapping footsteps of others echoed.

Without a beating heart, true Vampire death was hard to ascertain, unless the head was completely cleaved from the body. Not in this case. Lucien, aside from the missing arm, looked completely intact, with rags of his designer pinstriped suit covering his lower half.

The air, coiled with his dried blood and dead meat Vampire scent, now tasted twisted and bitter.

When I stepped forward, his eyes pinged open to tiny slits.

"Kitten." His voice, barely a husky wheeze, sounded more like shredded vocal cords than his former self.

"We thought you died."

He hacked. Trying to laugh, maybe? Instead, his hack lead to a coughing fit, spurting up a trickle of clotted blood that splattered his lips and dripped down his chin.

"Took my arm and burned it. Killed the rest." His raspy voice trailed off, and his head sagged down.

Neurons fired in my brain. A moment from the dilapidated ferry spiralled back to me. The loose thread I couldn't quite grasp and pull together. Clint and Allan had discovered Lucien's remains within a day of feeling their link with him break. Lucien was ancient. Maybe not as old as the Pharaoh, but he measured his age in centuries, not decades. Ashes a day after his supposed death was too soon for someone of Lucien's age. His remains should've lasted days.

"What about the link between you and the others? They felt it snap."

Lucien coughed up another dollop of blood.

Taking in his state of disrepair, he couldn't have much left to cough up.

"Bola..." he wheezed.

The last piece to the puzzle of Lucien's faked death fell into place. Of course, Bola. That sick bastard had an absurd wealth of scientific knowledge to tinker with drugs, and enough demonic power to snap bonds. He'd planned to do as much with Sid's mark on me. The Pharaoh and Bola had used Lucien's arm to create a pile of Lucien scented ash, and Bola severed Lucien's ties with his servant and horde.

A perfectly faked death. And instead of dead, Lucien had been here, the whole time, under our noses in a forced Hell.

I paused, and searched within again. Nope. No sympathy surfacing for this former Master either.

"Why'd you send Allan and Clint away?"

Allan shuffled behind me as the Vampires and Werewolves entered the room. Lucien's act of sending the two away had ensured their safety and survival.

"Had...had an agreement...with Pharaoh. Supposed to meet. Didn't fully trust..." His voice scraped against my eardrums.

Well, Lucien's spidey-senses had panned out.

Though, it hadn't worked out well for him.

"Why not just kill you?" Allan asked.

Lucien's head lifted briefly before flopping back down. "Ah, Akihiko..."

I shot Allan a dark look. He better not think of saving this guy, this tormentor from my past.

Allan shook his head. He might not have read my mind, but my death stare probably made my thoughts clear.

"Used me...used me for science." He coughed again. His whole body constricted and tensed, but no blood sputtered from his lips. His brows pinched in. "My blood...is old... Used for KK and SomaX."

Did that mean a little of Lucien's blood had pulsed through my veins? Maybe still did?

My skin crawled as Lucien's body convulsed again.

How long does a red blood cell survive? Wick asked me as he rubbed his blood-soaked body against my leg. He would've sensed or smelled my fear. Heck, it flowed off my skin in waves.

I ran my hands through his matted fur and shrugged. *A hundred to a hundred and twenty days.*

Then his blood no longer courses through you.

I sighed in relief, liking Wick's logic and wanting to

stick to it. *Let's hope none of those red blood cells developed the ability to divide and replicate.*

You'd smell of him. And you don't.

What do I smell like? I smiled, knowing the answer, my soul singing.

Like heaven. Like a pristine forest begging for me to run through it. And me. You smell like me. You smell like mine.

Lucien's body finished convulsing, and sagged.

Though his current state and power had been considerably depleted, and he wallowed in pain and discomfort, he could mend, with time and a lot of blood. He'd remain considerably vulnerable for a while, and he'd never regenerate an arm, but given protection and the means, he'd return to at least a portion of his former power.

The supes in the room grew restless, their feet scuffing against the dirt ground.

"We're not here to save you," I said and stepped forward.

"Good." His pained gaze met mine. "I hate... weak..."

Understanding hit me like a freight train. Lucien always hated looking weak. He lacked the courage and mental strength to overcome something like this. Hadn't he seen the brave soldiers who returned from battle with wounds and scars like his? How the men and women faced their new challenges in life with courage and carved out new lives?

Lucien didn't have that. He had nothing but pride,

backed with power, and now both of those had been ripped away from him.

Good.

Sickly sweet sweat clung to his pores, but I doubt Lucien feared what would come next. My possible inaction scared him. He feared *survival*.

I took another step forward. I could let him live. Have him survive and go through the torture of knowing the extent of his weakness and dependency on those around him.

I hesitated.

With only a foot separating me from the man who'd used Wick against me more than once, I weighed my options.

If I let him live, he'd find a way to kill himself, or he might somehow survive and come back to exact his revenge. And once recovered, he'd control wolves again, including Wick. I couldn't take that risk. Sure, under constant guard, he'd suffer months, if not years of recuperation. But...but, he'd already suffered for months and months in this condition.

His dark gaze met mine, recognition of my choice glimmering in his eyes. "Thank you."

I ripped his head clean from his shoulders, the tissue and bone weak from malnourishment. His body, still suspended from the beams, swayed from the force of my quick attack. Lucien's head, still gripped between my hands spilled only a little blood on the floor. He didn't have much left to lose.

I turned and walked to Allan, handing him Lucien's

head. The sunken features and glazed eyes a shadow of the attractive man he'd once been.

"Give this to Clint?"

Allan nodded.

"His Master is at rest now." Though I'd never understand why Clint cared deeply for his Master, he had. And although the feelings I held for Clint weren't exactly warm and fuzzy, I'd grown to appreciate the complexities of his personality, and the role he'd played in my rescue and revenge. He deserved some closure. After all, I'd found mine.

I shifted to wolf and leapt at Wick. *Let's run.*

Wick howled his agreement.

EPILOGUE

The wind whispered through the pine leaves and snarled branches lining the beach. Sonny soared over the waves with Tank, screeching delight as the summer sun reflected off their glistening feathers and the ocean water.

Wick sat beside me on the sand, holding my hand, breathing in the salty air, eyes shut in delight. His warmth beside me mimicked his expanding presence in my heart, the bond growing stronger, warmer and more content with each passing day.

We'd taken a break from all the hard work. Sonny finally quit his job at the lodge. His resort was shaping up nicely, and ahead of schedule, with the help of Wick's developer skills, and a pack of wolves taking vacation from their regular day jobs to help out with the manual labour.

It had been two months since killing Lucien, ATF,

Christine and the Pharaoh. Vancouver and the surrounding area had returned to normal with Allan as the head of the Vampire horde. He'd pulled back the influence of the Vampires in the Lower Mainland, ceding control over non-Vampire supes to create an environment of supe equality. Clint had taken Lucien's head and disappeared into the night without a word. Somehow, I knew we'd see him again, and not as an enemy.

With the corruption of the SRD and the evil plans of the Pharaoh and Bola revealed, the federal governments of Canada and the United States had dissolved the SRD in an epic knee-jerk reaction. Instead, specialized divisions within local police departments assumed control over monitoring the supernatural crimes in their jurisdictions.

Now, a lot of law enforcement agencies scrambled to hire qualified, capable, and honourable supes, strong enough to take down the bad supes. Because of this, or at least I suspected because of this, the upper brass of the Vancouver Police Department had forgiven me of my beastly outburst and expunged any pending charges or disciplinary actions they'd originally planned to dole out. Knowing I was part Goddess, and totally badass, they continuously attempted to lure me back to employment with promises of grandeur.

In other words, working with Stan.

I loved that man and still met him for beer & bitch sessions. Working with him would be awesome, and now that he headed the VPD's Supe Crime Division, it would be a lot of fun, too. Not all the super supes had been in cages. A few continued to lurk around the area and required extermination.

I hadn't made my decision, yet. Since I never attended any disciplinary hearings, and they hadn't finished the paperwork to fire me, the VPD was still technically my employer. I'd officially taken a Leave of Absence for extenuating circumstances, enjoying life as a newly mated supe, and as a glorified helper for my brother's dream.

Assisting Sonny with his resort had been rewarding and therapeutic, but as the summer came to an end, so too, did our sojourn. Tristan's inheritance provided me with the means to never work again. Mated with Wick, a very successful building developer, also ensured financial stability. But I needed something to call my own.

My cell phone vibrated, and I straightened my leg to pull it out of my pocket.

"Andy!" Ben yelled into the phone. "This one's for you."

The Witch coven crooned an 80s romance song into the receiver, and my smile broadened. The Witches had recuperated from their confinement and were back to their karaoke and joking selves.

Without the SRD, Ben and Matt faced unemployment. This fact led me to my brain child, a way to connect my new life with the old. When we returned to Vancouver, I planned to open an office for Sonny's resort. We'd do all the bookings, marketing, advertising, and arrange travel to and from the Haida Gwaii. With the office located in one of the busiest business sectors in North America, the exposure would be excellent. A one-trick travel agency of sorts. The Witches would work for me.

I'd get to travel back and forth between the Lower Mainland where I lived with Wick, my heart, and the Haida Gwaii, which sang to my soul.

When I told Sonny, his eyes had widened and glistened with what looked suspiciously like tears. The hug he gave me nearly crushed my bones.

The Witches finished their crooning, and without so much as a goodbye, hung up. To say they were excited about their new job and employer was a bit of an understatement.

I reached down and picked up the postcard from Donny, my old handler. He'd sent it from a tropical paradise with a simple message. "I'm proud of you." His chicken scratch handwriting stared back at me and brought a smile to my face. How the coyote Shifter discovered what transpired, or where I currently stayed remained a mystery, much like everything else about the old man. One thing I did know, I'd see him again, too.

Wick squeezed my hand, and I snuggled into the warmth of his side. His molten brown gaze melted mine as he dipped down to kiss me. A lazy kiss, with soft lips and a tease of tongue, the beast inside stirred as warmth expanded within me. I wanted more. I always did with Wick. His love didn't suffocate. Instead, it burned low and threatened to consume me with delicious heat. I wanted to melt. I wanted to turn to putty in this man's hands. Again, and again, and again.

Wick chuckled against my mouth. "Your brother is watching."

So am I, get a room, Tank crooned.

I ignored the featherhead and kept my gaze trained on my Werewolf. Wick's words might imply one thing, but his body said another. His gaze flashed yellow, and I reached down to grope the evidence. "Then let's find some privacy."

Wick stood up and offered his hand. The smooth chocolate of his gaze seared the inside of my soul with the warmth of his love.

A memory of a similar moment, from a lifetime ago, resurfaced and played with my neurons. *Whatever life threw at us, we'd face it together, and it would be all right.*

I smiled, recognizing the truth in my original thought from so long ago. The path to this moment was paved with pain and loss, but love bore me from the ashes, and made me a stronger, better person.

I gently placed the postcard on the towel and moved my discarded flip-flop to weigh it down from the wind. We'd come back for our stuff later. With a smile, I slipped my hand in Wick's and let him haul me to my feet. Our bodies slapped together, sending a jolt low in my belly. The corners of his mouth tugged up as he read my wicked thoughts and sent an image of his own, one of our naked bodies entwined on the soft mossy banks by the river.

As we ripped off our clothes to shift and run as

wolves together in the ancient forests of the Haida, as my birth parents once had, love flowed through my veins.

Yes, the fight against my enemies was over, but my life had just begun.

Did you enjoy the Carus Series?
Try one of my other urban fantasy series!

The Raven Crawford Series

A part-time waitress, part-time private investigator struggles to navigate the world of the dark fae and her growing feelings for one of the most dangerous members from the Underworld.

The Lark Morgan Series

A necromancer solves supernatural murder mysteries, dodges shifty vampires and breaks all the rules when her loved ones are in danger. Filled with a slow-burn romance, spice and gasp-worthy plot twists.

ACKNOWLEDGMENTS

Although I was born in Daajing Giids (Queen Charlotte City) and raised on the Haida Gwaii, I was young when I lived there and it was a long time ago (I might be dating myself here...). Any mistakes or errors are my own and I apologize in advance for them.

The one place in the story I haven't visited, much to my regret, is S'Gang Gwaay Llanagaay, also known as Ninstints. Although one critical scene is loosely based on this location, I took certain liberties to create a fictional area to fit my story's needs.

I grew up in a town called Port Clements (Gamadiis), about a ten minute drive from where the Golden Spruce, also known as Kiidk'yaas, once stood. We used to walk the short trail and sit across the bank to look at the magnificent tree.

When a man illegally cut down the Golden Spruce as a political statement, I grieved the loss. Kiidk'yaas has its own tale, but its story is not mine to tell. What I can share is the Golden Spruce was a three-hundred-year-old biological phenomenon, and to many people, including myself, it was so much more than "just a tree." I wish I could've taken my children to see it and to help create their own Golden Spruce memories. Now, I can only share photographs and tell stories.

Although scientists attempt to reproduce Kiidk'yaas from cuttings, saplings in pots will never replace the beautiful spruce that once stood majestically amidst ever-greens in a temperate rainforest off the west coast of Canada. If you ever have the chance to visit the Haida Gwaii, take it. It is a beautiful place.

In the making of this book, I'd like to thank my beta readers and critique partners: Charlotte Copper, Karilyn Bentley, Abigail Owen, Katie O'Sullivan, Nicole Flockton and Jana Richards. Thank you to my fabulous friends for location suggestions, especially Hannah and Lindsay. You'll see that I've incorporated a few of these sites into the story.

I'd also like to thank my editor Lara. She has been with me from the beginning and has always been fabulous to work with.

A huge thank you to Olga Sauchenia who designed all the new covers for the Carus series, including this one. She was amazing to work with and captured the dark vibes of the series perfectly.

I'd like to thank my friends, family and readers for their continued support and words of encouragement.

This book is about loss, but more importantly, it's about rising from the dark abyss of loss, the healing that comes from this growth, and how the love of friends and family can help heal these deep wounds.

Liam Neeson once said, "Everyone says love hurts, but that is not true. Loneliness hurts. Rejection hurts. Losing someone hurts. Envy hurts. Everyone gets these things confused with love, but in reality, love is the only thing in this world that covers up all the pain and makes someone feel wonderful again. Love is the only thing in this world that does not hurt."

Thank you to my husband and children for teaching me the truth in these words.

J. C.

ABOUT THE AUTHOR

J. C. McKenzie is a book loving, gumboot-wearing, unapologetic science geek. She predominantly writes urban fantasy and post-apocalyptic dystopian fantasy with strong romantic elements. When she's not spinning tales, she's in the classroom sharing her passion for science and mathematics while secretly warping the young, impressionable minds of our future to carry out her evil plans for world domination. She lives in the Pacific Northwest with her family.

Visit her at jcmckenzie.ca

facebook.com/j.c.mckenzie.author

instagram.com/j.c.mckenzie

tiktok.com/@jcmckenzie0

bookbub.com/authors/j-c-mckenzie